NEW YORK REVIEW BOOKS
CLASSICS

THE MIRADOR

ÉLISABETH GILLE (1937–1996) was born in Paris, the
daughter of Michel Epstein, a banker, and of the novelist Irène
Némirovsky. In 1942, both parents were deported to Auschwitz,
where they died, but Gille and her older sister, Denise, lived out
the duration of World War II in hiding. Gille worked for many
years as an editor and translator, especially of science fiction,
and she was over fifty when her first book, *The Mirador*, appeared
and was immediately recognized as a major achievement. Before
her death she also published *Le Crabe sur la banquette arrière*
(The Crab in the Backseat), a mordantly funny examination of
people's responses to her battle with cancer, and a short novel
that reflects her and her sister's life in the years after their
parents' disappearance, *Un paysage de cendres*, translated into
English as *Shadows of a Childhood*.

MARINA HARSS is a translator and dance writer living in
New York City. Her recent translations include Mariolina
Venezia's *Been Here a Thousand Years*, Alberto Moravia's
Conjugal Love, Pier Paolo Pasolini's *Stories from the City of
God*, and Dino Buzzati's *Poem Strip* (NYRB Classics).

RENÉ DE CECCATTY is a French novelist, playwright, and
critic. His most recent book is a study of Giacomo Leopardi.

THE MIRADOR

Dreamed Memories of Irène Némirovsky by Her Daughter

ÉLISABETH GILLE

Translated from the French by
MARINA HARSS

Afterword by
RENÉ DE CECCATTY

NEW YORK REVIEW BOOKS

New York

BOCA RATON PUBLIC LIBRARY
BOCA RATON, FLORIDA

THIS IS A NEW YORK REVIEW BOOK
PUBLISHED BY THE NEW YORK REVIEW OF BOOKS
435 Hudson Street, New York, NY 10014
www.nyrb.com

Copyright © 2000 by Éditions Stock
Translation copyright © 2011 by Marina Harss
All rights reserved.

First published in French in 1992 by Presses de la Renaissance

Library of Congress Cataloging-in-Publication Data
Gille, Élisabeth, 1937–
  [Mirador. English]
  The mirador : dreamed memories of Irène Némirovsky by her daughter / by
Élisabeth Gille ; translation by Marina Harss ; afterword by René de Ceccatty.
    p. cm. — (New York review books classics)
  ISBN 978-1-59017-444-9 (alk. paper)
  1. Gille, Élisabeth, 1937– —Childhood and youth. 2. Némirovsky, Irène,
1903–1942. 3. Russians—France—Paris—Biography. 4. Political refugees—
France—Paris—Biography. 5. Authors, French—20th century—Biography.
6. World War, 1939-1945—Jews—France. 7. Paris (France)—Intellectual life—
20th century. 8. France—Ethnic relations. I. Harss, Marina. II. Title.
  DC718.R8G5513 2011
  843'.912—dc22
  [B]

                        2011013384

ISBN 978-1-59017-444-9

Printed in the United States of America on acid-free paper.
10 9 8 7 6 5 4 3 2 1

BOCA RATON PUBLIC LIBRARY
BOCA RATON, FLORIDA

CONTENTS

PART I: Irène Némirovsky–*November, 1929* · 9

PART II: Irène Némirovsky–*June, 1942* · 145

Acknowledgments · 221

Notes · 225

Afterword · 227

Élisabeth Gille and René de Ceccatty
An Interview · 235

THE MIRADOR

To my sister, painful memories
To my children, life
To Natasha, the link

Qui pleure là, sinon le vent simple, à cette heure
Seule avec les diamants extremes?... Mais qui pleure,
Si proche de moi-même au moment de pleurer?*

—Paul Valéry, "La Jeune Parque"

MARCH 1937

*The child is born in a beautiful Parisian apartment. One imagines her
cradle surrounded by bright-eyed fairies: her mother, the famous
writer, her sister, who, with her blond curls and lacy white dress, is the
picture of a happy little girl (a picture for which the baby herself is a first
sketch), the servants, the nurse, the governess, the maid, and the cook;
and, of course, a prince charming: her father, wearing a light-colored
suit, with a tender expression on his face and a champagne flute in his
hand. A riddle: Who is the wicked witch? Under whose features has she
concealed herself? Many years later, the child will read these lines, by
Georges Perec: "Even if I have the help only of yellowing snapshots, a
handful of eyewitness accounts, and a few paltry documents to prop up
my implausible memories, I have no alternative but to conjure up what
for too many years I called the irrevocable: the things that were, the
things that stopped, the things that were closed off—things that surely
were and today are no longer, but things that also were so that I may
still be." And later in the same book: "Their memory is dead in writing; writing is the memory of their death and the assertion of my life."**

PART I

Irène Némirovsky–*November, 1929*

I

I HAVE always found the fragrance of linden blossoms aggressive, though it is in fact quite tender, at least in literature, inebriating the senses in the mild air of late-summer nights. Heady to the point of causing queasiness, it is the fragrance of village squares where young folk walk around and around in the evening air beneath the heavy-lidded gaze of old men perched on benches, fingers knotted over their canes. A tranquil fragrance from the provinces, dazed by the oppressive midday heat. The fragrance of the promenade in Charleville at sundown or of Turgenev's parks, where slender young women from the last century cling to their lovers' arms. And a fragrance which has always brought on my worst migraines and driven my heart to gallop and thrash uncontrollably.

Yesterday, at a crucial moment during labor, when my belly felt as if it were locked in a tight ring of steel against which I was aware of a violent kicking in my lower back, the curtains fluttered and the window burst open, pushed by a gust of wind, plastering my face with a suffocating blast of warm air. Something stuck in the bottom of my throat and I heard a whistling, the prelude to a great stirring in my chest, which by now felt like a hollow cavern. It was my asthma, my savage and terrible asthma, awakening at the worst possible moment. An image filled my memory: A small child, me, straining on tiptoe to peer out of the window of our dining room in Kiev. A powerful, intoxicating fragrance of linden blossoms. A murmur that grows and rumbles, becoming a clamor. In the blink of an eye, my mother picks me up and holds me to her chest. Engulfed by her breasts, my forehead pressed against her pearls, drowning in her perfume, I struggle and howl.

Was this the Kiev pogrom of 1905? The day the rioters crossed the forbidden line separating the lower neighborhoods from the upper city, snapping off branches from the linden trees along the way, trampling the leaves on the city streets, storming the protected districts of the city where rich families, like my own, believed themselves to be safe? I cannot possibly remember these scenes, which took place when I was two years old; they have surely been described to me. Even so, is it possible that on that day, in her terror, my mother picked up the first thing that stood in her path, me, and on this one occasion, never to be repeated, held me to her breast in a natural maternal gesture? The image lasted only an instant, like a spark.

The midwife, realizing that I was suffering an attack, immediately placed a mask over my face, and I fell asleep with a smile, surrounded by the smell of ether, a substance which my beloved English governess, Miss Matthews, inhaled by the bottle.

When I awoke, I had a tiny daughter with blond hair. I asked Michel to register her under the name Catherine, like the heroine of *Wuthering Heights*. He prefers the name France. He says he would like her to know from the beginning what she owes to the country that has embraced us and loves us and which we also love, where she will never have to know that her parents are Russian Jews; where she will not be exposed to persecution, or pogroms, or revolutions; and where our distant origins will dissolve quietly into the pleasures of the good life. It is November 10, 1929, and we are experiencing a marvelous Indian summer; the warm weather has revived the fragrance of linden blossoms that we had thought was dead and gone.

For me, if Finland is winter and St. Petersburg, with its yellow mists shrouding the shores of the Neva, is autumn, then Kiev is summer. We were not yet rich when we lived there, just well-to-do. My father's business took place mainly in the city, and he disappeared occasionally for brief stints to Odessa or Moscow. The complaints and quarreling had already begun; at the time it was still possible for my mother to see a necklace more beautiful than her own on the neck of one of her friends, or a more sumptuous fur on another friend's shoulders. She found our house too small, uncomfortable, dark, the maid too clumsy, the cook deficient.

I loved that house, especially after the arrival of my French governess, Mademoiselle Rose, who looked after me and only me, and protected me from my mother's screaming fits, recriminations, bouts of rage, and hysterical weeping. Unlike countless other Russians, I do not cherish tender memories of my wet nurse, or *nia-nia*; she was a peasant who wore a colorful kerchief over her blond braids and an embroidered blouse with puffy sleeves beneath a red apron. My father had found her, or so he said, in a small village on the Dnieper. She spoke only Ukrainian and probably reserved her love for the child she had left behind in her sister's care when she came to look after me. What could this fervent Orthodox Christian—raised to hate Jews and to fear all foreigners, and taught by backward priests to believe in the concrete existence of the Devil—possibly think of this tiny prune with frizzy hair that she was forced to hold to her pink breast and feed with her milk?

When I try to recover memories of my early childhood, I see myself sitting on a high chair in our dark, smoky kitchen, surrounded by the wafting fragrance of cabbage. At the other end of the long table, my *nia-nia* is speaking in an incomprehensible language with a bearded man wearing a smock cinched with a leather belt—her husband on a visit, perhaps. The fire rumbles. Pots and pans hang from hooks. There are garlands of onions on the wall. The samovar bubbles insistently.

The cook sighs at her stove. I see her massive back, her vast skirt woven from rough green wool, covered in red-and-black flowers and stiffened by petticoats so that it looks as if it were made of wood. She wears a shawl, and a kerchief, made of the same fabric as the skirt, covers her bun. My mother enters like a gust of wind, wrinkles her pretty nose ill-humoredly, waves her beautiful white arm as if to fan the smoke, barks a few orders and reproofs, and leaves once again without a glance in my direction. I start to cry.

I was four years old when, at my father's insistence, my *nia-nia* was replaced by Mademoiselle Rose. She was a small woman, round and gentle, and always wore pearl-gray skirts and blouses with high lace collars, white in summer, black in winter. He found her in Odessa, in the pretentious household of a business associate where she unhappily tolerated mistreatment by two bratty girls. She had overheard him declare that he was looking for a governess for his four-year-old daughter; after overcoming her shyness, she knocked on his door and offered her services. My mother would have preferred an English governess—it was more chic—but for once she bowed to his wishes without putting up much of a fight. I did not understand why until later, when she managed to convince him to allow us to spend a year in Paris, with the pretext that he was about to depart on a long journey to Transcaucasia and that she was too afraid to spend months alone with a young daughter in Kiev in such troubled times.

Mademoiselle Rose, who until then had seen only Moscow and the residential neighborhoods of Odessa, fell in love with Kiev. With my *nia-nia*, who was terrified of the city, our walks had been limited to the public gardens. We always took the same path, down one of those vast, silent avenues lined with large houses, invisible behind their tall fences, which intersected our street. Without letting go of my hand for even an instant, she would walk three times around the kiosk where a band blared fanfares, at a safe distance from the groups of secondary-school boys in uniforms, caps pushed back rakishly, shooting blazing glances at blushing girls in brown dresses and white pinafores, their ribboned braids hanging down to their knees. Women in straw hats, dressed in ankle-length skirts and clutching umbrellas, strolled slowly alongside gentlemen in boaters. The statues, released from the wooden shells that protected them from the icy winters, reached out to us with their marble arms. We avoided the spinning merry-go-rounds where children in shirtsleeves ran wildly around until, launched into the air, they floated, graceful as the angels in the cathedral of Saint Sophia, before once again returning to earth, waving their arms and tumbling like drunkards.

We barely even reached the esplanade, past rows of hedges and pro-tected by a guardrail, below which flowed the river's calm waters.

I owe to the Dnieper the greatest joy of my childhood. I was re-covering slowly from a case of whooping cough, complicated by asthma. I had spent most of the winter in the stifling heat of our largest room, presided over by an enormous Russian earthenware stove which heated the entire house. My bed had been placed above it. My mother was not able to convince my father to replace this stove with central heating until the following year. I was constantly bored, despite the best efforts of Mademoiselle Rose. Hostage to my passion for Napoleon, which she had instigated, she had grown tired of playing the role of the Austrians during countless battles staged with the small painted wooden soldiers I collected. She had read the *Memoirs of the Life, Exile, and Conversations of the Emperor Napo-leon* to me a hundred times, until I knew it by heart, and for her the final blow, after all the Emperor's endless reverses, must have been to hear me massacring his speeches.

The doctor, with his small beard, detachable collar, and pince-nez, came to examine me, finding me pale and in a weakened state. He decreed that I was well enough to travel and that a change of air was what I needed, even for a day or two. My parents discussed the idea of sending me to Odessa to visit my grandparents, but Made-moiselle Rose did not feel up to facing the whims of the Russian railways alone. There was no question of my mother leaving town; the season was only two months away and her seamstress, bom-barded by requests from all sides, was hard at work on the dress pat-terns that had just arrived from Paris, shrouded in mystery. She had scheduled a series of fittings that could under no circumstances be delayed.

In the end my father took things in hand, though not without a dramatic domestic tussle, during which my mother, blind with jeal-ousy, wrung her hands and screamed that he was trying to cloister her. The scene culminated in a fainting spell, during which my mother fell conveniently onto a pile of cushions on the settee. Even then, I was amazed that anyone could be taken in. And yet they all were, once again. There were tears, apologies, promises, and, at dinner, a jewelry case tucked under my mother's napkin. Its contents, once revealed, brought color to her cheeks. I can still see the stone, an emerald, showering its maleficent green sparks across the damask tablecloth amid Bohemian crystal goblets and Limoges plates decorated with pink flowers and a gold border. My father informed me during dessert that he would soon be leaving on a business trip and would take me and my governess with him. We would take a week-long cruise down the Dnieper on a steamboat.

This trip set the stage for my first tantrum. I decided that I absolutely must have a sailor suit. My mother, who was so extravagant when it came to her own attire, did not see the need for this. She was intent on dressing me in a hideous Scottish dress, paired with a linen cape and muff. I begged, cried, and finally screamed and rolled on the floor, to the dismay of Mademoiselle Rose, who had never seen me in such a state. Thanks to my father's intervention, my efforts were successful. I still have a photograph taken on the day of our departure, in front of the white-columned portico of our house. I am wearing an authentic sailor suit with knee breeches (the cause of a final conflict and triumph, for my mother pretended that I had requested a pleated skirt), a striped jersey, and a short navy blue jacket. With one hand on my hip, I stare out at the world victoriously, with the stubborn gaze, pursed lips, and crooked smile of one who has won a great victory and is ready to fight many battles, to conquer vast expanses and subdue hostile populations. I am Napoleon at Austerlitz! I love this photograph, which is seldom the case. I love my air of bravado, erect posture, and especially the effortless pose, my left hand in the pocket of my breeches, like a boy who would never even imagine wearing a dress. Only I know that in my pocket I clutch a bullet casing, black and tiny, my most prized possession, whose presence greatly magnified my courage.

I detest nostalgia. During the ten years I have lived in Paris, I have tried to avoid the musical soirées, teas, and charity balls to which my mother once dragged me, where one is constantly accosted by old fogies speaking in horribly accented French, misty-eyed at the wail of the first Gypsy violin. I cannot stand weepy evocations of "Our beloved mother Russia." Listening to a certain Prince Trubetzkoy—now working as a bank teller because he did not read the writing on the wall—as he exclaims about the splendors of the Russian land-scape and the rustic virtues of the serfs he once flogged on the slight-est pretext makes me want to vomit. And yet my memories of our weeklong cruise down the Dnieper are magical.

Kiev is a city built on a bluff dominated by St. Vladimir's Hill, with a giant statue of the saint brandishing his cross, illuminated at night with electric lights and visible from a distance of several versts. On the other shore, beyond forests and gardens, lies the vast steppe where, as a child, I imagined I could see Taras Bulba's pointy hat above the tall grass, bobbing up and down as he flew on his horse to join his Zaporishzhya Cossack brothers. We boarded the boat in the late afternoon. No sooner had we explored the hallways—a world of brass and polished wood—and settled into our cabins, where I sorely tested Mademoiselle Rose's patience by jumping on her bed in order to look out of the porthole, than my father came to escort us up to the deck. He had changed into a white tussah silk suit, stiff-collared shirt, tan cravat secured with a gold-tipped pin, silk waistcoat, two-toned shoes with buttoned spats, and, of course, the silver-handled cane he always used. He had it with him today when he emerged from his Buick, dressed in a dark gray suit, a cashmere coat, and a soft hat—he'd come to see his first granddaughter. These days he looks more and more like Charlie Chaplin, with his deep-set dark eyes and his fleshy, shapely mouth, the corner of which is marked by a slight crease of bitterness. One of these days he will spin his cane like a windmill to amuse her, as he did in 1914 after taking me to see one of Chaplin's first films. That evening on the boat he wanted to show us the moon as it began its ascent.

In the immensity of the Russian sky, the moon looked green, touched by the dying rays of the setting sun and crisscrossed by spec-tral clouds that slid over its white surface, leaving behind a trail of dark shadows. The silver domes of the church of Saint Andrew, which we had just passed, still glimmered faintly among the trees. The immense branches of the forest, which descended to the very edge of the river, draped the shoreline in darkness, but the middle of the current was dappled with metallic-colored spots as far as the eye could see. "All the Dnieper shimmered with silver like a wolf's skin in the night," my father murmured. Every Russian child, and especially every Ukrainian child, can recognize a quote from Gogol without being told its precise source. I, who had been read the stories from *Evenings on a Farm Near Dikanka* hundreds of times, was no longer looking at the river; with my nose tilted upward, eyes full of tears from staring at the moon—whose blurry edges were constantly transformed by the clouds as they were chased by a brisk breeze—I could see the Devil dancing.

In Gogol's story "Christmas Eve," the Devil decides to corrupt the inhabitants of a small village. Only one man, the blacksmith, fends off his advances. The demon has but a few hours left to seize the blacksmith's soul, because he must return to Hell as soon as the moon rises. When it appears, he decides to put it in his pocket. But the moon is hot and burns his fingers. He tosses it from one hand to the other, blowing on his fingers like a waiter juggling a red-hot plate, and the moon begins to fly back and forth across the sky, to the astonishment of an old man who has emerged from his *isba*, or hut, to relieve his vodka-logged bladder. The vision of the horned Devil rising up above the dark treetops and tossing the greenish moon from hand to hand frightened me so much that, sailor suit notwithstanding, I leapt into my father's arms, crying. He put his hand on the nape of my neck and waited, silently, for the attack to pass.

For someone who knew how to read the signs, everything in that late spring of 1910 foreshadowed the disaster that lay just around the corner, even though Halley's Comet, making its ominous return, had hardly been visible during its passage a month earlier and had precipitated none of the catastrophes that had been predicted. But our voyage through the towns, villages, and estates of Ukraine left me with an impression of terrifying decadence. Never had nature been so flamboyant; its vibrant freshness was like a satin-lined jewel box containing a precious stone corroded from within by a black chancre. Copses of beech with silvery trunks and tender green foliage engulfed dilapidated manor houses with roofs collapsing on abandoned rooms and broken windows, shutters torn asunder. The wheat, which was just beginning to turn golden, intermingled with the tall grasses of the steppes and with pink and mauve wildflowers, undulating around half-rotted *isbas* that crumbled on the edge of stagnant ponds. The limpid blue sky could not find its reflection in the muddy pools below, above which loomed ancient willow trees whose branches dangled into the water, filled with brambles that no one bothered to prune.

My father was there to buy wood: immense Russia was becoming industrialized and it needed ties for its railroads, timber for its factories, beams to build housing for its workers. On behalf of his bank, my father had made contact with several landowners and was planning to visit them to negotiate the purchase of wood. We departed in the morning in a horse-drawn carriage that was waiting for us at the loading dock. I had hardly slept and had trouble opening my eyes when the waiter brought my chocolate and pastries in the morning. I was too enervated by the excitement of the trip and the sound of balalaikas playing into the night for the entertainment of the poorer travelers crammed in the lower decks with their bundles. As soon as I laid my head down, I was tormented by the memory of one Jewish boy, about fifteen, with a thin face framed by long curls. His ardent eyes, engulfed by dark circles, had followed me for a long time after our arrival on board. He was clutching a bundle almost as large as he. I asked my father what it could possibly contain, and he answered that it was surely a consignment of carpets, imported from Turkey over the Black Sea, and that the boy was probably selling them at each stop along the Dnieper.

Mademoiselle Rose dressed me in white, low-waisted dresses with scalloped collars, black shoes and stockings, and a light quilted coat. I was only allowed to wear the sailor suit when we were on the boat. She spent an hour after breakfast battling my hair with a brush and a long-handled comb, around which she carefully twisted each lock in an attempt to transform the frizzy curls that made me look like a little savage into ringlets, which she then tied back prettily with a matching ribbon. Much as I protested against this getup, my father was anxious that his daughter make a good impression.

The troika clattered off over the wooden pavement. We traversed anemic little villages with a single street offering a few shops with old-fashioned signs, naïf images painted on sheet metal—a giant boot, a large golden loaf of bread, hedge clippers, giant scissors—meant to inform an illiterate clientele. Children chased after us demanding alms; some were able to hoist themselves onto the large trunk at the rear of the carriage, and the driver lashed at them with his long whip. I pressed myself against my father. Muzhiks wearing linden-bark sandals and ragged blouses and hirsute women carrying large bundles of laundry under their arms would turn and watch us with a vacant air. Everything spoke of poverty, decrepitude, neglect.

The uneven pavement disappeared, replaced by deeply furrowed dirt roads on which the horses sometimes stumbled. We rode past fields of wheat, buckwheat, and barley trembling in the breeze. Before us, scores of partridges and quail rose up with a fluttering of wings. I reached through the small opening in the leather hood of the carriage to catch large multicolor butterflies—their wings caressed my hand—or dragonflies that glided by within reach and flew off as soon as I tried to trap them. The larks sang. From time to time a shepherd's dog would chase after us down the road, barking furiously, only to be called back by a sharp whistle from a small boy who would stand watching us, shielding his eyes. We saw churches with white wooden walls topped by blue domes dappled with golden stars and visited by furtive little old women, bent and muttering, wrapped in shawls despite the heat; tiny windmills; and, rarely, standing neatly in the middle of a field of sunflowers, the house of a wealthy muzhik.

We cut down narrow lanes that descended into ravines filled with pine trees and birches, penetrated by cool air and shadows in which I took refuge from the blinding glare of the sun. The horses slowed. We could hear a stream bubbling nearby. Twigs caught in my hair when I poked my head out of the opening in the hood. Mademoiselle Rose tugged at my dress but I held on for as long as I could, watching a woodpecker hammering away at the trunk of a beech, a squirrel perched perfectly still in the bend of a branch, or a group of crows flying into the air, startled by the clatter of wheels. My father, absorbed in his papers, looked up only to deplore the terrible state of the trees; he explained that they were suffocating from overcrowding, that the density did not allow them to grow, that spots of mold on the bark revealed untreated blight. Here and there he pointed out a rare species suffering from lack of sunlight and space. Sometimes we came upon a clearing containing a pile of rotted trunks, cut down years earlier and abandoned, almost completely concealed beneath a tangle of moss and vines.

Soon a wooden gate would appear, announcing the entrance to an estate; usually it had been left open for so long that brambles and mulberry bushes made it impossible to pull closed. Mademoiselle Rose would comb my hair once again and place a wide-brimmed hat on my head. The road circled around a pond, where children fished in water up to their calves, and then continued past vegetable gardens and orchards filled with weeds where we often had to stop to push aside toppled railings, until finally it rounded the corner of a structure of yellowish stone and came to an end in a poorly kept courtyard. Our arrival sent birds scurrying in all directions. A black pig galloped off. Faces appeared in the windows and vanished just as quickly. We descended from the carriage. The adults would take me by the hand to keep me from stepping in puddles. A shy, shaggy-haired, barefoot little girl, wearing a dress several sizes too big that came down to her ankles, would dash into the house to announce our arrival.

There were surely estates in Ukraine where order and cleanliness reigned, like Konstantin Fyodorovich's estate, which so impressed Chichikov in *Dead Souls*, inspiring in him the fleeting desire to devote himself to the agricultural arts. The estates my father and I visited that summer belonged to modest country squires, most of them financially ruined, gentlemen who had been forced to return from

St. Petersburg or Moscow after spending their entire fortunes—for which they blamed the men who managed their estates—to eke out an existence from the fruits of the land. It was enough to step into the damp, dusty antechambers, to see the shaky stairs, the paintings so caked in grime that one could barely distinguish a golden epaulette in a family portrait or the silky reflection of a duck's plumage in a still life, to glimpse through a half-opened door, quickly shut, rooms furnished with rickety tables, their legs covered with thick spiderwebs, in order to understand that any attempt at maintaining these houses had long since been abandoned. The souls here were truly dead. The days of Oblomov were long past; if he had been raised in such a house, Ilya Ilyich would not have been compelled to loll about his whole life in his Oriental robe, dreaming nostalgically of a blessed time when white-elbowed cooks slaved in a kitchen fragrant with herbs, preparing meatballs, and ladies wove tapestries on waxed wood tables, lit by the candles of a crystal chandelier.

The owner of the estate and his wife would rush out to greet us. They cried "Leon Borisovich! What a joy! What an honor!" and showered me with compliments, praising my dress, my face. They called me "precious heart" and said they were amazed that I was only seven years old because of my good manners and graceful curtsy. They greeted Mademoiselle Rose with a simple gesture, because after all she was only a governess. They called the servants with great fanfare and pretended to attribute the state of the house to laziness and lack of foresight. A sulky old woman would light the samovar and, after we had been led into the parlor, bring in a tray of salted cucumbers and pierogi stuffed with cabbage and meat, cottage cheese and cream. Often the tablecloth bore the stains of the previous evening's meal, and crumbs dotted the frayed, faded carpet.

I pretended to eat, out of politeness. Our hosts exclaimed at my small appetite. In Russia, children are not fed, they are stuffed, and expected to be pink and round. My father did his best to partake of the bottles of spiced brandy the host had brought out from the depths of a cupboard. Michel, my husband, once explained to me why our ancient nation is Orthodox: The patriarch of Kiev, who had been tempted to select Islam as the official religion, was informed that this religion forbade alcohol, and not seeing how he could keep his people from drinking—and not wishing to forgo the pleasure himself—had chosen a more tolerant confession. Russian stomachs, be they of peasant stock or of noble lineage, are capable of imbibing enormous quantities of vodka, kvass, wine, or champagne. We gulp down food in order to empty glass after glass without doing ourselves too much harm, and we drink in order to wash down the food with which we gorge ourselves.

Eventually my father would drag himself away from the libations of his host, whose eyes were beginning to mist over and who was by now recounting tales of his misfortunes in a doughy voice. My father would lead his host outside to discuss business. Then I would be asked how I would like to pass the time. Since there were no other children to keep me company—the boys were off studying in the city and the girls were in boarding school—I usually requested a book, a notion that was always received with astonishment. They led me to a forlorn library which clearly no one ever visited, filled with piles of yellowing, flyspecked volumes with torn illustrations. When there was no library, I would ask to see the barn, where piles of old journals and rare editions rotted in a corner, consulted only by the goats and chickens. Mademoiselle Rose scolded me more than once for clasping these treasures to my breast; only my good manners and strict upbringing kept me from insisting that I be allowed to take these with us.

Then I would go outside. I visited the stables and caressed the muzzles of tired horses. I would often feed them a lump of sugar, which my governess kept in her handbag to be consumed with a drop of mint-flavored liqueur, in case of a dizzy spell. Children, dressed in tatters, peeked around corners and stared, sucking their fingers. Once, when Mademoiselle Rose left me alone for a moment while she asked our hostess about a certain type of embroidery, I followed one of the children all the way to his *isba*. At the door a small metal sign dangled from a piece of string; I grabbed it out of curiosity and saw that a ladder was painted on it. Later I asked my father about it, and he explained that it was there to remind the muzhik, presumed to be forgetful and stupid, of the tool he was meant to bring out in case of a fire. Each neighbor was responsible for bringing a single implement: a bucket, a hammer, or an ax. I stole a glance inside: the floor was made of black earth, there were holes in the thatched roof, straw mattresses lay piled in a corner, benches were placed along the walls, an old trunk contained a pile of dirty pillows, and an icon sat in one corner, embellished with a candle and a paper rose, the only touch of luxury. I ran away, my heart thumping. I did not get bored during these afternoons; the spectacle of such decrepitude astounded and captivated the city girl that I was. Then my father would return and I would run to him. He patted me tenderly on the head. We resisted the pleas of our hosts to stay for dinner, warning us of the great dangers we faced if we departed with an empty stomach, as if the meal we had devoured just a few hours earlier were not enough to keep us alive during the twenty versts or so we had to travel. We roused our carriage driver, who, after a few glasses of kvass, was out cold, and then we departed.

On our way back, we did not speak at all. I left my father to his ruminations, which appeared quite somber. Mademoiselle Rose dozed off. From time to time she would emit a soft snore, which, waking with a start, she would mask with a dainty cough before dozing off again. I contemplated the scenery. The dark forest looked more threatening now, and in my imagination I could see the outlines of animals, less friendly than before; I thought I heard wolves, and I avoided looking up at the sky, afraid I would see Baba Yaga on her giant mortar, with a pestle in her left hand and, in her right hand, the broom that she used to sweep away her trail. I, too, began to nod off. Then the jolt of the wheels against the wooden pavement would revive me; I knew we would soon return to the joyous effervescence of the boat, the comfortable lounges, the white tablecloths in the restaurant, the attentive staff, but most of all I knew that at dinner I would have my father to myself and that he would come to my cabin to tuck me in and tell me a story before going off with a cigar to rejoin the adult world.

MAY 1940

The child is three. She is chubby, with frizzy hair and dark skin. Her navy-blue shorts fit snugly around her belly and thighs. Her knees are dimpled, calves tanned. She stands on the tips of her toes, fanning them out in the dust. Her shirt, with puffy short sleeves and a blue-trimmed collar, rides up past her belly button, which is visible between her shorts and her Petit Bateau jacket. She pulls at her mother's sleeve; her mother is standing in the middle of the courtyard, reading. The young woman shifts the book, pushes back her glasses, and smiles. Her tender, myopic gaze caresses the child distractedly. The child wrinkles her brow, releases the sleeve, and moves away.

2

THE ADULTS hid many things from me and I knew it, even though I tormented them with questions and constantly reminded them that in February I had reached the age of reason. When we returned from the cruise, my father learned that one of his colleagues had been arrested. I knew this respectable-looking gray-haired gentleman, who often came to our house for lunch. Before removing his galoshes in the foyer and handing over his fur-lined coat, gloves, and melon hat to a servant, he always gave me a small package tied with a pink ribbon. It invariably contained candied fruit—prunes or cherries covered in glazed sugar—bought, of course, at Balaboukha, the finest confectioner in Kiev. I could not understand how one could throw a man of this sort in prison; I thought such measures were reserved for shaggy-haired nihilists, bomb throwers, or pale young women in threadbare coats and cheap felt boots, like young Dora Brilliant who, the year I was born, had taken part in the assassination of Grand Duke Sergei and whose picture I had discovered one day while flipping through old magazines.

My father seemed worried and shut himself in his study for a good two hours with the bank administrator who had come to bring the news. That night, when he came to my room to tuck me in, I asked in vain for an explanation. He told me that it was certainly an error and that very soon I would have my candied fruit again. I didn't believe a word of it. It was useless to ask my mother because she had banned all political discussions in her presence. If the gentlemen felt the need to discuss such matters, they could do so at their club; these topics gave her a headache and the vapors. Even my dear Mademoiselle Rose who, during our history lessons, had been happy to describe in copious and gory detail the horrors of French prisons during the Terror—like poor André Chénier writing his final verses on the damp straw in his dungeon—was flustered by my questions and said that a good little girl should not ask about such things.

I often listened outside of doors, especially during my governess's siesta, which she took in her room, adjacent to mine, after our mid-day meal. The servants were also sleeping, including the porter, or *dvornik*, even though he was not supposed to leave his post at the front door. I would tiptoe down the stairs in my bare feet and a cambric petticoat, hair loose over my shoulders, carrying my little cat, a blue ribbon around her neck. I would place my ear against the door of the smoking room, where my father lingered for one last glass of champagne with the male guests. My mother, who was only expected to perform the role of hostess in the evening, was never present. Often the discussions became heated and the guests raised their voices. I did not understand everything they said, but I could sense that they were uneasy, though seemingly to differing degrees. They also disagreed violently regarding the causes of the current situation and its potential remedies.

For the past five years, the autocratic government had been tightening its grip on the Russian people. The response to strikes and protests had been restrictive measures, arrests, sham trials, and deportations to Siberia. The czar took away with one hand what he had given with the other. People said that his prime minister, Stolypin, was favorable to reforms, but these reforms never came. Or worse, whenever a highly anticipated imperial ukase appeared in the papers, it was usually to announce the exact opposite of what everyone had hoped. Surveillance was exceptionally intense for intellectuals and students. I had already heard my father deplore the renewed emphasis on Latin and Greek in secondary schools to the detriment of economics and law, subjects he considered much more practical for the younger generation that would one day fill the ranks of business.

But what worried them the most were the new constraints placed on the Jews. There was a rumor going around that the quota of admissions to the university would be reduced further, and that families like ours, who were permitted to live outside the prescribed neighborhoods within Little Russia and Great Russia, families who lived in the most elegant neighborhoods in Kiev—such as the Pechersk quarter, just steps from the imperial palaces—even we might see limits placed on our freedom to travel, as well as higher taxes and other more significant obstacles. One day I heard a guest—somewhat the worse for drink—compare the atmosphere to that of 1905 and evoke the possibility of new pogroms, a comment that was greeted by a deep silence, followed by a cry of indignation. Terrified, my cat spat and squirmed as if possessed when I squeezed her tight against me. She jumped out of my arms and onto the staircase. I bounded up behind her, thus eluding my father's notice. I watched him from behind a baluster as he cracked open the door of the smoking room, alerted by the cat's howls.

This word—pogrom—was strictly forbidden in our house. I didn't know exactly what it meant, but it was surrounded by a fog of terror that linked it in my mind to either Pugachev's rebellious charge of Fort Belogorsk in Pushkin's story "The Captain's Daughter"—I imagined myself in the young woman's place, hiding behind an armoire, wiping away tears with my long hair as I waited for a young officer to save my life and my honor—or to the September massacres. In the latter scenario, I imagined myself in a white dress, being taken to the guillotine in a cart, from whose jaws the Scarlet Pimpernel, disguised as an executioner, would save me at the last moment. I knew, of course, that we were Jews, but this did not mean much to me. My parents were not religious. The year before, to please me, my father had taken me to the cathedral of Saint Sophia to witness the rituals of Orthodox Easter and the procession led by the priests three times around the church as the bells thundered loudly enough to make the walls shake. Like everyone else, I had been kissed three times by a stranger while crying out *Kristos voskres!*—"Christ is risen!"—candle in hand. Afterward, we went home to eat *kulich* and *paskha* and peel hard-boiled eggs that had been decorated by our cook. Only my maternal grandparents, Jonas and Bella Margoulis (née Chtchedrovitch), observed the precepts of Judaism, but when they were in Kiev, my mother, who was exasperated by such "foolishness," ordered her father to limit the use of his prayer shawl to his own room. Only once, at their house in Odessa, had I taken part in a Passover dinner. I was the youngest person present, so it had fallen to me to say, "Why is this night different from all other nights?" The answer had left me cold and, though I adored my grandparents, and their affection and special attentions still illuminated my memory of that night with a gentle warmth, it had been vastly overshadowed by the ceremony at Saint Sophia.

I was also acquainted with the Jews we encountered when Mademoiselle Rose and I descended, unbeknownst to my mother, into the Podol, the lower district that lies along the Dnieper. Not that my mother had actually forbidden us from going there; it had simply never occurred to her that we might prefer to walk down such disreputable streets rather than along Khreshchatyk Boulevard—the Champs-Élysées of Kiev—or in one of the innumerable parks which descend in terraces from the top of the hill where we lived down to the river. Despite her attachment to the Catholic faith, which classified lying by omission among the serious sins, my governess had carefully avoided requesting my mother's permission. We would leave the calèche behind, along with the coachman—who dressed in the Polish manner with a velvet jacket and peacock feathers, which I found ridiculous—and walk down the hill, taking either Vladimir's Descent or Andrew's Descent, which I adored because of its large wooden paving blocks. If we were tired, on the way back we would take the bus, which at the time was still drawn by horses, or the electric tram, which had the attraction of novelty.

The Jews of the Podol district were not reassuring to my eye: old men with whiskers and long reddish beards, dressed in cloaks beneath which one could make out the dirty fringe of their prayer shawls; sickly children with great black eyes and wispy curls; bewigged women standing in line outside kosher shops. I found them dirty and furtive, and I pulled away whenever a street vendor tried to slip a piece of sticky halva or cheese pastry into my hand. Our servants, insufficiently wary of my omnipresent ears, sometimes told stories in which these Jews committed the most horrible ritual crimes; the stories seemed no more unlikely than the fairy tales in which cruel witches pushed children into ovens and cooked them. In short, the Jews of the lower district scared me and made me uncomfortable. I could feel them staring at me with their dark eyes, like the young carpet salesman on the boat. I preferred the blond Ukrainian women at the market who reigned over buckets filled with brine-marinated anchovies or stood behind stalls heaped with enormous piles of watermelons, small hills of cherries, or large armfuls of marigolds. I never refused when they sweetly offered me a glass of ice-cold milk, which I sipped as I watched a blind beggar singing folk tunes, accompanied by a young boy on an accordion, bandura, or lyre.

Even now, deep down, I have the same reaction of mistrust and, to be honest, almost of revulsion when by chance I find myself in Belleville or the Marais and, for the first time in years, see these immigrants dressed in rags, these pious Jews with sidecurls, so like the ones in the Podol. They have been arriving in increasing numbers from their Polish shtetls and German ghettos, driven out by persecutions and poverty. As I walk, I overhear fragments of conversation in Yiddish, that forgotten dialect. A vague anxiety comes over me, often followed by an asthma attack upon my return home. I am conscious of the fact that my attitude is harsher toward them than, for example, the French beggars who hold out their hands on Sundays near my house, on the steps of Saint-François-Xavier. And when it comes to the wealthy Israelites, I don't know how my parents and their friends will react if one day they happen to read the novel I have just completed. It is entitled *David Golder*, after the main character, and it must be said I am not kind to this milieu. The same is true of a novella I recently began writing, which I will call simply

The Ball. In it, I flay the thing which I dread and detest the most: the immoderate passion for money and splendor, the mentality of the nouveau riche who display their wealth with arrogance and lack of taste—in other words the atmosphere in which, it must be said, my mother and her entourage are immersed.

We are fortunate to live in France where, since the Revolution, Jews have been allowed, when they desired it, to assimilate with ease. My husband feels no more Jewish than I do, even though in Moscow his father, who assiduously practiced his religion, was a member of the Council of Jewish Communities and obliged his children to at least respect appearances. Three years ago we were married in a synagogue, so as not to shock him. In Michel's view, such beliefs belong to the past and it would be much better if the older generation behaved more discreetly. He believes that ever since the successful outcome of the Dreyfus affair, which was obtained in large part thanks to Frenchmen like Zola and Péguy, the Jewish problem no longer exists in France. He often says in jest that one of the reasons he is so happy we had a daughter is that he will not have to argue with his father about circumcision. When I come upon a hateful or merely suspicious article, I am upset and point out to him that even today, in our time, there are anti-Semitic publications and movements, such as Charles Maurras's organization. Michel laughs and says that freedom of the press is well worth a few annoyances.

He is right, of course. I mustn't forget that Pope Pius XI condemned Maurras's Action Française three years ago, in 1926, and that now the vast majority of Catholics condemn it. It would be dishonest to claim that people like us are affected by xenophobia of any sort. But there is a price: We feel the obligation to show at all times that we are French before we are Jewish. And what does Jewish mean to us, beyond an obscure filiation which will soon be lost in the mists of time? We are surprised at the anxiety felt by some of our friends ever since people began to talk incessantly about the National Socialist movement in Germany, which is truly anti-Semitic; to us it all seems very exaggerated. My father argues that we should be the first to counsel moderation toward this defeated nation and in order for reason to prevail there as it does here, allow it to reestablish its economy instead of strangling it with our demands. Let us of course take in these unhappy German and Polish refugees who are faced with the pogroms that are born of a resurgence of this primitive hatred, but let us also hope that the exodus will soon come to an end so that French workers do not feel threatened by the refugees' presence. And most of all, let us advise these refugees to show the discretion that we ourselves would do well to practice.

Thanks to my aunt Assia, I finally found out in 1910 what exactly this word "pogrom" signified. Only ten years my senior, she showered me with a tenderness that her elder sister, my mother, was incapable of. Assia had recently finished her secondary studies at a private boarding school in Odessa, and at her request her parents were about to send her to Paris to study medicine in the care of a cousin. The limits of the quota had made it impossible for her to complete her studies in Russia. She was planning to leave in the spring in order to familiarize herself with the city and perfect her French during the months before the beginning of the school year. Meanwhile, she came to stay with us, since we would not be seeing each other for quite some time. All this made me very sad. I had great respect for Assia, so stubborn in her desire to study despite her family's reservations. My mother, in particular, found her wish to become a doctor to be indecent in a young girl. Inspired by Assia's example—along with Florence Nightingale's adventures, which Mademoiselle Rose had read to me, and the tears I had shed while reading a book about the horrors of the Boer wars, *The Boer Boy of the Transvaal*—I had secretly decided to follow in her footsteps when I grew up.

One afternoon in early November, Assia invited me to come along to meet a young man outside the high school on Bibikov Boulevard; she had not seen him since her last visit to Kiev, the previous year. The three of us would go for tea at the Kircheim pastry shop.

Extremely flattered by the offer, I ran to my mother to ask for permission, which she granted. I called out insistently to Mademoiselle Rose, who helped me put on my boots, coat, hat, and muff. Then I joined Assia in the front hall where she stood elegantly dressed in a fitted coat with a beaver-fur collar and hat. Since we had ample time, we walked down Aleksandrovskaya Street by the imperial palaces. The weather was exceptional for the season. The sun bounced off of the marble façades, transforming the windows into crystal prisms; it gilded the auburn leaves and sent sparks flying off the helmets of the guards who stood stock-still in front of their black-and-white-striped sentry boxes.

We turned onto Khreshchatyk Boulevard, crowded as usual with carriages, hackney cabs, and horse-drawn buses, its yellow-brick sidewalks swept by the long skirts of ladies trailed by servants burdened with enormous piles of parcels. We continued on Khreshchatyk to the corner where it intersected Bibikov Boulevard. A group of boys in school uniforms amused themselves by knocking leaves off chestnut trees with caps that they always wore as sloppily as possible. The leaves formed rustling golden piles that covered my boots, and I kicked them up into the sky, which was a deep Prussian blue. All of a sudden a group of youths rushed out of the large building housing the school. The buttons of their peacoats and their belt buckles gleamed in the sunlight. They wore black armbands. No sooner had they appeared than a detachment of cavalry galloped in from Vladimirskaya Street, dispersing them. Aunt Assia took my hand and pressed me against the iron gate of Nicholas I Square, just in time to avoid being crushed by the hooves of one of the animals. I could smell the hot, peppery fragrance of its sweaty coat as its rider's spur brushed against me and his saber caught the light. Then everything returned to normal.

Once our fear had subsided, she sat with me on a bench and explained that despite a ban these students had attempted to publicly mourn the death of Count Leo Tolstoy, which had been announced that morning. Though I had not yet read anything by the man whom the Russians consider the greatest writer of all time—I doubted that he could truly outshine Dickens and especially Hugo, whose *Les Misérables* Mademoiselle Rose was then reading to me—and though the Orthodox church, with the government's support, had excommunicated him because of his subversive writings, I was aware that his name had been in all the papers and on every tongue for weeks. On the night of October 27, at the age of eighty-four, Tolstoy had secretly left his estate of Yasnaya Polyana and gone to the nearest train station, where he boarded a train for an unknown destination. His desperate wife, children, and friends searched for him. On November 1 it was reported that he had been found, suffering from pneumonia in the small village of Astapovo. The press was filled with news of his health day after day, but the signs were not good; as he lay bedridden in the home of the stationmaster, his health declined, despite the care of his doctor. Finally, on November 7, his death was made public.

Assia had tears in her eyes. She stood up, looked at me, brushed off her shoulders, adjusted her fur hat and my own, and led me by the hand to the doors of the school. The bell had just rung, but I did not see the usual unruly pushing and shoving. The boys descended in order of seniority, walking silently and with measured steps; all at once, in perfect synchronicity, they pulled black armbands out of their pockets and tied them onto the sleeves of their uniforms, which were gray with gold buttons. I saw a group of men standing in the doorway, probably the director of the school and a few teachers, conversing with a worried air.

My aunt caught sight of the young man she had come to meet, and when he spotted her, he left his friends and joined us. He was a skinny, pimply boy with a red neck chafed by his stiff collar and a prominent Adam's apple that was constantly in motion. She introduced him as Konstantin Georgevich Paustovsky,* known as Kostik.

They immediately began a heated discussion about me, little Irina. Assia regretted having been thoughtless enough to take me out on such a day, and begged her friend to remove his armband before accompanying us to the Kircheim pastry shop as planned. Otherwise we would have to return immediately to Pechersk. There could be no excuse for putting a seven-year-old child at risk. Horrified, I protested: I was not a baby, and my father had recently judged that I was old enough to travel with him on the flooding Dnieper, an extremely perilous journey during the course of which the ship had almost sunk at least ten times. In addition I was well known by the police due to my close friendship with a revolutionary, who was currently wasting away in Siberia. The young man began to laugh and dutifully removed his armband, placing it in his pocket. Still deeply offended, I refused to take the hand Assia held out to me, stubbornly plunging both hands into my muff and following them sullenly toward Khreshchatyk Boulevard.

Contemplating the almond meringues and frothy cups of hot chocolate on lace tablecloths amid the stucco and gilding of the pastry shop, my anger melted away. I let Assia and Kostik catch up for a long while, describing what they had done over the past year and laying out their plans for the future. I began to grow bored. Then something Kostik said roused my attention: "Don't stay in Kiev for too long, Assia, and look after yourself. Remember what happened five years ago. Everyone thinks the same could happen again."

"Do you really think that a pogrom is still possible in this day and age?" my aunt asked.

I interrupted with my eternal question and, this time, I got a response. In October 1905, Kostik had been thirteen, Assia twelve. They did not know each other yet. On October 17, the director of the school had given the students three days off to celebrate the publication of the czar's manifesto, which at last granted his people certain freedoms, including freedom of religion, freedom of assembly, and freedom to express one's views in public or in writing without having to submit to censorship. He had also created an assembly, an elected Duma with a say in the creation of laws. Kostik, wearing a red cockade in his boutonniere, ran into the street with his friends and rushed down toward the university. A crowd of students poured out, singing "La Marseillaise."

Then, like now, hussars had appeared, but that time they were carrying guns. Shots rang out. Pushed back by the crowd, Kostik had almost been crushed and was separated form his friends. He felt himself being pulled down Volodymyrska Street just as another squadron of police appeared there, hoping to trap the students in a pincer maneuver. He ran to Khreshchatyk Boulevard and glanced right, toward home, but, overcome by curiosity, turned left toward the town hall, past Nikolaevsky Street.

The square was full of people waving red flags. Protesters climbed up the walls of the town hall, dangling from the colonnaded balcony with one arm. And that was how he had met Assia. She had lost her governess in the crowd and was crying; they were on their way to the Idzikowski Library to borrow books when the troops rushed in, sabers drawn. Taking the young girl's hand, Kostik led her back in the opposite direction and, without stopping for breath, down side streets toward his home, where his mother waited, crazed with worry.

I listened to this story, captivated by his every word.

"But Assia," I asked, "how did you get back to our house? Did mother scold you for going to a stranger's house without your governess?"

She picked up where he had left off, describing the attentiveness and generosity with which Kostik's parents had treated her. His father had refused to let her go outside. He had sent a servant to our house to reassure our family about her safety and to ask for permission to keep her overnight because the streets were still unsafe and would most likely become even more so after dark. He promised to escort her home himself the following day, once the danger subsided. But the next day the pogrom began.

Now I know that a pogrom has followed every significant occurrence in Russia. The year I was born, one of the worst pogroms caused the death of hundreds of inhabitants of the Jewish quarter in Kishinev. Like most, it had been, if not planned by the police, at least tolerated. But on this occasion it was not limited to the Podol. A business associate of my father's, Alexandre de Gunzbourg, later described in detail what had happened to him. He was in Kiev at the time for the funeral of his grandmother, Madame Rosenberg, which was attended by the city's Jewish haute bourgeoisie. His cousin's house, on the corner of Sadovaya and Aleksandrovskaya streets—an area filled with official buildings, including the governor's mansion, the national bank, and the central post office—was attacked first by rioters and then by the Black Hundred. The occupants of the house were saved only by the proximity of the British consulate, to which they escaped after slipping through some loose boards in the garden fence.

The same thing had happened on our peaceful residential street; my parents and I had escaped the violence only because the authorities, after allowing the rioters to run free most of the day, had decided that enough was enough. The police intervened when the crowd was already at our fence; we could see they were carrying clubs, hastily fashioned out of tree branches. Despite the fact that Kostik's family was not Jewish, and that their servants had taken the precaution of placing icons in the windows facing the street and drawing an Orthodox cross on the back door, drunken peasants had demanded to know whether by any chance they were hiding any "Yids." They only agreed to leave after being provided with vodka. Finally, when order had been restored, my young aunt had been escorted home, where she was greeted by my mother's hysterics and the news that her governess had been fired as punishment for losing her charge.

A month and a half later, on the day she was preparing to leave Kiev to spend the holidays at home, the city was once again filled with fire and blood. The authorities had decided to dismiss all the employees at the Department of Post and Telegraphs, who had been on strike for several weeks in Kiev and all over Russia, and replace them with a battalion of sappers. The sappers revolted, turning against their own commanders and parading down the streets with red flags. They were soon joined by other workers and were headed toward the Jewish market when the first salvos rang out from the barracks: the confrontation killed and wounded hundreds. My parents' driver, who was on his way to the station with Assia, had just enough time to turn around and return home.

This story made such an impression that I did not utter a word on the way home, which was not like me at all. Night was falling, gray clouds were beginning to appear, and a cold northern wind pricked my cheeks. I did not tell Mademoiselle Rose anything about my day, and she ascribed my lack of appetite to the cakes I had devoured at Kircheim and gave me cherry-stem tea to aid my digestion. Something kept me from pursuing the question further with my father, who was surprised by my silence and by the despair with which I gripped his jacket as he left my room. After he gingerly pulled away, I lay with my cat on my chest in the glow of the night-light, mulling a difficult question beneath the rose-colored canopy of my bed. I turned it over and over in my head: What did I have in common with those louse-ridden Jews of the Podol which could inspire the same people who smiled at me and bowed before my parents in normal times—carriage drivers, porters, servants, soldiers, and muzhiks of various types—to attack us on that day in October 1905?

When I awoke the following day, the sky was white. A squall blew the leaves from the trees. In the late morning, the first snowflakes began to fall. My mother ordered the servants to install the double windows. Winter had arrived.

JULY 1942

The child climbs a wall and follows the harvesters down into the fields. At the end of the day, she drags herself back, drunk with the pleasure of jumping on bales of hay all day long, red from the sun, with blades of straw in her hair, snot-nosed from the dust, her dress torn, socks drooping in her sandals. Her partner in crime, Lulu, also five years old, walks her to the door, then departs to face her own mother's fury. She, too, is afraid of the scolding that awaits her. The child's father, usually so charming, has been tense lately and recently spanked her for the first time for an offense that had something to do with spinach. As she enters she finds two officers standing in the foyer and the family, pale-faced, gathered in the sitting room; a terror seizes her and she prepares to apologize. But her mother kneels down and embraces her, whispers that she must be good and obey her father and her sister, kisses her many times, stands up, and, suitcase in hand, leaves with the officers.

3

ONE SEPTEMBER night in 1911, I was awoken by a terrible commotion. I ran to the window and flung it open: someone was pounding furiously with the brass knocker on the wooden door of the carriage entrance. Our *dvornik* ran into the courtyard, hopping as he pulled on a boot with both hands. One sleeve of his jacket dangled down his back; his tousled shock of red hair showed clearly that the clamor had torn him from a deep slumber, generously doused in kvass, which, despite repeated reprimands, he indulged in most evenings as soon as his services were no longer required. The other servants soon joined him in a similar state of alarm and undress, carrying lamps.

Once the gate had been opened my father's calèche burst into the courtyard. The bay, which the driver was having some trouble controlling, danced in place, its hooves creating sparks against the paving stones, its coat glimmering in the muted glow of the lanterns. My father—wearing a black coat with a beaver-fur collar over his tails, top hat in hand—leapt down from the carriage, and I heard him yell to the *dvornik* to fetch a doctor. Then he leapt back into the carriage and, assisted by a servant, carried out my mother, limp beneath her sable coat. He gathered her in his arms and brought her into the house, the ostrich plume in her hat dragging on the ground. I rushed down the stairs followed by Mademoiselle Rose, who had also been jolted awake by the noise and was wearing a shawl over her nightgown; with her hair hanging loose over her shoulders and wide-eyed with curiosity, she looked ten years younger.

Our elderly family doctor took some time to arrive. Apparently all the ladies in Kiev required his services that night. By the time he finally appeared, the servants had gathered around and the housekeeper had loosened my mother's corset; the cook was applying smelling salts while Mademoiselle Rose sprinkled my mother's cheeks with camphorated alcohol. She was beginning to come to with languid sighs. My father, who probably did not feel up to carrying her all the way to her room, had placed her on the sofa in the sitting room, her blond hair, now loose, gracefully complimented by the wide collar of her sable coat.

This fur coat, which my father had brought back two months earlier from Siberia, along with a short ermine coat and muff for me— "What an idea, an ermine for an eight-year-old who is always so sloppy and takes so little care in her attire!"—had been the object of minute calculations over the course of the previous week. After an arduous campaign—including surprise attacks, strategic retreats, unexpected alliances, sudden changes of heart, and negotiations as subtle as they were dogged—my mother had managed to obtain an invitation to the opera on the night of a special gala in honor of the czar, who had come to Kiev to unveil a very ugly monument glorifying his father, Alexander, and to attend the races. The city's high society had fought bitterly for tickets. Though it must be said that these hard-won seats were located at the rear of a loge, behind a column that partly blocked the view of the stage, it is also true that my mother's first priority was to be seen, for which she would have ample opportunity during the three intermissions. She was only vaguely aware that Rimsky-Korsakov's *The Tale of Tsar Saltan* was on the program that evening.

Once the fortress had been conquered—in other words, once she had obtained an invitation to the gala—the real preparations began. The selection of a dress, its fabrication, the fittings, the parade of milliners, the errand boys burdened with unstable piles of hatboxes, all of this had exhausted the entire household. Mademoiselle Rose and I fled as often as we could for long walks in the gardens of the Cave Monastery, bathed in sunshine and overflowing with ragged pilgrims who came to pray in the churches and visit the catacombs.

We went to concerts in Pechersk Park, where lovers jealously defended the fragrant groves, and gobbled giant cherries sold out of buckets of ice by young Ukrainian women wearing white kerchiefs. We walked up to the plateau in the royal gardens and looked out over the harbor with its confusion of masts, white sails, and smoke from the steamboats. When it was too hot, we spent hours in the cool halls of the Idzikowski Library, each of us emerging with our four-book allotment before setting off to enjoy a sorbet on Khreshchatyk Boulevard. Sometimes we took the ferry to Trukhanov Island, where we rented a beach tent and I pretended to swim in my calf-length bathing bloomers, trying to impress Mademoiselle Rose, but with one toe secretly touching the bottom.

That summer, we crisscrossed the sunbaked city. Some days the air was filled with dust blown in by the dry winds from the Caucasus. We climbed stairs and steep streets, the sound of our footsteps echoing off the wooden pavement. We walked down boulevards beneath a canopy of plane trees and chestnuts, between rows of yellow-brick houses. We visited each of the city's squares, from the Contract House to the Golden Door, from Saint Sophia to town hall, with our noses in the air, straining to catch a glimpse of Saint Michael's sword glistening in the sunlight as we chewed on sunflower seeds from little paper packages and gulped down tumblers of ice-cold milk. It was as if a frenzy had come over me; in my mind those days are like a giant merry-go-round. I see myself dizzily spinning, giddy from the heat, with the bright foliage and blue sky flashing by, along with palaces, columns with white marble capitals, blue towers with silver or golden onion domes, pyramid-shaped poplars, and clumps of multicolored flowers. Every day I forced poor Mademoiselle Rose to leave the house as soon as we had taken our last bite of breakfast; she followed me around the city, suffocating in her tight lace collars, cheeks pink despite the parasol she always carried in one gloved hand. Perhaps I knew somehow, though there were as yet no warning signs, that I would never again see my beloved Kiev in summer. When, on our return, disheveled and sweaty, we peeked into my mother's room, she would be there in her corset, surrounded by mountains of shimmering fabrics and rustling tissue paper. In the middle of her room stood a mannequin with her measurements, austere and naked. She peered in our direction, barely recognizing us, her brow furrowed, and sent us away with an irritated wave of the hand.

The hat she finally selected was an enormous still life covered with more varieties of fruit than existed on this earth, even in the most exotic regions, and shaded with trembling feathers gathered at one end like a palm frond. Overcoming his astonishment, my father had remarked tactfully and sensibly that he was grateful their seats were in the third row of the loge, against a wall, thus avoiding complaints from spectators obliged to twist their necks uncomfortably to bypass the enormous obstacle. Now the issue of the coat had to be resolved. My mother had only allowed a few of her closest friends to glimpse her new sable coat and was hoping it would become the instrument of her ultimate triumph. But can one wear a fur in summertime? "Come now, you will be ten times too warm, Fanny!" my father protested. She argued that the season was turning and that the air was becoming decidedly cooler, especially toward evening. She scoured the sky for the slightest hint of a cloud to veil the accursed sun. A sudden change in the weather confirmed that God himself was on her side.

Invited in to admire her before their departure, I saw my mother encased in sea of green silk edged with pearls, savagely corseted, her bosom protruding like the bow of a ship, the sable draped over her shoulders, pink-faced with excitement beneath the geyser of feathers that hung over her eyes. There was no question of my kissing her—it would have spoiled her makeup—and instead she held out a plump hand for me to kiss. I felt the cold, hard surface of her emerald beneath my lips. As I raised my head I was forced to admit that I found her very beautiful, so blond, plump, and pale, encased in glistening fur. I envied her, especially the protective arm that my father placed around her shoulders and his satisfied, proprietary look. But on that particular night, I did not hold it against her.

Earlier that afternoon she had allowed me to go with her to the races to catch a glimpse of the czar, the grand duchesses, and especially the little czarevitch, Alexis. Dressed in white muslin, my hair mercilessly pulled back under a wide-brimmed hat with a large ribbon that tickled my cheek and cascaded down my neck, calves sheathed in black stockings which I had to pull up incessantly, I craned my neck to see the imperial carriage, curtsying each time my mother greeted an acquaintance with a graceful tilt of the head. In the roar of fanfares and applause I saw a young girl, dressed even more elegantly than I, present a bouquet to a pale little boy wearing a uniform bedecked with epaulettes and gold, medals and stars. He took a step back with a frightened expression and hid behind one of his sisters. My mother explained later that he suffered from a serious illness and could die from the slightest scrape; he had been instructed not to allow anyone to come closer than three paces. The surprised girl returned to her spot in the crowd, still clutching her flowers, and I thought how silly she was for not giving the flowers to the czar, whose face seemed so paternal with its blue eyes, upturned mustache, and beautiful brown beard. We went home early so that my mother would have several hours to prepare. After having dinner as usual in my room with Mademoiselle Rose, I went to bed and dreamed about this sad little boy who could neither skate nor sled, nor even play catch.

The scene that caused my mother's malaise and sudden return from the opera has been described to me in such detail that I feel as if I had been present. The setting is the magnificent hall of the Kiev Opera, still new at the time, with its crimson velvet seats, crystal chandeliers, and blue-tinted cigar smoke. In the audience one can see officers in their white uniforms and the sparkle of diamonds on ladies' necks. There are whispers and laughter, as well as much to-ing and fro-ing. It is the third intermission and most people are in their seats. Suddenly two shots ring out. Someone cries: "He's been shot!" Everyone turns toward the czar's loge. But below and to the left, in the third row of the orchestra, a tall bearded man, also dressed in white and wearing a wide blue sash, slowly crumples to the floor. Blood begins to spread across his tunic. As he falls, he has just enough time to shake his hand toward Nicholas, whether to bless him or to warn him no one will ever know. It is the prime minister, Stolypin. (Like many others, I spent the following day standing on the straw-covered sidewalk in front of the clinic where he lay dying for three days.) The czar, after leaning over the balustrade, disappears into the shadows. His guards surround him and his two daughters.

A young man walks calmly down the center aisle. A voice cries out: "It's him!" An officer jumps down from the dress circle and, with a blow, knocks him to the ground; he does not defend himself. He is dragged outside. Later it is revealed that he is a university student, Dmitri Grigoriyevich Bogrov, a graduate of High School Number 1 and a famous troublemaker. As Stolypin is carried out of the theater, the orchestra plays the imperial hymn three times in a row. The singers return, holding out their arms and calling "Hurrah!" toward the imperial loge. Someone in the audience cries "God save the czar!" and the rest of the audience rises and does the same. Nicholas does not reappear, and the police give the order to evacuate the house. When there is nothing left to see, the ladies remember that in such cases it is customary to faint. Their cavaliers carry them to their carriages or hackney cabs, which crowd into the square, creating chaos.

My father was supposed to leave in January on a long voyage. He was being sent by his bank to buy petroleum in Transcaucasia, in Baku, on the Caspian Sea, and I was worried about his safety. I thought of the 1905 riots that Assia had told me about. People said that the Armenians and the Tartars, who in 1905 had attacked each other in the shadow of the enormous, snowy Mount Elbrus, were ready to go at it again. My mother was concerned about me, or pretended to be. Kiev was in a state of agitation. At the beginning of the year, a Jewish laborer, Mendel Beilis, had been arrested and accused of stabbing a thirteen-year-old boy. People called it a ritual killing. Terrible details circulated. The man declared himself innocent but I was not convinced, so disturbing did he appear in the newspaper photographs, with his ferocious eyes set in a thicket of shaggy whiskers. Over the course of the long trial, it would eventually be revealed that Beilis—defended by such figures as Anatole France and Jean Jaurès—was in fact innocent and that the boy had been murdered by his mother's lover. But in 1911 this crime fed the furor of the anti-Semites, backed by the police and the government. Soon pogroms inflamed the city.

Stolypin's murder once again lit the fuse. The crime was attributed to the Israelites even though, as was said in liberal circles, the student had been armed by the police. Punitive expeditions ravaged the Podol district; men's throats were slit, women were raped, babies killed, shops pillaged. The administrative noose was tightened more than ever. The number of Jews admitted to the university was further reduced. Even a protest orchestrated in their defense by a group of students from this same High School Number 1—which I learned of from Kostik during one of our walks, and which I revealed to my parents—did little to reassure the Jewish population. In reaction to the restrictions placed on their Israelite schoolmates, who were required to obtain the top score in every subject in order to be accepted at university, the senior class had agreed to respond incorrectly to one Latin question in order to concede the highest marks to their Jewish classmates. My father admired their generosity but worried nonetheless.

Finally he gave in to my mother's supplications. She was too scared to stay in Kiev during several long months in this distressing atmosphere, alone with a child, a French governess, and a staff whose loyalty she claimed to be unsure of. She requested that he send us to France, where he would join us after he had completed his business. I was conflicted: on the one hand, I was frightened to leave my world—I had never seen anything beyond the Crimea, my native city, and its immediate surroundings—but on the other hand, I was curious to finally see the country Mademoiselle Rose had described to me at length, whose language I spoke perfectly, and whose literature I devoured in the small yellow volumes of the Bibliothèque Universelle. She looked forward to showing me around the city, and I must admit that at that age the adventure tempted me.

It was decided, then, that we would go to Paris, where my father had enough friends and relations to look after us. My mother was in a hurry to leave. He explained to her that some time was required for us to get organized and, in any case, he demanded that we travel first to Odessa in order to celebrate the New Year with my grandparents. He, who had lost his parents at a young age, was determined that we should maintain close family ties. All I knew about his parents were their names, Boris Némirovsky and Eudoxia Korsounsky, and their hometown, Elizabethgrad. He had never wanted to tell me more, and to this day, I can only weave obscure hypotheses regarding their origins. It was decided that he would accompany us to Odessa and that we would depart at the end of January; he would go to Baku, and we to Bucharest to board the Orient Express for Paris. My mother grumbled—the idea of spending an entire month in this provincial backwater in the middle of winter did not appeal to her in the least—but she had obtained so much that she did not make too much trouble.

We departed in December, leaving behind an empty, echoing, ghostly house draped in dust covers and steeped in the fragrance of mothballs. The train that greeted us on a glacial evening—wrapped in our furs, hats pressed down over our ears, and hands thrust into muffs as porters fussed over our mountain of luggage—was the famous *Courrier*. It traversed the six hundred and fifty kilometers between Kiev and Odessa overnight, at the then unheard-of speed of sixty-five kilometers per hour. The luxury of this train was also extraordinary; it contained only first-class carriages and one needed a special permit to be admitted on board. The seats were deep white-velvet armchairs with ample headrests and wide armrests which, when folded out, became soft beds. The rose-bouquet motif on the Aubusson carpets was echoed on the domed ceiling, and the compartment included a real bathroom with a porcelain tub, mahogany paneling, and crystal bottles. Each car was divided in two, with a sitting room in the middle. Furious, I dined there with my governess, while my parents headed off to the dining car in their chic evening attire.

When we arrived at ten in the morning, Odessa was completely white, buried under snow. The sleigh my grandparents had sent for us went down by the seafront, which was visible only as a steely gray mass beneath a sky filled with snowflakes. In 1925, just before it was banned, I saw Sergei Eisenstein's *Battleship Potemkin* in Paris but was unable to recapture the sense of wonder I experienced when I first saw the enormous staircase of ninety-two steps, dominated by a statue of Richelieu. In my mind it will never again be as deserted as on that day but rather overrun by boots, engulfed by the smoke of rifles, a baby carriage endlessly rolling down the stairs. At the time I noticed that several buildings still bore the traces of shells fired six years earlier by the mutinous sailors.

My mother did not enjoy visiting her parents, mainly because their house—however spacious and comfortable—was situated in the Jewish quarter, on the edge of the Moldavanka ghetto. It was not unusual to see portly ladies in wigs standing in the street with their hands on their hips, loudly calling out to each other in Yiddish, or cap-wearing louts with blue boots and crimson vests under sheepskin coats. There were bearded men everywhere, always rushing, carrying packages on their shoulders. My mother found all this to be the height of vulgarity, and I must admit that it frightened me. At first I stayed indoors, but the family library did not offer much distraction. It was full of somber volumes with ancient bindings and yellowing pages covered in Hebrew script, which inspired in me a kind of dark terror.

But I loved going down to the port with my grandfather to see the warehouses filled with wheat waiting to be loaded onto the gaping hulls of ships by a fleet of carts. I stood there for hours, despite the cold, my hand in his, watching the swarm of boats with their funnels and masts filling the water and sky as far as the eye could see. There was a deafening clamor by the quayside, with every language imaginable being spoken at once. Enormous stevedores passed by, bent under their heavy loads. French, English, and Russian officers struck them with a flick of the crop if they happened to accidentally cross their path. Turkish, Greek, and Malaysian sailors swayed, arm in arm, drunk on vodka or Jamaican rum, as they howled incompre-

PART I · 49

hensible songs. Boats came into the harbor filled to the brim with
glistening fish and were quickly surrounded by crowds of merchants
loudly discussing prices as the lilting fragrance of tea, oranges,
spices, and cigars disappeared beneath the more pungent, violent
fragrance of brine. When he noticed that I was frozen, my grandfather took me, despite my mother's strict instructions, to a smoky
tavern for a glass of scalding tea, after which we returned home. As
always, he was impeccably turned out and carried a cane, and I returned pink-cheeked, my eyebrows white with frost. Mademoiselle
Rose, who hated the cold and never joined us on these excursions,
cried out in horror on our return and promptly submerged me in a
scalding bath.

We celebrated the Russian New Year in Odessa. My grandmother, the sweet-natured Bella, had prepared a feast. We had an
enormous meal preceded by zakuski—salmon, caviar, smoked stur-
geon, salted cucumbers, and pâtés of all types—washed down with
vodka, followed by a series of dishes that combined traditional Russian Jewish cuisine with French and Russian recipes, from a pie
made with carp to boiled chicken, accompanied by a series of wines,
culminating in several bottles of champagne which we drank, as one
should, so cold that tiny icicles chimed against the crystal glasses. I
was allowed to take a few sips—after all, I would be nine in only a
month. I enjoyed the champagne so much that I discreetly finished
off what was left in several flutes and was able for the first time to
experience one of the pleasures of the adult world that was usually
denied to me. This love of champagne, of its sharp bubbles that
tickle the nose, is something that I have retained to this day: when I
was eighteen, it spiced up my crazy nights at the casino in Nice, as
well as my first flirtations, and it still sparkles every evening in the
glasses Michel places on a tray of delicacies from the pantry lorded
over by our cook, Kra, and which we consume in bed.

On that particular day, the champagne surely contributed to my
tantrum during dessert, when I was presented with my present.
Everyone watched expectantly as I removed, at first with care and
then with impatient abandon, the many layers of wrapping paper

decorated with mistletoe and holly encasing an enormous white box. The more padding I removed, the more anxious I became. I no longer remember what it was I so desired: books, probably, or perhaps a toy train. Instead what I discovered inside was an enormous porcelain doll, almost as big as I but different in every respect, with elegantly waved blond hair, unintelligent long-lashed eyes that opened and closed, and lace bloomers peeking out beneath a frilly pink dress. And there were more boxes, which I opened with increasing apprehension. They contained a tea set, a complete wardrobe, and even a tiny toiletry set with miniature perfume bottles, brushes, and an ivory nail buffer. My heart broke. I began to sob. That my mother might give me such objects, representing her idea of the perfect little girl, I could understand. That my grandmother, with her old-fashioned notions, might approve her choice, I could easily forgive. But that my grandfather, with whom I had spent so many hearty hours "among men," in places forbidden to children and especially to little girls, and, even worse, that my father, whom I constantly sought to impress with my precocious observations, could have been so blind, was truly intolerable. They ascribed the tears to my great joy—the doll had been ordered from Paris and cost a fortune—and to the champagne, compounded by exhaustion. I was sent off to bed. Only Mademoiselle Rose, who tucked me in that night, understood the real reason for my distress.

I confess, to my embarrassment, that I threw the accursed doll out a window of the Orient Express somewhere between Vienna and Munich. I may be forgiven for not remembering exactly where, for in midwinter the landscapes I saw as I stared out, scratching away at the frost on the windowpane, were all the same—white fields and pine forests—during the entire trip of fifty hours. I remember I undertook this criminal act on the second night, taking advantage of Mademoiselle Rose's absence while she performed her ablutions in the bathroom. I had seen my mother wearing a low-cut dress, opening the door to her compartment to an elegant young man with pomaded hair and taking his arm as they headed toward the café car. Our eyes met and I watched her walk away, after which I took the repulsive object by the hair, lowered the window, and with great difficulty because of her size and the cold wind that rushed into the compartment thrust her overboard, followed by the tea set, the wardrobe, and finally the toiletry set. I hope that some little daughter of a German or Austrian crossing guard found her intact in the snow and was able to love her.

If I am honest I must admit that the mistrust I felt toward my mother and the violent gesture it inspired in me poisoned our entire stay in Paris. Our difficult relationship came to a head six or seven months ago when I announced that I was pregnant and she begged me to have an abortion, using every possible argument, from the mess my life would become after the birth of a child at such a young age—I had just turned twenty-six!—to her eventual admission, mingled with tears, that she was not ready to become a grandmother. As a child in Paris I felt a vague sense of unease, and my feelings toward her were conflicted. I did not like the way men looked at her, and I had a secret desire to see her constantly in tears, enveloped in thick mourning during her separations from my father. I felt compelled to play the role of warden, though of course no one had asked me to.

This dark mood and compulsion to spy meant that I would not harbor the typical lyric memories of our journey on the Orient Express, the kind Valéry Larbaud would sing of in his *Barnabooth* the following year: "Lend me your vast noise, your gentle speed, your nightly slipping through a lighted Europe, O luxury train! And the agonizing music that sounds the length of your gilt corridors, while behind the japanned doors with heavy copper latches sleep millionaires..." I did not awake from my sullen torpor until our arrival at the Gare de l'Est where a liveried chauffeur, sent by the friend my father had asked to watch over us in Paris, organized our luggage and invited us aboard his motorcar, my first. At my request, he allowed me to sit next to him in the open air, enveloped in a goatskin and wearing a leather helmet which I had to hold with both hands so it would not slip down to my shoulders. My mother and Mademoiselle Rose settled in behind us. The speed and noise of the motor intoxicated me.

A furnished apartment had been rented for us in the neighborhood of Auteuil. I found it bright and comfortable compared to our old house in Kiev and especially compared to my grandparents' even older house in Odessa. Mademoiselle Rose and I had three rooms to ourselves: my bedroom, hers, and a schoolroom where she immediately began the job of making up for the time we had lost over the past few months. She established a very strict schedule, which we constantly violated due to my ardent desire to explore the city and her eagerness to point out the monuments we had so often spoken of during our lessons. I would recite my history or geography lesson at lightning speed and then we would jump into a cab driven by a man in a top hat or onto a horse-drawn bus (as in Kiev, except that here they did not ride on rails), steam bus, or double-decker.

Mademoiselle Rose was proud of my French, which was already very good and quickly improved even further through contact with the little boys in sailor suits whom I engaged in conversation at the Bois de Boulogne where I played with my hoop, or at the Luxembourg Garden where, despite her remonstrances—she reminded me that I was a girl and already nine years old—I lay on my stomach to tap with a stick the sailboat we had rented for five centimes, or perched for hours on the wooden horses that went up and down in the carousel, before quenching my thirst with licorice water from Père Clément's shop.

Even more than the "old" Paris—the Louvre, Notre Dame, and even the Eiffel Tower that loomed above the rhinoceros at the Trocadéro like a giant shepherdess with steel petticoats—I loved the Grand Boulevards, the crowds, the brightly lit cafés, the sidewalks heated by braziers and lined with merchandise overflowing from the shops, and the street singers who, after exhausting their repertoire and inviting their onlookers to join in the chorus, sold sheet music all around. At first we obeyed my mother, who spoke little French and perhaps for that reason never wandered farther than the Faubourg Saint-Germain or the Champs-Élysées, but gradually we began to stray beyond the boundaries she had set for us. One Sunday in April, just after the bloody arrest of the Bonnot Gang, we went for a walk near the prison, where I felt a delicious frisson as I watched the young gang members, their arms around their companions' supple waists.

I committed my greatest infraction in the company of Assia, my young aunt who was studying medicine and had already become a Parisienne after a year in the city. She often came to visit us, unrecognizable with her chignon, swing jackets, and gold wire-rimmed glasses. She escorted me one afternoon to the Closerie des Lilas where, sitting quietly with a cup of hot chocolate, I watched a strange and scraggly crowd moving about in the back, among whom I was still too young to recognize Soutine and Modigliani, Max Jacob and Ilya Ehrenburg, though the echo of Russian voices floated to my ears.

My mother went out often. In early spring she discovered the inadequacy of her wardrobe, which was quickly becoming more and more dated, with its ample outfits burdened with lace and pleats. For a time she adopted Japanese-style kimonos and Paul Poiret skirts, but she hesitated to throw away her corset as so many Parisian women were at the time, doing so only after one of her friends initiated her into a new dance that was all the rage in the dance halls of the capital, the tango, and which necessitated a supple waist and bare calves visible through a slit in the skirt. She began to frequent tea dances and went to the races. She seemed agitated; the *Titanic* disaster, which deeply affected the high-society circles to which many of its victims had belonged, excited her all the more. One day when I was walking with Mademoiselle Rose down the Corso in the Bois de Boulogne, I thought I caught a glimpse of her wearing a veil, sitting in a motorcar, head tenderly resting on a stranger's shoulder.

After the Grand Prix races, we left for Le Touquet, whose immense beaches, wind, wild grasses, and cold water I detested as much as I did the goat milk from the small herds that trotted across the beach, which was served at teatime. I still have a photograph from this holiday: I am standing in front of a painting depicting a furious storm at sea. In the midst of the waves, the mast of a boat lists dangerously; I am barefoot and standing upon a pale surface that looks more like a bear skin than an expanse of sand. In order to make the scene appear more realistic, I have rolled up the pant legs of my ever-present sailor suit. With a shrimp net thrown over my right shoulder, a wicker basket in my left hand, and a bucket bearing the words "Paris-Plage" at my feet, I look as somber as the stormy gray sky and as turbulent as the raging waters behind me.

At the Hotel Westminster, where children of course dined before their parents in a separate dining room, I never saw my mother. She awoke at approximately the hour when I was going to bed. Sometimes I caught a glimpse of her, looking ravishing on the arm of a young man, on the way to the casino. She bought a horrid Pomeranian, and one afternoon when she awoke earlier than usual to have tea with a Russian friend, I asked her if she was planning to go on playing the "Lady with a Lapdog" for long. She did not immediately understand the reference but her friend, who blushed and opened her eyes wide with horror, must have explained it to her because that night she appeared during dinner and announced in front of everyone that I would be punished, consigned to my room for forty-eight hours. I took advantage of the confinement to read the Chekhov story, whose subject I knew only secondhand.

Back in Paris, after two months of glum thoughts rendered only darker by the approach of a second winter, I wrote a long letter to my father in which, without going so far as to denounce my mother, I begged him to come for us, arguing that I hated Paris, which was untrue, and that I missed him terribly, which was true. He did not receive it: by then he had left Baku for St. Petersburg. We received a letter from there, in December, announcing his impending arrival. That same day, when I was bringing the letter to my mother, she announced that, having surrendered to the affectionate pressure of her friends, she would be leaving for Nice where a new palace—the Hotel Negresco—would soon be inaugurated on the Promenade des Anglais in the presence of seven sovereigns, including Queen Ranavalona of Madagascar. In an act of jealousy and hatred, the extreme cruelty of which still shocks me and fills me with shame—and which I have tried to analyze through the actions of the little girl Antoinette in my novel *The Ball*—I hid my father's letter. Sitting at her dressing table, my mother did not notice anything amiss; she left without realizing that my father was about to arrive. But the grand opening was postponed until January, and she was still in Nice when he showed up.

My bad behavior did not have the desired effect. Instead, it spoiled my reunion with my father. I did not have the courage to admit what I had done and was forced to simulate surprise when he appeared. White with anger at the idea that my mother had abandoned Mademoiselle Rose and me, he took the train to Nice the following morning. He did not return until two weeks later, assuaged and in love, his radiant wife on his arm. That night at dinner he announced his plans, which he had already revealed to my mother to her great joy. I was able to express neither sadness nor uncertainty, so suffocating was my remorse. We would not be returning to Kiev—he had already sold the house and all our furniture—and instead we would all move permanently to St. Petersburg where he had been sent for business.

OCTOBER 1942

Two officers have gone to the village school for the girl and her older sister and are taking them to the police station, at the end of the main road. All the windows facing the road are closed. In every house along the way, curtains are pushed aside as they go by. A two-year-old plays on the sidewalk. A door cracks open, an arm appears, and the child is pulled inside. The younger girl is proud to parade down the road in total silence, like a princess being escorted to her kingdom. She would like to hold the officers' hands. She knows them: three months earlier, they took her mother away on a trip. But her older sister, who walks beside her, very pale despite the beautiful yellow star sewn onto her lapel, stares down and bites her lips, gripping her hand firmly. Feeling the little girl wriggle, her sister grabs her wrist and squeezes it, twists it. The little girl whimpers a bit but then, seeing that no one notices, tries to wander off to play hopscotch along the way.

4

IN ORDER to love St. Petersburg, I believe one must be born there. During the four eventful, terrible years we lived there, even though I experienced more than a few poetic moments, especially in the spring and summer beneath the whispering foliage of its many islands, and even though I sought out the capricious shadows of Pushkin and Gogol in its crystalline beauty—before they were overwhelmed by the dark, convulsive shadow of Dostoyevsky's *Crime and Punishment*—I would never fully embrace the city. In part this was due to the sadness I felt at leaving, without forewarning and against my wishes, my beloved, ancient Kiev, my toboggan of a city, warm and gay, crisscrossed with alleyways and staircases. My heart bled. And secondly because my first contact with this cold, geometric, flat capital had been chilling in contrast to the liveliness of Paris, where I had spent many long months.

The train deposited us at the Nicholas Railway Station on a glacial day in early February. After watching the cortege of porters load a sleigh with our many suitcases, topped by my mother's hatboxes, our driver, chosen by my father from a thicket of whips brandished in the air to attract our attention, helped us climb onto his sleigh and covered us with furs. He was a giant, as wide as he was tall in his long, quilted, midnight-blue coat cinched at the waist with a red cloth belt under which he had secured his gloves. He wore a three-cornered velvet hat that covered his entire forehead. As he settled into the sleigh, he pulled a leather apron over his knees. Staring at his back, I felt a pang of nostalgia: he reminded me of the Michelin Man, who had recently begun to appear on advertisements in

France. Just a few days ago, in a Paris that now seemed so far away, this image had made me laugh.

A leaden sky bore down on the city. It had snowed overnight and we could feel a heavy layer of clouds above us, ready to burst once more. My parents, giddy with happiness, fidgeted in the sleigh, chattering and teasing each other; my mother fished for details about our new lodgings, but my father refused to reveal anything. I was silent. The Parisian boulevards had seemed wide compared to the narrow streets and even the main roads in Kiev. But the immensity of the Nevsky Prospect, thirty-five meters wide and rendered even more impressive by the absence of trees or fences, lined with buildings with lights shining inside, like beasts with yellow eyes, deserted and covered with a thick layer of white snow, chilled my heart. Mademoiselle Rose, unhappy under her fur hat, pressed against me in her long coat; she knew what I felt and took my hand. The sleigh flew over the snow. The blades rustled in the silent city. The horse snorted and shook its mane to remove the frost. From time to time, a block of ice dropped from a drainpipe to the ground with a dull thud.

We crossed elaborate metal bridges with creaking struts, over three frozen rivers—the Fontanka, the Catherine Canal, and the Moika—passing spectacular buildings which my father pointed out one by one. Here was the baroque Beloselsky-Belozersky Palace, with its vigorous Atlases supporting cream-colored pilasters against a red façade. And the town hall, housing the Duma; he told us that in the case of a fire, balloons of different colors were raised on its spire, each color indicating the neighborhood that had been affected. The spire was also used as semaphore to exchange messages with the czar at his palace at Tsarskoye Selo. My father pointed out the massive Roman colonnades of the Cathedral of Our Lady of Kazan in the distance; on our right we could see the Church of the Savior on the Spilled Blood, built on the exact spot where a bomb had shattered Czar Alexander II's legs. Everything here spoke of violence, fire, and murder.

Irritated by my father's gleeful chattering, furious that he did not seem to notice my depression, and determined to make him aware of it, I closed my eyes. I did not open them again until my governess whispered to me that we were about to pass No. 18 of the Nevsky Prospect, the address of Wolf and Béranger, the pastry shop where Pushkin had met his friend Danzas on January 27, 1837, before heading off to his fatal duel with the Frenchman Georges d'Anthès. "As for you, you arrogant descendants / of fathers famed for their base infamies,"* I hissed through clenched teeth, invoking Lermontov's booming words on the death of Pushkin, whom all of Russia had mourned and was still mourning seventy-six years later. In this terrible city of bronze, granite, and marble, pressed to the ground under a sky like a funerary slab, how long, I wondered, would I survive?

The Winter Palace and the enormous square at its center out of which loomed the Alexander Column, taller than the obelisk in the Place de la Concorde; the endless row of ocher-colored façades with their greenish roofs peeking through the snow here and there—all this chilled me. It looked like a cemetery filled with frozen elephants covered by a layer of ivory. I had begun to study our history after the autumn afternoon in Kiev when my aunt Assia and her friend Kostik told me about the Revolution of 1905. I was unable to hold back a shiver as I imagined the events of Bloody Sunday unfolding in this grandiose setting. On that day the army had fired into a crowd of workers who had come to present their petition to their "little father," the czar, led by Gapon, an Orthodox priest. My memory of the chocolates and meringues laid out on lace doilies at the cozy Kircheim pastry shop merged with a surge of emotion and I almost burst into tears. The golden arrow of the Admiralty building stabbed the gray sky. Some verses by Osip Mandelstam returned to me:

> Stone, became a web,
> A lace fragility:
> Let your thin needle stab
> The empty breast of sky.‡

We turned left onto Bolshaya Morskaya Street and caught a glimpse of the bronze statue in the middle of Mariinsky Square: a horse prancing on its granite pedestal beneath the weight of Nicholas I, sitting heavily in the saddle. Finally we came to a stop. It was on this wide avenue, on the bank of the Moika between the Yusupov Palace and the Conservatory of Music, one of the most elegant streets in the city, that my father had located a vast apartment occupying the entire first floor of a private house. Once the luggage had been unloaded with the help of a very urbane *dvornik* and we had climbed the beautiful staircase, we rang the bell and a servant opened the door. I was frozen with amazement as I entered the tiled vestibule. Before me lay a long series of luminous white-and-gold rooms, their number further augmented by countless mirrors. Persian carpets covered the parquet floors, which gleamed with wax. Saffron-colored curtains, elegantly tied back, hung in graceful folds on either side of the tall windows. The rooms were filled with tables, armoires, vases, couches and chairs upholstered in silk and velvet, and lamps with painted glass shades. I even caught a glimpse of a lacquered white piano.

My mother was also frozen. Suddenly putting down her enormous muff, still wearing her dripping fur coat, she began to rush from room to room, now touching a bibelot, now taking a few steps back to admire it from a distance. She disappeared in a whirlwind, her high-pitched squeals of pleasure echoing from the sonorous depths of the apartment, and then returned to throw herself in my father's arms, embracing him effusively before exploding into sobs of joy. He placed his chin on her dripping-wet sable toque and patted her back as he looked at me ecstatically.

"And you, Irotchka?" he asked in Russian, despite my mother's directive that I should be addressed only in French. "You have said almost nothing since our arrival. What do you think of your new home? Do you like it as much as your mother does?"

I fiddled with my gloves. The sourish smell of fresh paint and varnish tickled my nose. Mademoiselle Rose gave me a little shove with her elbow. Faced with my parents' expressions of happiness, which were so rare when they were together and almost never simultaneous, I could no longer sulk. And though the art-nouveau style of this apartment pleased me less than it did my mother—I had heard her exclaim over a very similar decor in Paris at the home of one of her friends—I was still dumbfounded by its extravagance. There was no comparison between this luxury and the bourgeois comfort of our old home in Kiev.

"So, Father, have you become very rich?" I asked naïvely.

"I've done some good deals," he answered. "And one could not dream of better conditions for business. Russia is becoming modernized more quickly than one could have imagined even a few years ago. The world is calm, except for these insignificant quarrels in the Balkans. They say that the czar has realized that he must place the reins of power in the hands of industrialists. We are heading for great times, my darling, I can feel it. With a little courage, work, and good luck, I'll build a brilliant future for you."

I gazed at him with admiration. My mother embraced him even more tightly. They wandered off, arm in arm, to explore their new domain. Mademoiselle and I followed them to discover ours.

We had arrived in St. Petersburg in time to take part in the lavish ceremonies marking the tercentenary of the Romanovs. Like everyone, we went to applaud the imperial family on the square in front of the Winter Palace, where they stopped on their way to a thanksgiving mass at the Cathedral of Our Lady of Kazan. The wings of the golden angel atop the rose-colored Alexander Column seemed to shield the soldiers of the Pavlovsky Regiment as they stood with their rifles held obliquely across their chests, wearing their blue wool uniforms and strange mitres whose origins date back to the time of Frederick the Great. Against the backdrop of the imperial palace, the czar, flanked by two rows of soldiers with bayonets, drove by in an open carriage drawn by two white horses whose nostrils emitted clouds of vapor; little Alexis sat next to his father. Behind them, in another carriage, traveled the empress and the grand duchesses. Their faces were pink with cold beneath their sparkling tiaras.

The crowd began to cheer. I stood on my tiptoes, straining to get a better view, until my father took pity on me and gave me permission to climb onto a stool carried there by a prescient young man who was kind enough to share its tiny surface with this frozen bundle of fur—me. The snow on his long hair melted and dripped down my neck. The czar waved his hand and cried out to the soldiers "Hello, children!" A chorus of bass voices replied with a thunderous "Good health, your Imperial Majesty!" I was transfixed. The noisy echoes of trumpets and drums ricocheted against the yellow walls of the palace. At my insistence, we followed the procession. The clamorous, lurching crowd went completely silent in front of the cathedral as Nicholas, pale and serious, descended from the carriage and gestured toward one of his Cossacks. This giant, dressed in red with a cape flung over one shoulder, bent down to pick up the pale, thin czarevitch, obviously unable to walk on his own, and carried him inside.

An almost palpable shudder went through the crowd before the ovations and singing recommenced, like a warning of the upheavals to come, despite my father's optimistic predictions. His opinion, however, seemed further confirmed by the events of that year, 1913. As I walked along the quays and canals, through petrified gardens and down the immense rectilinear avenues, pressed against Mademoiselle Rose's muff for warmth, it seemed to me that nothing could imbue this artificial city with life. I thought of Hermann, the murderous gambler outdone by the diabolical maneuvers of the spectral Queen of Spades. My parents were swimming in happiness.

My father had taken a leap into the world of large-scale speculation. Admittedly, political reform did not come as quickly as he had predicted, and one strike followed another just as in 1905; the Czar's secret police, the Okhrana, arrested people left and right, sending them into exile or locking them up in the already overcrowded Peter and Paul Fortress; the Dumas came and went, dissolved as soon as they fell in line with the liberal majority; and the scandalous Beilis trial revealed the profound anti-Semitism of the Russian justice system. But at that time in Russia everything—oil, forests, textiles, furs, grains, and especially stocks—was bought and sold at a frenetic pace.

At home in our sumptuous apartment, we often had guests. Almost every night I came downstairs to curtsy to oily, cigar-smoking businessmen flanked by their young wives sheathed in silk, wearing pencil skirts with box pleats like Oriental pantaloons and tiered tunics with flounces, their small heads wrapped in feather-adorned turbans, necks bedecked with several strands of pearls, long cigarette holders at their lips. They caressed my cheek, in a cloud of Turkish tobacco, while an amateur pianist plucked out the notes of a tango, surrounded by a swarm of chattering girls, champagne flutes in hand. The men played cards and talked about money in an incomprehensible language in which foreign-sounding words—many of them American—were strung together nonsensically.

I know almost nothing about Yiddish literature, though I've been told that it contains some gems, but I've recently discovered a Russian translation of a hilarious novel by Sholem Aleichem. It tells of the tribulations of a Jewish man, Menahem-Mendl, the optimist, who leaves his hometown of Kasrilevke in order to invest his wife's dowry of 1,500 rubles in the markets of Odessa, and later in Kiev. In his missives to his wife, the imprudent man describes the "*hausses*," "*baisses*," "variations," and "stallages" that affect the markets for "Londons" (pounds sterling), "Berlins," "Petersburgs," "Potfolios," and other "papers" of various sorts for which the unfortunate man spends real cash on the self-interested advice of corrupt brokers. Like Mr. Menahem-Mendl and his unfortunate wife, I understood none of my father's feverish business discussions with his friends. At one point Mrs. Menahem-Mendl writes to her husband begging him to return to his family: "Even if you were to chop my head off, I still wouldn't understand what kind of merchandise it can be if it's invisible. A cat in a sack?... Listen to me, Mendl, I don't like it. In my father's home, I wasn't accustomed to such airy affairs, and may the almighty continue to preserve me from them. As mother says, God bless her, 'From the air, all one can catch is a cold.'"* More recently, during the last month since news of the crash in the United States reached us, I have often thought back to that time. The newspapers are filled with horrible stories—ruined bankers throwing themselves out of the windows of New York skyscrapers, families reduced to poverty—but my father, husband, and the rest of our relations have assured me that the crisis will not reach Europe and that the frenzy of speculation worldwide belies no danger of catastrophe.

I was slightly ashamed when I heard of Beilis's innocence, and blamed my quasi-certitude of his guilt two years earlier in Kiev on my childish ignorance and the servants' salacious gossip. I who had never set foot in a synagogue—not even in Odessa where my grandfather longed to take me but was prevented from doing so by my mother—and who was showered with presents on every Orthodox holy day, I who had seen so few Jews (no surprise since St. Petersburg was open to only a tiny number, most of them bankers, important business owners, industrialists, or lawyers, and almost all of them atheists since the Enlightenment), I could not understand why this dangerous label of "Israelites" still applied. One day I suggested to my father that he convert and have us all baptized, a straightforward, commonsense solution which I naïvely imagined had never occurred to him. I remember he had just returned from the Egorov baths, where he had gone to freshen up after lunch at his club. He ran his hand through his wet hair and went pale, contemplating me in amazement and mumbling something about my saying silly things, but without offering a single contrary argument. This conversation left me very confused; normally he made an effort to take me seriously and answer my questions.

When my parents were not receiving guests at home, they went out. My natural curiosity overcame my instinctual misgivings about the city, and I quickly agreed to join them whenever given the chance. In June 1913, at the property of some friends on the Gulf of Finland, I experienced my first white night. That afternoon on the lawn of their little rococo château I had played an intense game of croquet amid gesticulations and cries that left my throat dry and my voice ragged despite several glasses of lemonade, followed by a game of badminton. In the evening we ate a sumptuous picnic in a forest of larches and pines, the trees in silhouette against the eternal twilight, while shrieking seagulls streamed by. Tired of running in the dunes with the other children, I collapsed on a plaid blanket and rested my head on my father's thigh; without seeming to note my presence, he balanced his champagne flute on my head. As far as the eye could see, gray sand merged with the pearl-colored sea in which here and there patches gleamed like giant flat fish with shimmering scales. The wooden stilts of the bathing huts were black stripes in the mauve sky and the cranberry bushes rustled in the breeze. The warm air was fragrant with sap, heliotrope, and tidal waters. I fell asleep amid the murmur of conversations and did not awake until the next day, at home in my own bed.

Several times I went with them to lunch at elegant restaurants, such as Donon on Morskaya Street. The silverware and crystal sparkled beneath a flood of electric light and one could order Portuguese oysters, French wines, and exotic fruits no matter the season. That year my parents did not take their holidays in France as usual because they were so happy in St. Petersburg. They took me to cheerful open-air cafés on the islands where Gypsy orchestras played. I cannot say whether I loved or hated these Gypsies; the men were small and thin, their gaze reduced to a narrow yellowish slit beneath heavy lids. They would come to our table, so close that they almost touched me, their chins pressed against the blond wood of their violins. The women had dark eyes and black hair pulled back into a chignon held in place with combs; they wore crimson skirts and gaudy shawls. Their heavy sandalwood perfume went to my head as they sidled toward me, holding out a glass of vodka on an overturned saucer—which of course I did not touch—and dedicating one of their savage songs to me. Even though I knew they did this at the behest of my father—he would discreetly slip a hundred-ruble note into their bodice—the intensity of their large pupils, the brutal acceleration of their cadences, the painful crescendo of their deep, nasal voices brought tears to my eyes while at the same time pinning me to my seat in an attitude of submission.

It is hard to imagine now the musical, literary, and theatrical ferment that existed in Russia during that time, later baptized the Silver Age, when even a ten-year-old girl like me could relish the message of Alexander Blok's song:

> The tempest roars,
> The ocean sings,
> Snow whirls,
> The Century
> A receding blast,
> We dream of a happy shore!*

At the Mariinsky, I saw *Swan Lake* danced by Anna Pavlova. My parents gave me season tickets to the French classical plays at the Mikhailovsky Theatre. I went every month with Mademoiselle Rose. I heard Chaliapin, wearing a brocade caftan, sing *Boris Godunov*. I was even lucky enough to see *The Cherry Orchard* in the incredibly modern Moscow Art Theatre production staged by Stanislavsky, who came to the city every year. I emerged stirred by a profound melancholy that has burrowed shamefully deep into my soul and still lingers there, rising to the surface in moments of irrational panic when I stare distractedly at my husband, children, belongings, and the entire cocoon I have built around me. I imagine that I can hear Varya's voice saying, "The place will be sold in August."

My mother frequented the Eliseev Brothers' department store and the elegant Morskaya Street boutiques, but I preferred the covered market of Gostiny Dvor, whose two hundred stalls offered—amid emanations of perfume and spices—a formidable collection of bric-a-brac, much of it from the Orient. Beneath the market's arcades, among a dizzying variety of national costumes, one encountered all the peoples of Russia. A thousand dialects intersected, accompanied by the crackling of abaci. There was a hint there of my old Kiev.

I still did not love St. Petersburg but was no longer completely resistant to its charms. The autumn, dripping with mist and damp smoke, and the winter, helmeted with ice, had driven me shivering into my shell. But now I noticed that the slightest glimmer of sun shimmered like a playful flame against the windows of the palaces. The domes of the cathedrals were slowly beginning to reappear, green and gold, from beneath their white covering, and the squares began to reveal trees that had been invisible the day before. What had felt like a melancholy city seemed to wink gaily, transforming itself magically into a giant toy box. Once again I began to venture out, staring up at the sky and all around me.

I have a particularly strong memory of the spring of 1914. One day, I went with Mademoiselle Rose to watch an extraordinary spectacle: the ice breaking up on the Neva. She had permitted this distraction because we had been making steady progress in my studies. She was responsible for most of my lessons, complemented by Russian, in which I was tutored by a university student. The only thing missing were piano lessons, which I refused despite my mother's scolding, perhaps because I feared the abominable exhibitions in friends' drawing rooms that were often imposed on piano pupils wearing little white dresses, their hair tied back with ribbon. On that day, all of St. Petersburg crowded the shores of the river. Lugubrious crackling was the prelude to the breaking up of the ice. Enormous blocks, veritable icebergs like the one that had destroyed the *Titanic*, crashed into each other like polar bears standing on their hind legs, abandoning themselves to epic battles before being swept away by the current, their course marked by sudden hesitations, waltz-like swirls, uncertain leaps, and unexpected accelerations. A faint odor emanated from the liberated waters, as if an entire drowned population were rising to the surface. I remember how, turning away from the waters in disgust, I was seized with fright as I saw, rearing up before me, small, nauseous, and weak in my ocelot fur coat, the terrifying statue of the bronze horseman, Peter the Great. The steed's front hooves clawed the air, seemingly about to come crashing down on my head.

There is no more famous or more often recited poem in the entire history of Russian literature than Pushkin's "The Bronze Horseman." With its violent, jerky rhythms, it tells the story of an unfortunate man who rushes through the city after losing his family to a tragic flood. Overcome with madness, he dares to rail at the czar who decreed that St. Petersburg should be built on a marsh.

> He shivered with bitter fury, then
> took headlong flight. He had the impression
> that the grim czar, in sudden race
> of blazing anger, turned his face
> quietly and without expression . . .
> and through the empty square he runs,
> but hears behind him, loud as guns
> or thunderclap reverberation,
> ponderous hooves in detonation
> along the shuddering roadway—
> as, lighted by the pale moon-ray,
> one arm stretched up, on headlong course,
> after him gallops the Bronze Rider,
> after him clatters the Bronze Horse.
> So all night long, demented strider
> wherever he might turn his head—
> everywhere gallops the Bronze Rider
> pursuing him with thunderous tread.*

This image often returned to me, thwarting my surges of affection for the city as that fatal year of 1914 progressed. In June we were preparing to leave for Nice when the heir to the throne of the Hapsburgs, Archduke Francis Ferdinand, was assassinated. Despite the fact that the "insignificant quarrels" in the Balkans my father had spoken of upon our arrival had not been resolved, that the world had divided itself into two hostile camps—the Triple Entente and the Triple Alliance—and that all of Europe was arming itself, no one believed there would be a war. My mother considered the cancellation of our trip to France a kind of personal affront. The foreign minister, Sazonov, made one soothing declaration after another. When Austria, soon supported by Germany, presented Serbia—a Russian ally—with an unacceptable ultimatum, practically none of the newspapers imagined that the kaiser would send his soldiers against his beloved "cousin Nicky." The czar, for his part, was only mildly alarmed and ordered a general mobilization, then changed his mind and called it a partial mobilization. In early July, Petersburgers greeted President Poincaré with a parade down the Nevsky Prospect, with Cossacks on horseback wearing belted red tunics, baggy trousers tucked into their boots, and Astrakhan hats. The bravos and laughter of the crowds further illustrated that no one, or almost no one, expected the worst.

And then, on August 1, the bombshell fell: Germany had declared war on Russia. The following day offered an unforgettable spectacle, a lesson in destiny's tricks and the instability of peoples. The czar gathered the entire court and all the foreign ambassadors and functionaries, five or six thousand people in all. They stood in the enormous St. George's Hall in full evening dress. After a mass celebrated with all the pomp of the Orthodox liturgy, during which the protodeacon called upon the soldiers to fight "with sword in hand and the Cross upon your heart," the czar read a manifesto that ended with these words: "I hereby take a solemn pledge not to conclude peace so long as a single enemy remains on Russian soil... Through you I address my armies, united in nation and spirit, strong as a granite wall, and bless them in their historic task." With these words he echoed the declaration made in 1812 by his ancestor, Alexander I. I proudly taught this declaration to my governess, having learned it from my Russian tutor with whom I was reading *War and Peace*. The hall exploded in cheers, echoed by the cheering of the crowd that had gathered beneath the palace windows. All the bells of the city rang with a deafening clamor; thousands of people knelt down as one to sing "God Save the Czar!" and waved banners reading "Help the poor people of Serbia!" People cried and jumped with joy, they kissed; a stranger picked me up in his arms and I succumbed to a terrible asthma attack. Mademoiselle Rose had to struggle to get me home in the midst of the celebrations.

This was but the first of many manifestations of allegiance to the czar and the beginning of an extraordinary period during which all members of the opposition, including striking workers, liberals, Socialist Revolutionaries, and even Marxists and anarchists seemed to melt away as if by magic or at the very least to blend into the crowds acclaiming the sovereign. The press proclaimed: "The president of the Duma has said to our enemies, 'You thought that discord and hatred were everywhere in our land, when in fact all the peoples of this vast Russia and all the political parties have merged into a single fraternal family to save the endangered fatherland.' Whatever trials he faces, the Russian bogatyr will not be brought down; his brave shoulders will persevere and when the enemy has been driven back, our fatherland, united and indivisible, will blossom in peace, happiness, and fulfillment in the glow of its inalterable glory." I had the growing sense that I had been transported to the time of the Napoleonic Wars and sometimes I secretly imagined myself to be not Natasha Rostova crying at the deathbed of Prince Andrei but rather her younger brother Petya, chomping at the bit, eager for the smell of gunpowder.

It was marvelously exciting to walk around the streets of the city that summer—at least for me. But it was becoming increasingly difficult to drag Mademoiselle Rose out of the house. The spontaneous demonstrations that formed around the imperial banner and the impromptu processions behind the young men who had been mobilized made her extremely uneasy. As in France, the soldiers went to the train stations with flowers in their rifles, laughing and making grotesque threats against the Austro-Germans. I spent the month of September negotiating our outings, sulking, cajoling, haggling. Wearing a little checked cotton dress and a light summer coat, a large straw hat cocked insolently on my head, I dragged Mademoiselle Rose across an unrecognizable St. Petersburg in which all sorrow and coldness seemed to have disappeared forever. Her reluctance to go out made me regret that I no longer had playmates my own age, as I had in Paris and Kiev. I had made little effort to acquire friends: I automatically detested the daughters of my mother's friends, and the spectacle of young students from the Smolny Institute—inaccessible to me in any case due to my Jewish origins—in their white pinafores, short canvas capes, and pleated muslin bonnets, or of the sneering schoolboys in their blue Russian blouses with silver buttons and caps pulled down over their foreheads, inspired a certain disdain in me after my Parisian experience.

This delicious state of intoxication lasted until early autumn. It was fed by our initial victories, credited to the Grand Duke Nicholas, a friendly colossus, uncle of the czar, who was in charge of Russia's armies. My father—whom I barely saw during the day because of his many business engagements but who came to my room at night to tuck me in and give me what he quite seriously referred to as my "daily briefing"—lived in a state of exaltation. We had pushed the Germans back into western Prussia, reassured the French—who were in great need of reassurance—and attacked Galicia. Even our crushing defeats in Tannenberg and in the Masurian Lakes region, followed by further setbacks in the south, did not trouble him. A surprisingly calm climate of optimism and kindness reigned. Strangers greeted one another in the street, impromptu orators launched into patriotic tirades that were received with enthusiastic applause, and street vendors handed out flowers to soldiers so that they could place them in the buttonholes of their greatcoats. Never have I been on better terms with my mother, neither before nor since. When she returned from her shopping excursions, arms laden with packages, newly svelte in her close-fitting dresses, blond hair curled at the temples, accompanied by the jangle of dancing pearls, she would come up to my classroom and warmly inquire after my progress, caressing my hair before disappearing again to change for the next party.

The weather was beginning to cool. There were scattered rain showers. A yellowish fog began to rise from the Neva, like a hallucination: One night, I thought I saw Gogol's nose rushing off in the frayed coils of fog, wearing a plumed tricorne as it fled from its former proprietor, Major Kovalyov. Another time, I caught a glimpse of the overcoat belonging to the unfortunate titular counselor Akaky Akakievich, flying through patches of mist. The mist merged with the stinking fumes of the factory chimneys over by the French quay, beyond the Nicholas Bridge, on Vasilievsky Island, inhabited by workers who were beginning to stir as they slept on their uncomfortable mattresses in sweaty dormitories, and to whom no one gave a thought.

JANUARY 1943

The child roars with laughter, bouncing up and down under a starry sky. The nun who is carrying her to the cellar scurries across the cobbled courtyard, her wimple rustling and rosary beads clicking. Sirens moan like cows waiting to be milked. The even drone of airplanes overhead changes pitch and rhythm and becomes the buzzing of a hornet in her ear. Dark packages fall slowly from the sky. They see flashes in the distance. The little girl stares at the lights, sighing with wonder, watching the sparks through her fingers. Something is burning. "Don't be afraid," a farmer's daughter says to the child's sister. "It's nothing at all."

5

ST. PETERSBURG — "Peter" to insiders — was renamed Petrograd at the start of the war in an attempt to erase its Germanic origins. From the first months of 1915, the atmosphere in the city had changed completely. The previous autumn, the few injured soldiers returning from the front were received at the train station by large crowds and celebrated with great fanfare, decorated, acclaimed, covered in flowers, and then led with great pomp to the hospitals, where they were received by doctors and nurses happy to make use of their brand-new facilities. Then, suddenly, there were too many of them. The trains arrived, filled with decrepit young men on stretchers, boys with sunken chests or hopping on one leg, leaning on the shoulder of a comrade wearing head bandages. Now only old women in shawls scurried to the quayside to stare avidly into the faces of the returning soldiers and beg for news of their own sons. The regular passengers averted their eyes.

I was twelve years old and had begun to read the newspapers, with my father's approval and despite my mother's displeasure. She thought it was dangerous for young girls to be exposed to the lurid "news in brief" items, which she herself consumed with relish. I complained that she treated me like a child, dressing me in outfits which were too young for my age and insisting that I wear ribbons in my hair. She refused to acknowledge that I was beginning to develop breasts, and the previous year I had not even bothered to tell her that I was pubescent; long before, Mademoiselle Rose had explained what it all meant and what measures I should take. I discussed the events of the day with my father, in the few moments I had with him; most days he shut himself in the parlor with his colleagues or his business partners as soon as he returned from the stock exchange or the bank. The reports in the press were still triumphant, but the dry tone of the official communiqués belied the truth. We were being beaten back on all fronts: in Galicia as well as in Poland, where General Alekseyev was retreating—though he did so with panache—and where the local population had been evacuated. We did not know the numbers of casualties, but we imagined them to be enormous. Little by little, the truth seeped out. We heard that there was a shortage of weapons and supplies, that the government had foreseen a short war lasting at most twelve weeks, that soldiers were arriving at the front without weapons and were receiving orders to arm themselves by stripping enemy cadavers. People spoke more and more openly of the incompetence of the minister of war, Vladimir Sukhomlinov, who had been relieved of his position by the Duma when it convened briefly in August. A short time later, an article appeared in the *Russian News* entitled "A Tragic Situation: The Pilot Has Gone Mad." It was a transparent metaphor for the state of the country under the leadership of the czar. The pamphlet, which my father brought back from his club, was passed from hand to hand, eliciting scandalized and delighted exclamations.

Among my father's usual guests, several joined one of two organizations created by Prince Georgy Lvov, president of the Provisional Government: the Union of Zemstvos and the Union of Towns. They did their best to offset the official shortages and coordinate efforts. My father was invited to join the War Industries Committee, which attempted to speed up the production of and, more important, the delivery of arms to the front. The pitiful state of the railway system was creating havoc with the supply routes. My mother, encouraged by her friends who tried to outdo one another in their patriotic zeal, decided to volunteer for the Red Cross; now when she invited her friends to tea, no one was idle and the piano remained silent. The ladies shredded linen for bandages while they ate petits fours. In the evenings, when the gentlemen arrived to escort their wives home, I passed around an alms purse with an embroidered cross for those who lingered in the sitting room with a glass of port; they dropped in a few rubles. They applauded my sense of duty and pretended to be amazed at my transformation into a serious young lady who would soon be pinning up her hair and wearing long dresses. My mother laughed, reminding them of my age, which she seemed to forget with surprising ease, obstinately shaving off at least a year. I quietly corrected her and thanked them with a curtsy, but I would have liked to do more: wear a nurse's uniform, for example, like Florence Nightingale. I longed to sit with injured soldiers, encouraging them with my warm words, or to console the dying with an angelic smile. When I spoke to my father about this, he would shrug his shoulders and advise me to focus on my studies. Desperate to do something useful, I decided to knit wool socks for the soldiers but was constantly dropping stitches. The cook, who was the only person in the house who knew how to knit, soon grew tired of seeing me rush up to her with flailing needles, and suggested that I try something simple, like a scarf.

Mademoiselle Rose worried about her family in France, especially her nephew, who had been mobilized in August 1914 and about whom she had no news; the mail arrived with long delays, if at all. According to the newspapers, things were going as badly there as they were here. I could feel her withdrawing from me more and more. Sometimes during our lessons she forgot the topic of discussion. She would stare vaguely into the distance as I went on and on about Zola's *Germinal*, which I was reading at the time and which had inspired generous liberal feelings in me. She would finger the medallion she wore on a black velvet ribbon, and which, I knew, contained a photo of the young soldier. She was less and less interested in what was going on in the city. It was as if Russia, to which she had become so attached over the years—though she had never managed to learn the language—was becoming a foreign place. I would furtively observe her when she was lost in thought and she, who had always seemed ageless to me, looked older now, not only because of the increasing number of silver threads in her chestnut hair but because her complexion was beginning to lose its freshness. Though she always powdered her face coquettishly, I could see that it was now covered in fine lines.

As I walked around the city, I noticed that the shop windows were beginning to look empty. Gone was the extraordinary abundance of recent times, stores crammed with exotic merchandise, cherries framed in snow in midwinter, giant Turkish grapes at Easter, piles of braided, sculpted breads decorated with cardamom or ginger, cakes and brioches. The pastry cart that arrived with our ritual Viennese hot chocolate at Krafft had become less opulent. It was becoming difficult, my father said, to find good cigars at Ten Cate or shoes for two hundred rubles at Weiss. The windows of Fabergé on Morskaya Street still featured a row of serene gold-and-enamel eggs, an extravagant specimen of which the czar still gave the empress each year, as well as bouquets of flowers made up of emerald leaves and sapphire petals with a diamond in the center. But these were like the remnants of another world, enduring in the midst of the penury that was beginning to set in. Even at the Gostiny Dvor covered market, the deliveries of French perfumes, Siberian furs, and Chinese tea were beginning to taper off. I had overheard the servants saying that in the poorer neighborhoods like Narva and Vyborg there were lines outside the shops and that people often left empty-handed. Once again there were strikes; at the Putilov Factory, twenty thousand workers took part, and there were barricades, though they were soon swept away.

And then there was the monk Rasputin. It was to him that three-quarters of the Russian population attributed the blame for all these disasters. People whispered that he claimed he could heal the czarevitch's hemophilia, and thus had enormous influence not only over Empress Alexandra but over the czar himself. I had heard terrible stories of his debauchery. It was said that he had been accused of several rapes; in 1914, before the start of hostilities, a prostitute had shot and wounded him. It was clear that he played an important role in the affairs of state: ministers came and went, all of them ineffectual and all appointed on his advice, or so people claimed. My father supported Professor Milyukov, leader of the Kadet Party in the Duma, with whom he had several friends in common. He explained to me that after much hesitation Nicholas was leaning more and more toward a harsh stance and was refusing to cooperate with the Progressive Bloc. In particular the negotiations regarding the status of the Jews, which this group of deputies had proposed liberalizing, had fallen apart despite the support of right-wing ministers who argued with a certain cynicism that international aid would be easier to obtain if the laws restricting the activities of the Jews were abolished. Nicholas's wife, Alexandra—who, we were constantly reminded, was German by birth—was pushing him to further reinforce his autocratic stance. The final straw came when the czar forced the still-popular Grand Duke Nicholas to give up his post, taking over his role as supreme commander of the armies. There were rumors of plots within his entourage, and some said that an officer from the air force had concocted a plan to crash a plane into his carriage. For the first time I heard people in my parents' house openly pronounce the word "revolution" unchallenged.

I didn't know what to think. I remembered Turgenev's *Virgin Soil*; I had been deeply touched by Nezhdanov's suicide, and especially the postscript to his final letter to his beloved: "Oh! Something more: you will think, perhaps, Marianna, 'He was afraid of the prison where they would certainly have put him, and he thought of *this* expedient to escape it.' No; imprisonment's nothing of any consequence; but to be in prison for a cause you don't believe in— that's really senseless. And I am putting an end to myself, not from dread of being in prison. Good-bye, Marianna! Good-bye, my pure, spotless girl!"* Was this a cause one could believe in? I mulled the question during my walks, which had become an obsession. I gazed at the sinister Winter Palace, at the monumental, grime-covered Saint Isaac's Cathedral, and across the river, at the imposing Peter and Paul Fortress with its dismal Trubetskoy Bastion where so many revolutionaries had been—were still—imprisoned. I lowered my eyes as I passed before the bronze horseman and noticed details that had escaped me before: the lash marks on the faces of coach drivers, the stubborn expressions of the beggars in whose hands I dropped a few kopecks, the gaunt cheeks of the young delivery boys who brought telegrams to our house. The men I saw in the street had Raskolnikov's features and perhaps, like him, they too concealed an ax in the lining of their overcoats.

I tried to discuss my observations with Mademoiselle Rose, but she avoided my questions, answering vaguely. Of course France was a republic and people lived well there, but the violence that had brought about the fall of the monarchy had occurred so long ago that it was the stuff of history books, its bloody episodes reduced to mere images and stories. The fear I had experienced in 1910 on the day Tolstoy died, when the hussar brushed against me with his horse, was still vivid, and I wished Assia were with us now. Younger, closer to me in age and spirit, she would surely have been able to explain many things. Was it really right to hope for the departure of the kindly-faced czar and the downfall of the grand duchesses, whose great generosity and beauty had until recently been extolled by all? And what of the poor boy, Alexis, already so sick? At my house discussions of the situation led nowhere. Even my father, whose expression suggested a kind of exalted terror, all too often sent me away with an impatient gesture if I brought up the topic.

But reality is insistent and has no time for the troubled conscience of a little girl. Though there was a surge of hope in 1916 after Romania joined our side in the war, we soon realized with its defeat that the front, already too vast for our forces, had been extended even farther. The successes of the Brusilov Offensive in Galicia were followed by painful reversals. Soldiers began to desert en masse. It was said that they had nothing, neither rifles nor bread, and that even the promise of execution no longer deterred them. A large number were turning against their officers and killing them. They robbed trains and returned to their lands, further aggravating the chaos with the railways. They raped, pillaged, and burned everything in their path. At our house, we lacked for nothing, but the atmosphere was so oppressive that I often suffered asthma attacks. I had a particularly serious one the day Mademoiselle Rose announced that she had decided to leave while a few trains were still running.

I helped her pack and accompanied her to the station with my father, who handed out fistfuls of rubles in the struggle to purchase a ticket, after which he pushed his way through the crowds to make a space for her on the packed train. We passed her luggage through the window. All this took place in a rush and in an atmosphere of such agitation that I did not even have the chance to say goodbye. My final memory is of Mademoiselle Rose's black straw hat, held in place with one hand as she waved a white lace handkerchief with the other, her small pale mouth crying out into the smoke of the locomotive and the noise of the axles, words that I was not able to hear. I never saw Mademoiselle Rose again; when I arrived in Paris in 1919 I found that the address she had given me was a gaping hole surrounded by equipment laying the foundation of a new building. None of the numerous notices I placed in the newspapers ever produced any result. I will never forget our return through a depressing Petrograd; I sobbed, and my father kneeled down before me in the middle of the street, pushing back my bangs and drying my cheeks with his handkerchief. Trying desperately to console me, he proposed tea in a pastry shop, but I was unable to swallow a bite. His hot hand held mine all the way home, and that night, for the last time, he tucked me in.

It was just next door, at the Yusupov Palace, that Rasputin was assassinated. Later his murderer described the events in great detail: The cyanide, generously sprinkled on petits fours which the *starets*—a force of nature—gulped down without the slightest effect. The bullet that appeared to kill him, followed by his sudden resurrection. The prince, who believed Rasputin was drawing his last breath, crouching over the bear rug where he lay in order to administer a coup de grace. The monster rising up, eyes burning, beard bristling, and grabbing his arm. Rasputin fleeing, staggering through the frozen gardens, leaving a trail of blood in the snow. The terrified accomplice finding the courage to shoot him again. The body, still alive, shuddering inside the rug in which it had been wrapped. The bundle was carried to Grand Duke Dmitri Romanov's limousine, a Delaunay-Belleville, and was found the following day in the Little Neva, encased in a thin film of ice. All this had taken place only a few meters from our house. When she heard the news, my mother suffered one of her hysterical attacks. She blamed Yusupov and considered the fact that he had chosen to kill the monk in his own palace to be a personal affront, deliberately concocted to injure her person. She waited all day for the arrival of agents of the Okhrana, but they never came.

I myself did not feel very reassured by the turn of events. That night, to help me sleep, I was given two drops of the opium that the doctor had prescribed for my mother. I had a nightmare: I was a contemptuous siren like the ones in Gogol's stories, crowned with roses, cleaving the waters of the Dnieper beneath a bright moon and holding out my pale arms toward the youths on the shore in order to bring them down with me toward the river's liquid gardens. But a hand grabbed my ankle and pulled me to the muddy bottom. The clear water became cloudy, then froze. I lost my crown and my hair came undone. Viscous seaweed wrapped itself around my neck. An animal with thick fur drew close, its black muzzle and fetid breath suffocating me as pools of blood swirled in the waves. A heavy eyelid opened, revealing a yellow eye that grew and grew and began to engulf me. I woke up screaming and called out for Mademoiselle Rose. When she failed to come, I suffered an asthma attack which the doctor had great difficulty subduing.

The widespread joy that greeted Rasputin's assassination confused me. No matter what crimes the *starets* had committed, I was not accustomed to the idea of rejoicing at a man's death, even less at his murder. But everything had become so strange that I no longer tried to distinguish good from bad. I missed my governess terribly. She had been replaced in all areas but French by my Russian tutor. Every day I wrote to her, letters which she probably never received and which, in any case, were never answered. Sometimes I thought about little Alexis and wondered whether the disappearance of his miracle worker would bring his early demise. I did not dare discuss my fear with anyone, not even my father, knowing that my questions would seem incongruous amid the general exaltation. I took refuge in my reading, but even in this I lacked an interlocutor. Though I had been a voracious reader from the age of five, I had always had a guide to direct my choices and share my discoveries, my pleasures, and my disappointments. Now I was forced to cast about blindly in my parents' library and the shelves of secondhand bookshops. I read more and more and ate less and less. After a series of persistent migraines, I was found to be severely nearsighted and began to wear small metal-framed glasses which my mother begged me to remove when guests came, making it eminently clear that the glasses did not improve my appearance. I obeyed without a fuss: I much preferred the haze in which I had lived since infancy to the harsh edges of the world as it truly was. This fluid state suited my dreamy nature so well that it had taken me fourteen years to admit that it was the result of impaired vision.

After Mademoiselle Rose's departure, my mother had given me her maid, Maroussia, who now looked after me and accompanied me when I went out. Mother considered this servant to be clumsy and brusque; her coarse peasant hands scraped her neck when she undid the buttons of her dress. Maroussia's replacement, who had been given the French name Lili despite her flattened Slavic features, had suspiciously bright blond ringlets and overly red lips that gave her a slightly disreputable look. But my mother found Lili's gossip entertaining and she ironed lace beautifully. Maroussia wore a taciturn expression beneath her white bonnet, which sat slightly askew atop the oily hair that she combed up into a bun. Her lips were always chapped, and her hands, it is true, were large and red, with thick fingers and gnawed fingernails. Whenever she came into my room, she insisted on bowing awkwardly despite my friendly gestures toward her, and her feet would get tangled in her long black skirt. The strings of her lace apron were perennially coming undone. Outside, she walked with her eyes down and spoke to me only in monosyllables. One day when we were walking along the river, she brusquely told me that she had to go visit her sick mother across the Neva on Vasilievsky Island. I did not have permission to go to that neighborhood. I had only been there once, when we traversed it in a carriage, and I remembered it as a desolate area, crisscrossed by streets. There were still a few cottages surrounded by farmyards and dusty gardens, like the old house Oblomov lived in after breaking off his engagement. I hesitated for a moment and then, intrigued, agreed to go with her.

After a long walk that took us around the walls of factories belching waves of black smoke, down paths of beaten earth on which bony chickens pecked at pebbles, by shop windows covered in thick grime and taverns out of which emerged groups of staggering men spitting long streams of brown saliva, Maroussia invited me into a hovel nestled at the back of a fetid courtyard. We climbed a flight of stairs that reeked of urine, and where two skinny children played, wearing only tops, their behinds and legs bare. My companion pushed on the half-open door. An old woman lay on a mattress on the floor, like a pile of rags, her sparse, tousled gray hair revealing patches of pink skin. She flashed me a toothless grin. Without a word, Maroussia pulled a canvas bag out of her cape and turned her back to me so that I would not see its contents. I stood on my tiptoes and caught a glimpse of bread, bits of pâté, a paper envelope containing a few tea leaves, and other assorted leftovers. As I looked away, the sick old woman suddenly reached out and took my hand, which she brought to her moist lips and kissed. I was barely able to control a reaction of disgust. Afterward we crossed the bridge again; we would never mention this escapade, either on the way back home or later.

In early 1917, Petrograd gathered its resources for a final hurrah on the occasion of a visit by the future president Wilson, Gaston

Doumergue, and other foreign delegations. The electric streetlamps glowed, their light softened by flurries of powdery snow on the Nevsky Prospect. A parade went by in the cold air. I was there with Maroussia. She seemed less mistrustful of me since our expedition and I was able to induce her to utter a few words, though when I asked her certain overly personal questions about her feelings, she responded only with a strange look and quickly lowered her eyelids. The haggard crowd, freezing on the gloomy sidewalks—only a few shop windows were illuminated and it had been a long time since anyone had set up braziers—was taciturn and tired, and at times seemed shaken by a turbulent wave. On the orders of Prince Obolensky, commander of the capital, armed guards disbanded the small groups that had formed around individuals who spontaneously held up banners demanding coal and bread. That evening the Mariinsky was illuminated in all its blazing glory, and accompanied by my father, my mother, wearing a ball gown under her sable coat and a brand-new river of diamonds at her throat, attended a ballet performance organized for the illustrious visitors. Unable to sleep, I awaited their return, and came down to greet them in the sitting room. Happy and excited, they finished off a bottle of champagne before going to bed. Perched on the armrest of the couch in my robe, I listened as they described the endless ovations that followed the curtain calls of the *étoiles*: Pavlova, Karsavina, and Kschessinska. They bourréed back from the front of the stage en pointe, hand in hand, bowing so deeply in their white tutus that their hair, decorated with flowers, skimmed the floor. They came forward again and again as the houselights were turned on and off. Neither my parents nor anyone else in the hall that night realized that the curtain was closing definitively on the world as they knew it.

On February 21 there was a shortage of flour and General Khabalov, commander of the Petrograd District, introduced rationing cards. Long lines began to form outside the empty shops. A few windows were smashed, a few shop owners killed. The temperature went down to minus twenty degrees Celsius, and there was no coal coming into the city. Even our house was affected. We hired chimney sweeps to clean out the flues and the old wood-burning stoves. We bought gas lamps because the electricity was constantly interrupted. Several rooms were sealed off. We no longer removed our coats and shawls inside the house. There was a series of protests, many of which became riots. On February 23, the day traditionally dedicated to women workers, there was a parade, which grew quickly and was joined by the laborers who had been locked out of the Putilov factories. For the first time, shop owners, government functionaries, and people in the street joined their ranks. I was not allowed to go outside, even in the company of Maroussia, who would never have dared to disobey her masters. Trapped in our sealed apartment, I watched from behind a yellow velvet curtain as the events unfolded. That day the atmosphere on the street was good-natured, almost joyful; the trams stopped in their tracks and the conductors climbed out, cheered on by the crowd, to join the marchers. Everyone noted the strange inaction of the police and the passivity of the dreaded Cossacks. That evening, when my father returned from work, he was optimistic and exalted, full of praise for the ancestral wisdom of the Russian people and their instinctual recognition of "elemental rights." In his opinion, everything would turn out well, the revolution would be bloodless, and we would march toward a new golden age free of interdictions and exclusions. My mother, wrapped in her furs, shivered as she listened to him.

The next day, February 24, the bridges that connected downtown Petrograd to Vasilievsky Island were filled with people. I was still not allowed to leave the house. Too anxious to study or even read, I was bursting with curiosity. I begged Maroussia to go out and gather news. Finally she relented, wrapped herself in a shawl, grabbed the basket she always carried with her, and disappeared. For hours I awaited her return. An enormous crowd, she informed me, had inundated the Nevsky Prospect. People were carrying red flags and singing "La Marseillaise." They marched up the avenue all the way to Znamenskaya Square, in the middle of which loomed an enormous equestrian statue of Alexander III on a pedestal of pink granite. The crowd cried out: "Long live the Republic!" The police charged, halfheartedly, injuring a few people. On February 25, Maroussia described another incident, shaking her head distractedly; this moment changed the course of events. In that same square, a member of the Cossacks—the guards who, in the past, had so often put down protests with enormous violence—suddenly leant forward in his saddle and, with a swish of his saber, severed the head of a policeman who was aiming his rifle at a spontaneous orator. Two days later, soldiers had begun fraternizing with the protesters and joining them on their march to the Tauride Palace, the seat of the Duma.

Unable to tolerate my imprisonment any longer, I snuck out of the house, taking advantage of Maroussia's absence—she had been given permission to visit her family—and one of my mother's migraines, which confined her to bed in her darkened room under a pile of covers, on top of which lay her sable. I knew that my father was out there, along with all the city's notables. The wind had died down. I stopped near the military esplanade to catch my breath; a pale winter sun cast a pearly sheen on the milky clouds, and suddenly, as if magically transformed, the city revealed to me its theatrical allure. The square seemed to grow even larger as I gazed at its ocher façades, its colonnades, and its capitals. It all looked like a painted backdrop awaiting the arrival of the main characters. The czar was at his headquarters in Mogilev, reading Caesar's *Gallic Wars*, more concerned with the measles afflicting his children at their Tsarskoye Selo residence than with the insurrection in Petrograd. Suddenly the scene was flooded with black ants. The protesters, carrying rifles, poured in from every street. The Pavlovsky Regiment appeared in tightly formed battalions, carrying banners. I thought the soldiers would stop and take aim at the insurgents, but instead they surged forward, entering the Winter Palace with the permission of the sentinels at the door. A few moments later, the imperial standard was lowered, replaced by a red flag. A wave of cheers shook the crowd.

I kept running. At the Tauride Palace there was chaos. Twenty thousand people were attacking the building. The deputies fled, unsure whether the civilians and soldiers were there to massacre them or to protect them. Only Kerensky came down to greet them. The Duma formed a committee with the purpose of restoring order while, in another hall, members of the many outlawed organizations—the Socialist Revolutionaries, anarchists, Bolsheviks, and Mensheviks—met to constitute a Soviet. My father explained this to me later. Obviously I did not know what was happening as I stood there in the crowd. Frightened by the noisy, heaving mass which seemed unaware of my existence, I headed home down streets filled with dirty snow. My mother was still asleep. The following day the papers informed us that during those frenetic hours Nicholas, who had refused to replace the elderly and incompetent prime minister Golitsyn with someone who had the confidence of the deputies, had instead granted dictatorial powers to General Ivanov and decided to return to Tsarskoye Selo, from where the czarina had been inundating him with letters inciting him to stand firm. Unable to reach his destination because the lines had been cut by striking railway workers, he was forced to return toward Pskov.

Events accelerated further. Telegrams flew between the Tauride Palace and Pskov. The czar was informed that the riots had spread to Moscow and other cities, that the naval fleet was mutinying in the Baltic and at Kronstadt, and that soldiers everywhere were turning on their officers. He received missives from his generals, all grand dukes, demanding his abdication. A Provisional Government had been formed in Petrograd, presided over by Prince Lvov, with Kerensky in charge of the Justice Ministry. My father was jubilant. Finally, on March 1, the czar abdicated, at first in favor of his son, Alexis. Then, after demanding that his doctors tell him the truth about the czarevitch's health and learning that under no circumstances would he survive beyond the age of sixteen, the czar named his brother Grand Duke Mikhail Alexandrovich as his successor. This was the same brother he had exiled from the court years earlier for marrying a divorcée. The grand duke declined the honor. A red flag flew above the Yusupov Palace next door. I saw Grand Duke Cyril returning home with a red cockade in his buttonhole. Czarism was dead in Russia.

The city was overcome with delirium. People began to go out into the streets again. We went to see American films at the Piccadilly Cinema. My father was the chairman of the board of the Commercial Bank of Voronezh, administrator of the Moscow Union Bank, and a member of the board of the private Commercial Bank of Petrograd. He was making money hand over fist. For a belated celebration of my fourteenth birthday he took me to the Grand Hotel Europe—behind my mother's back—where the black bartender had a Kentucky accent. I tasted my first Manhattan and took a puff of my first *papirosi*. That night, he escorted me to the Nevsky Farce Theatre where Sacha Guitry's *Fall of Bergen op Zoom* was enjoying an enormous success. I sulked a bit because I had not been allowed to fulfill my dream of wearing a long dress or a décolleté, however modest. Instead I was encased in a flood of blue taffeta with a wide collar of Valenciennes lace which, I was convinced, accentuated my olive complexion. It took all of the French theater company's comic talents to convince me to crack a smile, until finally I relented and burst out laughing.

We went to Yar, to Chez Ernest, and to Chez Constant, where the stocks of caviar and champagne were still plentiful. A parade of people came through our house. Everyone had a plan for modernizing the country; there were animated discussions, with much yelling and screaming. Liters of vodka were consumed. My tutor had disappeared at the beginning of the uprising and it no longer occurred to anyone to send me off to my ice-cold room during these debates.

But in the following months the euphoria was becoming tinged with anxiety. My father and his friends found the funerals for the victims of the revolution that took place in March to be a bit excessive. There was an enormous secular ceremony on Palace Square, with red coffins and enormous scarlet banners flapping like sails, giant urns spewing clouds of incense, flaming torches, and cannon salutes. I saw clearly that the situation was tenuous, hanging by a thread: either the moderates would hold on to power and people like us would continue to prosper in a world liberated from the yoke of the czars, or the Bolsheviks would take over and the wealth would be redistributed. We might well lose everything, including our lives. There was already talk of pillaged estates, torched crops, and aristocrats and wealthy merchants attacked, robbed, and killed in the streets. My mother was instructed not to wear jewelry outside the house and to replace her sable with a simple padded overcoat.

In April, Lenin emerged from his sealed train at Finland Station. Inflation had begun to reach fantastic proportions. Like its predecessors, the Provisional Government was unable to secure the delivery of sufficient supplies to the city, and it was said that in the poorest neighborhoods large numbers of children were dying of hunger and thirst. The war dragged on. Kerensky became minister of war and of the navy, but the officers in the armed forces no longer seemed to have any authority over their soldiers; entire regiments had begun to desert. New figures, terrifying in their enormity, began to emerge: more than 1.5 million men killed on the battlefield, almost 4 million injured, and 2.4 million held prisoner. In July, the Bolsheviks attempted a hostile takeover of the government. It failed, and Lenin was forced to flee to Finland. In September, they tried again and the news went around that General Kornilov's forces, supported by the conservative elements in the country, were planning to retake Petrograd and establish order. A rail-workers' strike blocked the offensive. Kerensky, who had been named prime minister at the end of July, held on to power as well as he could, constantly shuffling his cabinets and negotiating with the Soviets. All my father's hopes hung on Kerensky's success. I remember heartbreaking sunsets in Petrograd during those weeks, purple clouds that opened like a stage curtain to reveal the moon, round and golden in a velvet sky. At the Smolny Institute, the former convent for daughters of the aristocracy, where copper plates still indicated the use of each room—BURSAR'S OF-FICE, YOUNG LADIES' DRESSING ROOM, etc.—the burgeoning Soviets prepared their witch's brew. There were armored cars draped in red flags that flapped in the wind; ragged men rode on the running boards, their Brownings and Colts drawn. Maroussia avoided me. My mother seemed to be in a permanent stupor, barely speaking and clutching her husband's arm as soon as he walked through the door, not leaving his side for an instant. On October 25, Lenin, who had secretly returned to St. Petersburg, and a group of friends, including Trotsky, unleashed the soldiers of the St. Petersburg Garrison, the Kronstadt sailors, and the worker-soldiers against the legitimate government. The cruiser *Aurora* pointed its guns at the Winter Palace where the government was headquartered, the ministers were arrested, and Kerensky fled. We were doomed.

We left our beautiful Petrograd apartment very early one damp, cold morning for Moscow, which was calmer and where my father planned to consider his options before making a final decision. Once again we drove down the Nevsky Prospect, but in reverse; again it was deserted and even more sinister than the day we arrived, slick with oil and lined with broken shop windows. Street signs had been torn down, posters blew in the wind, armfuls of soggy leaflets coated the wooden paving blocks, and piles of trash lay on the sidewalks. No one spoke. We crossed Znamenskaya Square, where Alexander III's statue had been covered with hideous inscriptions. Several panes of glass were missing from the glass of the Nicholas Railway Station where we waited for hours in the cold, my mother and I sitting on our luggage, until my father was able to purchase tickets for the train, a wheezy locomotive lugging wooden cattle wagons.

October 1943

All one can see of the little girl are two swollen eyelids, red from crying, framed between a wool hat that has been pulled down over her forehead and a scarf that has been pulled tight over her mouth to keep her from chattering like a magpie as she walks along the wet paving stones of Bordeaux. The street is empty because of the curfew. Moments earlier she was awakened brusquely in the freezing dormitory, her hands tucked into the warm spot between her thighs, despite the nuns' prohibition. Then she and her sister were thrust out into the cold drizzle. Her sister whispers something in her ear to keep her quiet: "The Germans have found us!" The little girl grabs on to a leg with both hands; it is a strange leg, and it belongs to Julie. Julie is the tall, thin woman who has been looking after them ever since their parents left. She was in a shipwreck—perhaps the Titanic?—*and ever since then, instead of a soft calf, she has had this thin layer of brown skin covering her tibia. The sniveling child chews on her scarf, and it tastes of wet wool and salt.*

6

BECAUSE of the Bolsheviks, I never celebrated my fifteenth birthday. In the distant past, now submerged beneath pools of stagnant water, tinted red with blood and guarded by a barricade of bayonets, pikes, and rifles, as forbidding as the brambles that concealed Sleeping Beauty's castle from the world, Mademoiselle Rose had dreamily described this shimmering event to me. It would be like the strike of a gong, announcing my metamorphosis. No longer a little girl, I would become a young lady and enter the state of adulthood while at the same time preserving for a while longer all the privileges of childhood. And now, even though my beloved governess was no longer there to celebrate the moment and to officially comb my hair up as she had done once in Kiev after repeated requests—back in the days when I dressed up in my mother's old gowns—I was eager to turn this corner and be instantly transformed.

However, in February 1918 the government decreed that the Russian calendar, which lagged two weeks behind the Roman calendar recognized in the rest of Europe, would be accelerated: my birthday, February 11, disappeared into the growing trash heap of history. By the time the day had almost arrived, it had already passed. I obstinately refused to adopt February 24—my new official birth date—in exchange. This grievance may appear childish in the midst of the many calamities we suffered. But I was inconsolable nonetheless and I admit that I still hold a personal grudge against Lenin for having slighted me in this way. I can imagine him in his study, caressing the blue vein that pulsed beneath his bald pate and, with a cruel glint in his slanting Mongol eyes, leaning over a register with his pointy beard, slashing Irène Némirovsky's fifteenth birthday with a mark of the pen, just as a few months later he would order the czarevitch's death. I decreed that my age should never be mentioned again, which I'm sure secretly pleased my mother.

We had many reasons to be upset with the Bolsheviks. Because of them, our arrival in Moscow in October 1917 was quite eventful. My father had reserved two rooms at the Hotel Metropol while he continued his search for an apartment and a maid. No sooner had we begun to settle into this luxurious ultramodern establishment than we heard shots. The negotiations that had been going on for several days between the moderates at the Kremlin and the revolutionaries ensconced at the Governor-General's Palace on Skobelev Square had broken down. The Dvinsk Regiment, which several months earlier had been confined to barracks on Kerensky's orders for refusing to leave for the front, had joined the Reds. The only soldiers left to defend us were the Junkers, junior officers or even cadets recruited for this purpose. This was explained to us by the director of the hotel, who invited all the guests down to the billiard room in the basement. It was considered safer because it had no windows.

I had to be dragged away from the spectacle I was watching from our window, torn between terror and excitement. Decapitated by the bullets, the lanterns on the square spurted streams of burning gas in the dark night. Shells traversed the sky and when they landed in the distance, burst into a spray of sparks followed by a hesitant yellow glow and then the scarlet blaze of fires. Cannons peeped out from between the white columns of the theater. The enormous building, which had been empty and silent since we arrived, now revealed the smoking barrel of a machine gun behind every statue on the rooftop and in the embrasure of each dormer window. The chariot atop the pediment looked as if it were about to fly off in the fusillade, with a sharp kick of steel-tipped hooves, ready to carry the armed men who lay flat on the horses' necks into the stars that glimmered among the clouds. Orders, cries, and shouts of rage mingled with the crackle of rifle shot, the whistle of shells, and the bells which had just begun to ring in the city's four hundred churches.

I picked up a book, Bely's *Petersburg*, which I had bought before our departure but had not yet had time to read, and followed my parents down the stairs. The vast room was packed: prattling dowagers with tortoiseshell lorgnettes, their housekeepers standing behind them and a toy terrier in their arms; potbellied gentlemen blotting their foreheads and double chins, compressed in their stiff collars; young men with bandaged heads or an arm in a sling, in order to explain why they were not at the front; doleful young girls shivering under their Orenburg shawls and fussed over by young men. They gathered in small groups, asking questions, arguing, gesticulating. It was like being trapped in a henhouse.

Leaving my mother in her husband's care, I found a stool and pulled it to one side of the room. I put on my glasses and dove into my book: I have always had the ability to become completely absorbed in my reading, even in the midst of noise and agitation. I had just reached the passage where Sofia Petrovna meets the red domino on the shore of the Neva when the maître d'hôtel came over to invite me to sit at one of the tables set up by the staff amid the chaos. My parents were already there. This extraordinary book had transported me to the ghostly, foggy city I had just left behind; a ballad that reverberated in the mind of the heroine began to go round and round in my own consciousness: "Gazing at the rays of purple sunset, / You stood upon the banks of the Neva."*

The three days we spent trapped in the Metropol gave me a foretaste of immigration as I would soon experience it, even though the people gathered at the hotel were only there temporarily and most of them would eventually be able to return home. I lost myself in my book. This was partly because even a revolution and the clamor of crossfire were not enough to distract me from my passionate curiosity regarding the destiny of young Nikolai Apollonovich, with his colorful dressing gown and his Tartar skullcap, and the mystery of whether he would or would not be able to defuse the bomb in the sardine can which was meant to blow up his luxurious apartment and kill his dear father, Senator Apollon Apollonovich. And partly because of my shyness, especially around people my age, whom I was not accustomed to spending time with. Even so, I kept my eyes and ears open.

On the first evening, I remember there were recriminations and boasts: before long the legitimate government would subdue the hooligans, which were bands of army and navy deserters commanded by idiots who soon would be drunk out of their minds in the streets after some pillaging. People treated the staff of the hotel and housekeepers who had come with their mistresses brusquely, suspecting them of complicity with the thugs. The staff was overwhelmed with orders and counterorders, as if their masters were trying to test their loyalty. They obeyed, eyes lowered. At dinner, people complained and sent back their veal cutlets à la Pojarski, which had grown cold on the long voyage from the kitchens; the wine was corked, the champagne was not sufficiently chilled.

On the following day, after a night spent sleeping on the green felt of the billiard tables or cushions and overcoats on the floor, a few energetic souls attempted to establish a semblance of order. Young society ladies tore the fabric off of chairs and made armbands, offering their services to an amiable doctor who was nursing several dowagers suffering from feigned fainting spells. A prince took it upon himself to remove all the lapdogs to a nearby room because their barking had become intolerable. His aristocratic title proved essential in obtaining the owners' cooperation; even so, there were heartbreaking farewells and tearful exhortations. Card games, literary salons, and magic shows were proposed. Committees were organized, most notably a defense committee, which gathered an impressive arsenal that included silver table knives and pocket knives, not to mention fireplace pokers and curtain rods. At lunch and dinner we consumed enormous quantities of caviar and vodka, for the hotel seemed to have infinite reserves of these, though bread was beginning to grow scarce.

By the third day, the energy and good humor had faded several degrees. It was difficult to find a partner for a game of whist, preference, or poker; the volunteer nurses showed less enthusiasm for loosening dowagers' corsets and holding smelling salts up to their noses; the invitations to participate in music and poetry recitals went unheeded. People's treatment of the domestics began to change; now they wooed them assiduously with the relatively obvious aim of obtaining small favors: a basin of warm water in which to wash or shave, an extra pillow, a cup of tea, or blini on which to spread their caviar, which eventually becomes inedible if consumed by the spoonful. The staff complied with growing ill humor and effrontery; their uniforms lost their crispness and they began to disappear one by one, never to return. Like the other ladies, my mother removed her jewels and asked me to conceal them in my blouse, believing that no one would think to look for them there. There were long stretches of silence amid the general commotion. Soon, even the most long-winded gossips went quiet.

That night, when the Bolsheviks arrived, noisily knocking down the double doors in the purest revolutionary tradition, they found a taciturn assembly of wild-haired, haggard folk who put up absolutely no resistance to their orders. Under the command of a uniformed officer, they were an ill-assorted group of factory workers in jackets and caps, peasants in filthy coats and moth-eaten fur hats, and soldiers in tattered uniforms, all more or less bloody but festooned with red cockades, ribbons, and armbands. They did not search us but, after a brief speech in which they announced that the hotel had been requisitioned by the revolutionary forces in order to house the revolutionary war committee, simply ordered that we vacate the premises within fifteen minutes. After gathering our luggage we emerged into the night, stepping over a river of wine that poured out of the hotel's basement windows. The officers had ordered that all the reserves be destroyed in order to avoid temptation. The air was filled with the fragrance of Bordeaux and fine champagne. On the square, the fusillades had come to an end but flames still licked the walls of the theater and the first snowflakes powdered the blankets that had been hastily thrown over piles of cadavers.

The apartment that my father found for us near the Dolgorukov Palace—home of Tolstoy's Rostov family—belonged to a young cavalryman of the Horse Guards who had departed for the front. It had the advantage of being discreetly located at the rear of an internal courtyard and had two entrances, like many buildings in Moscow, especially in the Arbat neighborhood, which is full of alleyways and gardens. The young man's mother had furnished the four rooms with family antiques, which in her own home had most likely been replaced with more modern furnishings. It was full of divans upholstered in faded velvet, dusty wall hangings and tasseled curtains, portieres of threadbare brocade, chipped Chinese screens with flaking varnish, gilded candelabras and frayed lampshades, faded carpets, plaster busts of generals with chipped noses, and portraits of elderly countesses, white lace gone gray with the passage of time.

All the windows of this ramshackle place looked out onto the courtyard, and it was so dark that even in the mornings we had to turn on all the electric lights, which were sometimes replaced by sinister candlelight because of increasingly frequent power cuts. My parents were not pleased by the decor, but I was aware of only one thing: the well-stocked library. I owe to this collection one of the great discoveries of my early life: *The Picture of Dorian Gray*, by Oscar Wilde, in a Russian translation. This book left an indelible impression on me.

The day after we settled in, my father found a maid, Theodosia. She was one of those "hard-headed" Muscovite women whose cynicism is equaled only by their bluntness. She firmly believed, like most of the inhabitants of this ancient city which soon would once again become the capital, that God and the czar would one day reestablish order in Russia. Her hair fastened in a kerchief which she pulled down to her eyebrows, belly wrapped in an enormous apron whose colors had faded after innumerable washings, and skirts rigidly held up by many petticoats, she waved her broom at the Bolsheviks, predicting all the torments of hell, and made the sign of the cross whenever Lenin's name was uttered. As the building's caretaker, she gritted her teeth as she scraped graffiti off the walls with rags drenched in bleach: "Peace to the cottages, war to the palaces," "Either with us or against us," "Blood will have blood."

Because my father had once again instructed me to stay indoors—the city was full of deserters, vagrants from the countryside, and armed bands, and skirmishes flared up on the slightest excuse—I had only Theodosia to talk to. My mother no longer spoke when my father was not around, and simply gazed at me with a distant air if I tried to draw her into conversation. Old Theodosia, who had no idea we were Jewish, pampered me. She thought that I bore a resemblance to the youngest of the "young ladies" she had looked after before entering our service. She gave me recipes for lightening my complexion: cucumber compresses and honey-based brews. "Barina," she would say, "my little dove, my sugarplum, the priest said at mass on Sunday at Saint Basil that if the Whites do not return soon to massacre these Red hooligans, bandits, and criminals with God's help, a cloud of locusts will descend on our little mother Russia for thirteen years. During the Feast of the Dormition this year Our Lady of Vladimir bled." I watched her closely; to me, she was a perfect embodiment of the Russian people in all their misery. Her face was as wrinkled as a sprouted potato, her eyes were blue and watery, and her hands were covered with brown spots. She cursed the revolutionaries and lamented the days when she had served as an assistant to the cook in the home of an aristocratic family who had gone into exile. I remembered a line from Chekhov's story "The Steppe": "They were all people with a wonderful past and an appalling present. To a man they spoke ecstatically of their past, but almost contemptuously of the present. Russians like to reminisce, but they don't like living."*

My father brought discouraging news from the outside world. The Constituent Assembly, in whom the liberal bourgeoisie had placed such high hopes, had been dissolved because it refused to go along with the Bolsheviks' demands. Businessmen and bankers, who after much resistance and many fierce discussions had for the most part been willing to support the new government by investing money in national industries crucial to the success of the Revolution, had begun leaving the country one by one, sometimes secretly, sometimes openly. My father, too, had begun liquidating his assets and discreetly transferring them piece by piece to foreign markets, to Stockholm in particular. He described the plunder that was taking place in the city. The anarchists, who had occupied the mansion that had once belonged to the millionaire Morozov, covered the façade of the house with a black sheet. They held orgies and indulged in champagne and cocaine, surrounded by Morozov's collection of impressionist paintings. Strelnya, the most luxurious restaurant in Moscow —encased in glass, in winter it looked like a block of ice, but inside it contained a shimmering greenhouse with tropical palm trees and exotic plants surrounded by whispering fountains—now housed the press club. Slovenly men fondled Bolshevik sirens in its artificial rock gardens; drunkards used the curtain rods to fish the last sturgeons from its ponds. The Philippov bakery on Tverskaya Street was no more: its storefront had been shattered during a fusillade on the first night of the coup, showering glass over the poppy-seed and raisin buns. My mother, who had often visited these places with my father in the past, almost sobbed as she listened to his reports.

My own experience, thanks to Wilde, was altogether different. His novel had produced a new exaltation in me. Dorian Gray asked himself whether "some red star had come too close to the earth." He was referring, of course, to his own era, the "fin-de-siècle," which was full of debauchery and violence, further bespattered by his own crime, the murder of the creator of his magical portrait. What could one say of the times I was living in, plagued by revolutions, pogroms, and interminable wars, so much mutilated young flesh buried forever beneath the cold dirt or doomed to the torments of infirmity and misery? What of my own destiny? I thought of the grand duchesses and the czarevitch, exiled in Siberia. I was seduced by Lord

Henry's cynicism, his reckless defense of beauty, youth, and happiness even at the price of sin, like the "poisonous book" that had ensnared Dorian Gray. (Later, when we arrived in Paris, I was determined to identify this book and asked my French tutor about it during our very first lesson. He referred me to Huysmans's *À Rebours*, which I immediately devoured.) I attempted to counter his mentor's arguments with my own moral reasoning, but his brilliant paradoxes seemed to pull the rug out from under me and I allowed myself to sink deliciously into the voluptuousness of decadence. "You have a wonderfully beautiful face, Mr. Gray...Yes, Mr. Gray, the gods have been good to you. But what the gods give they quickly take away. You have only a few years in which to live really, perfectly, and fully...Time is jealous of you, and wars against your lilies and your roses...Don't squander the gold of your days, listening to the tedious, trying to improve the hopeless failure, or giving away your life to the ignorant, the common, and the vulgar. These are the sickly aims, the false ideals, of our age. Live! Live the wonderful life that is in you!"

I read and reread these pages all day long as I sat next to the cast-iron stove. In the absence of coal, we burned wooden boards pilfered from the rubble of destroyed houses in order to keep warm in these chilly early days of spring. In times of plenty my appetite had always been small, but now I often went hungry. I was sorely tempted to turn my back on Tolstoy and his sermons, on Dostoyevsky and his guilt, and to avert my eyes from the suffering of Anna, dying of tuberculosis in Gorky's *The Lower Depths*, and all her brethren, who teemed around me in the Sennaya Ploschad District and the Khitrov Market, these beggars dressed in stinking rags whom the Revolution was determined to save at my expense. Was this not the "sickly aim," the "false ideal" of my time? "The only way to get rid of a temptation is to yield to it," Lord Henry had said. I contemplated our landlord's photograph, the young cavalryman in the Horse Guards whose name, I had learned, was Maxim, and with whom I had fallen deeply in love: he was blond, with light eyes, a saber at his side in his dress uniform: black tunic and medals, braids, gold epaulettes and stiff collar, polished boots, white breeches and gloves. To me, he looked like Dorian Gray. He had Gray's pure expression, his "rose-red youth and rose-white boyhood." I imagined him losing an arm, bleeding, and calling out for his mother from the bottom of a muddy trench. Why? What ideal was worth losing one's youth and one's life for? I sighed as I looked out the window at the chestnut tree in the courtyard, whose tender green leaves and faint pink clusters of flowers reached toward the sky. Then I turned from the window and cried bitter tears over the photo. My father had miraculously found a large leather-bound notebook at a stationary store and given it to me; it had a lock, and I kept the key on a chain around my neck, to my mother's great annoyance. I feverishly filled its pages with elegiac poems, strewn with young, fair-haired corpses in black coffins amid lilies and tuberoses.

Such were my romantic reveries and such was my state of inertia when Assia showed up on our doorstep. She had just arrived from Paris where she had finished her final exams in time to rush off to take part in the revolution. We were terrified by the insistent ringing one balmy April afternoon, and it took me some time to recognize her voice as she begged us to open the triple-locked door. When she removed her cloche, her short hair stupefied me. She was wearing a fluid outfit made of jersey, with a skirt that ended a good four inches above the ankle. My mother, even more surprised, quickly came to and began to examine the stitching of the dress and to inundate her with questions. Did society ladies in Paris really wear their hair short? Had hemlines really risen so much? Were turbans no longer in fashion? Had Assia brought any magazines or catalogues, anything that might aide her, stuck in this backwater, to form a picture of civilized society, if such a thing still existed? The apparition contemplated us with a surprise at least equal to our own and bombarded us with questions. What was the status of the power struggle between the Bolsheviks and the Socialist Revolutionaries? What did people think of the Treaty of Brest-Litovsk, which had brought an end to the war in Russia but ceded vast territories to the enemy, including Ukraine? Did people here claim that Lenin and Trotsky were paid by the Germans? With some sense of shame, I looked at my mother. She knew no more than I did.

Assia swept into our house like a whirlwind. The windows were thrown open, the rugs shaken out; our elderly maid no longer knew where to turn, and even I was called upon to do my part with the duster. A gramophone was found in the back of a closet; we cranked the handle and it emitted nasal-sounding Strauss waltzes and Offenbach operettas. "*Le roi barbu qui s'avance, c'est Agamemnon, Aga, Agamemnon.*"* On my father's return that evening, he was dragged into a wild Charleston with Assia to a record that she had brought, carefully wrapped in one of her silk slips. After this, she sat him down, wiped his brow—he was pouring with sweat and pretended to be annoyed—gave him a cup of tea, and subjected him to a detailed interrogation. His report informed me as much as it did her, but she did not believe a word of the somber tableau he laid out. She saw the chaos that had overcome the country as an inevitable prologue to a new era that would bring an end to injustice. The early decrees nationalizing land and industries were just the beginning. She professed a mixture—typical at the time—of Marxist materialism and pan-Slavic humanism and defended her ideas with such enthusiasm that my father quickly gave up trying to dissuade her. Her conviction and optimism lightened his spirit to such an extent that, after weeks spent in a torpor which was quite contrary to his nature, he gave her permission to take me out into the city, so long as she took the necessary precautions.

Beginning the next day and for the three months that followed, she and I—my mother refused to join us—explored every street, every square, every public place in the new capital. It seemed as if all of Russia had arranged to meet in those streets, especially the soldiers returning from the front, with or without permission. None of them wanted to go back to their villages before touring the city. They strained their eyes staring at the joyous tumult of yellow, green, and red enameled domes shaped like pineapples, onions, pears, pine cones, and collared leeks atop the Cathedral of Saint Basil. Gawking upward, they looked as if they believed that the candy-colored sky with its slow clouds like spun sugar would open up to reveal an elderly giant with a blue tunic and a white beard, who would pour out the contents of his bag over the city, as in a Chagall painting. They walked in muddy boots across the marble and malachite floors of the palaces on Bolshaya Nikitskaya Street and Prechistenka Street, licking their fingers to test the gold leaf, squeezing the thick curtains. They elbowed each other and guffawed whenever they noticed a family portrait abandoned on the wall. They jumped on Directoire-style beds. In the street, they scratched their heads as they stared at the notices pasted on every surface and asked their less illiterate comrades to decipher them.

In the spring of 1918, everyone had an opinion, a story to tell, a picture to paint, or a poem to declaim. There were performances on Red Square, just outside the walls of the Kremlin. Lovers kissed in the shrubs of the Alexander Gardens as an orchestra played the revolutionary "Warszawianka" or "The Blue Danube." People went for boat rides at all hours on the ponds near Chistye Prudi Boulevard. They sunbathed on the banks of the Moscow River. At the end of Tverskaya Street, speakers climbed onto the pedestal of the Skobelev statue, which had been covered with a red peplum—the statue itself had been knocked down. The spectators, mocking or eager, interrupted the speeches with jeers or bravos, as likely to topple a speaker by pulling on the cloth as to cheer him on with a hearty rendition of the Internationale. In Pushkin Square, the bronze statue of the poet disappeared under flags and banners. Large wooden constructions were erected in front of monuments around town by groups of futurist and constructivist artists, and then plastered with slogans painted in electric script and incomprehensible, brightly colored designs. Emaciated laborers dressed in jute bags with holes cut out for their knotty arms; drunk soldiers in torn uniforms, an omnipresent flask at their hip; girls with pale faces and painted lips; fat housewives carrying shopping bags out of which peeked a few wan leaves of cabbage—each offered a wild interpretation of the artwork, in a language generously sprinkled with colorful curses, interpretations that even the artists could not have imagined.

The poets were the most enthusiastic of all. They were everywhere: in theaters, circuses, railway stations, and of course cafés. The adventurous Assia took me, her consenting victim, to some of the wildest of these spots, swearing me to silence. In the cellar where the futurists met, we saw Mayakovsky with a proletarian cap pulled down over his forehead, his jacket collar turned up, and a red scarf around his neck. He recited "A Cloud in Trousers," with a chunk of meat in one hand and a boot sole in the other. One of the greatest surprises of my life awaited me at the Poets' Café: it was there, sitting at a pedestal table and drinking the unidentifiable concoction that at the time passed for tea, that I saw my childhood idol, the romantic Alexander Blok, standing on a platform, half hidden by thick cigarette smoke. Like every Russian girl, I knew his "Verses to the Beautiful Lady" by heart; but I knew others as well, even sweeter and less famous:

> Not hurrying, my quiet friend
> and I walk through the stubble,
> and my soul is unburdened
> as in a village chapel.
>
> The autumn day is still and clear,
> a crow raucously scoffing
> at others is all you can hear,
> and an old woman coughing.*

There he was, declaiming in a booming voice, his complexion blotchy, and pulling desperately at his thick hair. He recited the fiery revolutionary verses of "The Twelve":

> The wind plays up: snow flutters down.
> Twelve men are marching through the town.

Their rifle-butts on black slings sway.
Lights left, right, left, wink all the way...

Cap tilted, fag drooping, every one
looks like a jailbird on the run.

Freedom, freedom,
down with the cross!

Rat-a-tat-tat!

. . . .

Let's have a crack at Holy Russia,
Mother
Russia
with her big, fat arse!

. . . .

Honey, honey, let him be!
You've got room in bed for me!

. . . .

Forward, and forward again
the working men!*

   That night I staggered home as drunk as if I had consumed an
entire carafe of vodka rather than the usual sugary water.
   At home, Theodosia had given up trying to keep the walls free of
the strange sketches, rough drafts of such powerful works as Malev-
ich's *The Knife Grinder*. She watched my young aunt grimly—who,
in her eyes, was the very embodiment of disorder and corruption—
suspicious of her sarcasm and proletarian sermonizing. She often

cornered me in the kitchen and muttered dark predictions while making the sign of the Orthodox cross on my forehead to protect me from danger. There was no time to write in my diary: every morning after our chores, Assia and I picked up our frayed jackets, our hunger barely sated by a slice of brown bread filled with straw, and rushed out into the street. During the celebrations of the Orthodox Easter at Uspenski Cathedral, we were not shocked to see elderly aristocrats in tears standing next to factory workers, soldiers, and Chekists all crying out "Christ is risen!," just as the day before they had yelled "Down with the bourgeoisie!"—as they would again the next day.

In July, the German ambassador, Count von Mirbach, was assassinated. The Socialist Revolutionaries attempted to take control of Moscow, but their uprising was violently put down. We also learned of the massacre at Yekaterinburg. The news of the death of the grand duchesses and the czarevitch did not provoke the deluge of tears it would have just a few months earlier before my tender soul had been hardened by privation, fear, and the daily spectacle of shootings and corpses. Nonetheless, this news did cool the revolutionary ardor that Assia had been working hard to stir up in her impressionable niece. For a moment I felt the same horror experienced by Dorian Gray at the sight of Henry Wotton's indifference to news of the suicide of poor young Sybil Vane after her utter humiliation. I remember Wilde's words about the pleasure which the strong feel when bending the weak to their will, and I wondered whether Assia was playing this role with me.

My father resolved this question. The failure of the July uprising, the increasingly oppressive presence of the Cheka—which had replaced the Okhrana—Theodosia's changed attitude since she had been named superintendent of our building and had converted to the Revolution, the White armies' retreat in the south and in the Urals, all of this had convinced him that the time had come to leave. One night after the maid had retired to her quarters, he gathered us all in his room with the curtains hermetically drawn and whispered that he had arranged our escape. He had obtained false travel documents that would allow us to reach Finland dressed as peasant women; he would join us there as soon as possible. His fortune awaited us in Stockholm, intact. He would take us there and from there we would travel to London or Paris, where he would once again be able to offer us the life we deserved.

My aunt balked and did her best to shame him by reasoning that his experience and money were indispensable to the successful outcome of the Revolution. She accused him of bourgeois individualism and criminal selfishness. But it was no use. He informed her that he would be putting her on the first train to Odessa the following day, by force if necessary, to rejoin her parents. The fact that she was of age meant nothing; given her lack of good sense, he refused to leave her alone in Moscow. Out of cowardice, I said nothing. She rejected my offer to help her pack, and departed at dawn. Our final farewell was cold. Her parents joined us in France the following year. I never saw her again.

After accompanying her to the station, my father stopped by the Khitrov Market to purchase some malodorous peasant garments— long skirts, felt boots, scarves—for our voyage. We spent the whole night concealing bills under the soles of our shoes and clumsily sewing jewels into our clothing. The next morning when we left the house, after Theodosia had departed for the market, it would have been easy to tell that we were carrying a treasure trove of jewelry simply from the sounds we emitted as we walked. My mother jingled, I chimed. Her river of diamonds, which had been sewn into the hem of my underwear, itched like a hair shirt. We were ridiculous and terrified.

We climbed into the train (it was the kind known at the time as a Maxim-Gorky, one of those shaky little things cobbled together out of planks that crawled behind wheezing locomotives through Russia's muddy wastes) and found that it was filled with farm laborers and peasant women carrying heavy bundles. When one of them opened a corner of a bundle to pull out a dried sausage, a hunk of lard, or a bit of brown bread, one could just make out the edge of a fine lace tablecloth, cashmere shawl, a pair of silver candelabra, or even an icon: all acquired, no doubt, from one of the elderly, exhausted aristocrats who had already begun wandering the streets, selling their last belongings for a scrap of food. When the travelers weren't eating, they slept. No one paid the least attention to us; we avoided speaking so as not to awaken suspicion. At one point, there was a silent battle between us when my mother pulled a collection of Maupassant stories out of my hands, just as I was innocently settling down to read. I had taken it from the cavalryman's library. She succeeded, and I was reduced to reciting poems to myself all the way to the border. A friend of my father's was waiting for us, and without the slightest difficulty, we left Russia forever.

JANUARY 1945

After being exhumed from the cave where they had hidden, in complete silence and in the dark, for weeks, they stand on a street in liberated Bordeaux, blinded by the fireworks. They run and jump to avoid the firecrackers, frightened as rabbits intent on evading a hunter's bullets. Then they are pulled onto a crowded truck. Legs still shaky, they are deposited outside the door of an elegant house at 24 Quai de Passy. Julie rings the doorbell and a latch turns. The door is cracked open. "Madame Némirovsky," Julie says, "these are your granddaughters. They survived the war and I've brought them back to you." "I don't have any grandchildren," a strongly accented voice growls, wolflike. "The eldest has pneumonia," Julie continues. "There are clinics for poor children," the wolf replies.

7

I BECAME an adult under my mother's jealous gaze. It was the night of my sixteenth birthday, at the inn in Finland where my mother and I stayed, waiting for my father's final return. He had left for Petrograd to liquidate his last remaining holdings and had made several visits, each time bringing with him small amounts of furs and clothing. All around us the civil war was tearing the country apart. The Bolsheviks and the White Guards under the command of General Mannerheim repeatedly took over and lost control of the villages around us. Even in our tiny hamlet in the forest, we could hear cannons and see the glow of fires against the black sky. In these parts, the sun set at three in the afternoon in winter. Groups of partisans wandered the forests and the acrid smoke of their campfires reached us, carried by the icy north wind.

The hotel, a long low structure built out of logs and fragrant with resin, had dark corridors and pine paneling punctuated by tiny windows, and was often half submerged in snowdrifts. It was furnished with narrow beds covered with goose-down comforters, bleached-wood chests and dressing tables, and large enamel stoves for heating. Clean and cheerful with its blue-and-white-checkered cotton curtains, before the Revolution it had hosted couples from St. Petersburg, people of modest backgrounds who came there for amorous weekends.

The atmosphere in the hotel was very unique. First of all, there were no men—they were all off fighting with the White Armies or seeking shelter for their families in Paris, London, or Stockholm. Meanwhile, here in Finland, their families were more or less safe.

From time to time a father would come to visit, as my own father did. Everyone would crowd around, eager for news as the man, haggard and visibly thinner, gulped down his lard soup and roasted reindeer. Many believed that the Bolshevik regime would not survive the winter; the armistice had reawakened hopes of an intervention by the Allies. Since December, the French fleet had been stationed just off the shore of Odessa and forty thousand troops occupied part of the Crimea under the command of Franchet d'Esperey. People spoke of the successes of Admiral Kolchak in Siberia and evaluated his chances of joining forces with the troops under Denikin, who had begun another offensive in the south and taken Kiev from the Poles. Some of the families who had decided to emigrate began to hope that it would not be necessary.

Except for these brief visits, the population of the hotel consisted of women, adolescents, and children. No more *nia-nias* or French, English, or German nannies; they had all long since returned to their respective countries. The hotel staff, young peasant women, many of them Red sympathizers who despite their cheerful and discreet manner wore red ribbons in their straw-colored hair, were only responsible for cooking and cleaning. The women guests, all married to aristocrats, prosperous businessmen, and bankers and accustomed to managing a large staff, were barely capable of dressing themselves. One might say that they and their children were learning the hard way. The mothers were completely absorbed with the care of their youngest children, who had been terribly spoiled by their *nia-nias* and were intolerant of the slightest delay in the gratification of their wishes. These women were exhausted by their crying, noisy games, and quarrels. Some of them were even forced to breast-feed, a behavior unknown for at least two or three generations. They completely neglected their older children who, left to their own devices for the first time in their lives, were having a grand old time.

Still quite shy, I spent the first few weeks on my own exploring the hotel's library, which contained a varied selection of tomes left there by past guests. In French, I read *Béatrix* and *Mademoiselle de Maupin*, as well as Maeterlinck, Verhaeren, and Henri de Régnier.

In Russian, I discovered a novel by Aleksandr Kuprin, *The Pit*, which my mother, had she been paying attention, would have immediately torn from my hands. It taught me much about Kiev and its more disreputable neighborhoods, about its *maisons de rendez-vous* and the habits of its student population, and about other things that Mademoiselle Rose had surely been unaware of on those afternoons when she took me to watch the boats in the harbor. But I had already read *The Maison Tellier*, which dealt with more or less the same theme, and I felt that Kuprin's very Russian style—full of digressions, sermonizing, and sentimentalism, tinted with ironic pessimism, to be sure—was nonetheless quite inferior to Maupassant's sober tone, elliptical language, cynicism, and ability to create an atmosphere or evoke a character with just a few words, as well as his extraordinary capacity to describe a man's downfall. I imitated his style in the stories I was writing at the time, but I lacked experience. I did not know how to sketch behavior and types because I had not yet had the opportunity to observe people, and I knew I would have to do so if I wanted to become a writer. I began to write two or three pages each day, describing the occupants of the hotel, their attitudes and their habits, their manner of dressing and speaking, their everyday activities and gestures.

Because of this, my literary curiosity eventually trumped my shyness. Without any conscious effort I started to approach others at the hotel and to behave in a less unsociable manner, and soon people began to make overtures. Two girls, only slightly older than myself, Hélène and Marie Obolensky, were the first to approach me. They told me all about their lives and demanded to hear about my own. The adolescents at the hotel formed a tight-knit group. They had all been torn from their easy, pampered, golden existences, and thrust, unprepared, into the revolutionary storm. They had emerged, blinking absently like young birds with a wing torn off, disoriented by the perils they had only barely survived, the privations and sorrow, the bloody spectacles, the scenes of panic. They had lost confidence in the wisdom of their parents, whose improvidence, blindness, and indecision had been revealed. No one knew what the future held.

They all wanted to enjoy life, to seize the moment. Intoxicated by the pure, icy air of Finland after the putrid fumes of Petrograd and the stuffiness of Muscovite apartments where they had remained concealed for long periods, they now rushed outside immediately after gulping down their breakfasts. They spent their days skating and launching themselves downhill, screaming, on luges and sleds—sometimes simply wicker chairs fitted with blades—and at the end of these wild descents they piled into the white, powdery embankments. I had watched them during my solitary walks but had never joined in. They returned red-faced, wild-haired, and hoarse, dripping with melting snow. In the evenings they were overcome by a kind of nervous gaiety that quickly turned into hysteria; they laughed and cried uncontrollably and became involved in crazy schemes that soon became dangerous escapades or were forgotten as quickly as they had been hatched. They left their mothers to their worried discussions and ate together in the hotel's large dining room at a cluster of tables near the enormous fireplace in which entire fir trunks glowed.

On February 24, the night of my birthday—which I still refused to celebrate—I was sitting with my mother and a group of adults who, as usual, were discussing the situation in Russia, exchanging tiny shreds of information gleaned from a rare letter or a visit by one of the husbands. No one paid the least attention to me. I enviously watched the table of young people, their fresh faces and shiny hair illuminated by the playful glow of the flames. Their cries, arguments, and laughter reached the area where we were sitting, causing the ladies at my table to raise their eyebrows. I noticed that three of them, Hélène, Marie, and a boy my own age with delicate features, a dark complexion, and black hair that fell in thick curls over his forehead—his name was André Mikhailovich—were looking in my direction and whispering. I blushed, convinced that they were making fun of me. Suddenly the lights went out. The room went silent and the chef appeared, wearing his white toque and carrying a cake decorated with sixteen candles, plus one in the center in accordance to Russian tradition, to guarantee the survival of all present for another year. Bright voices began to intone "Happy birthday to you,

Irina, happy birthday to you!" With tears in my eyes, I blew out the candles, cut the cake, and timidly offered slices to everyone.

When I eventually returned to my seat, André walked over to our table and bowed to my mother, kissed her hand, and asked permission to take me to their table. Permission was granted. He led me by the hand. Someone ordered champagne. We drank liberally that night, but I was able to hold my drink. I looked around happily. These nervous bodies brushing against each other roughly, these youthful, animated voices, the exclamations and laughter, all this was beginning to go to my head and bringing out the pink in my cheeks. We spoke a mixture of Russian and French, switching easily between *tu* and *vous*. The mothers had long since abandoned the dining room for the sitting room. André had seated me to his left. He proposed toast after toast, praising the charms of each young lady at our table. Then he toasted the czar and the empress, the members of the imperial family, and the White generals. He emptied each glass of champagne with a single gulp and after a while began to break the glasses, throwing them behind him in the Russian manner. Soon everyone was doing the same, overcome by a wave of joyful intoxication. He, on the other hand, was becoming more somber and pale as the libations continued. With a nervous gesture he kept pushing back a lock of hair that fell into his eyes, revealing a sweaty brow and dark circles beneath his eyes. Suddenly he stood up, pushed back his chair, and slammed his fist brutally on the table. Two bright red splotches rose on his cheeks.

"Listen," he announced in the sudden silence, "it's all well and good to laugh and play like babies in swaddling clothes, but we're fifteen, sixteen years old, we're not children anymore! Doesn't it bother you that even as we vegetate here, people our own age, secondary-school students and schoolboys even younger than us are being killed by the Red swine? Don't you want to fight to save your homes, your properties, everything that was once your life? Would you rather leave this task to the old?"

The others were shocked into silence. The only sound was a few people clearing their throats.

"I won't have it," he went on in a hoarse voice, a voice that had only recently cracked and which was becoming more and more high-pitched, riding the wave of his emotion. "I won't stay here, I have plans, I have information. I'll join the Whites, I won't stay here with my arms crossed, you'll see, you'll see..."

He slumped down heavily in his chair, his face pale. No one spoke. People looked away as if this sudden mention by a member of our group of the drama that so preoccupied the adults were a betrayal. Finally, Hélène broke the ice.

"Come on now, we're not going to behave like our parents, are we? Enough serious talk for one evening. After all, it's Irène's birthday. She can't go to bed at ten o'clock on her sixteenth birthday! None of us wants to go to bed. How about a sleigh ride? Let's empty our pockets, I'll go rouse the drivers!"

Her words were greeted with an ovation. With a sigh of relief, we threw our napkins on the soiled tablecloth and poured bills and coins into Hélène's hands. Then with a great clamor of chairs, boot heels, and slammed doors, everyone ran off to find their overcoats. I waited to see André's reaction. He remained slumped in his chair, watching the fire and trembling. I touched his hand. After a moment he raised his head, looked at me, picked up a bottle, finished it off, threw it to the floor, and indicated that I should follow him. Without even thinking to ask my mother for permission, I ran to my room and grabbed my coat, muff, and Astrakhan hat, a gift from my father. We met at the service entrance, put on our boots, laughing and whispering as we leaned against each other. Outside, the cold cut like a blade. The four sleighs were waiting in the silent night, bathed in the pale light of a great white moon and a thousand stars. I saw André, his head bare and wearing a jacket, standing on the running board of one of the sleighs. He hoisted me onto the seat and covered us both in a sheepskin.

The sleigh bells rang softly. The lamps flashed brightly as we covered them with their glass globes. The blades made a creaking sound on the icy path. We followed along the edge of a small pond that was covered by a thick layer of bluish ice. A few meters farther lay the forest. As we were about to take the road that went through the forest, I glimpsed a row of pine trees and larches, delicate sculptures of spun sugar. In the light of the sleigh lamps they became Christmas trees hung with cut crystals and mirrored spirals made of silver paper. Bundles of snow fell softly ahead. The moon played with the pearl-gray bark of the birches, creating constantly shifting silvery shapes. Icicles fell from the branches, like so many multifaceted mirrors or arrows, sparkling before our eyes. There were traces of paw prints in the white sheet spread out before us.

Our horse, the leader of the caravan, picked up speed. The sleigh swished quietly in the soft snow as flakes sprinkled down on us, falling on my cheeks and powdering my eyelashes, making me blink. André was silent. He slid his arm around my shoulders and his warm breath tickled my nose as he leaned toward me. The frost on his eyebrows and his nascent mustache made his skin look darker and his watery eyes blacker. He smiled, and his white teeth knocked against mine. I felt a hot tongue enter my mouth and a hand slip under my coat and then my dress. The sleigh bells rang like chimes. The hand had grabbed hold of my breast and pressed it through the silk of my blouse. The other hand pulled at my hair. A rough chin pressed against mine. My heart beat in my chest like a gong.

I don't know why, but when we returned to the hotel, I ran into my mother's room without removing my coat, impulsively throwing the door open. She was sitting at her vanity table in an ivory-colored satin robe, resting her elbows on the marble surface, without makeup, pale, her eyelids heavy, staring at herself in the mirror and pinching at the slightly rumpled skin of her neck. I took a few steps toward her and leaned against the back of her chair. Her blond hair, spread out over her shoulders, revealed thick, dark roots. I raised my head, and the mirror revealed my reflection above hers. Beneath my fur hat, still gleaming with white crystals that sparkled in the light, two dark, triumphant eyes stared back at me. The cold air had turned my skin the color of a velvety peach. My lips, recently nibbled, were deep red and swollen. The raised collar of my fur framed the perfectly smooth skin of my neck, beneath which one could make out the throbbing of a bluish vein. My mother's lips trembled, like a child who is about to cry. Suddenly she looked very old to me, and at the same time very young. I took a few steps back and closed the door softly behind me. The next day, André was gone. They searched for him in the forest without much hope. The woods were filled with Reds, and the search was abandoned after twenty-four hours.

Eight days later, early in March 1919, we left Finland for Stockholm. We were planning to stay for three months. I have only a vague memory of that leaden, gray city. I can only remember the riot of lilacs that bloomed in spring in all the gardens, courtyards, and streets, and how they drove away the smell of winter. I was still in love with André and would be for a full year, partly out of a sense of honor: At the time it would have been quite reprehensible to let oneself be touched and kissed by a boy without the justification of a wild passion and terrible unhappiness. I replayed our brief story in my head, inventing earlier chapters and persuading myself that a fatal attraction had drawn us together from the moment of my arrival at the little hotel in Finland. I blamed myself for underestimating his resolve and felt hurt that he had not asked me to come with him. I imagined our heartwarming reunion months later, when he would finally reappear, heroic in his officer's uniform, arm in a sling and chest covered with medals.

My parents had quickly become part of a small circle of Russian émigrés that was surrounded by a buzzing swarm of journalists, who eagerly pumped the latest arrivals for news of what was happening across the border. Things were still very much in flux. Areas of opposition to the Bolsheviks rose up here and there, and for a while it seemed that Kolchak might finally join forces with Denikin, though we also heard that part of the French fleet had mutinied on the Black Sea, instigated by André Marty, a mechanical engineering officer. While the adults were feverishly discussing such issues, I focused on cultivating a dark, mysterious aura, playing the part of the victim of a doomed love. When we went for tea at the home of this

or that young lady, I would write cryptic romantic verses dripping
with despair in the visitors' book:

> In a month, in a year,
> What suffering must we endure?
> Driven apart, oceans divide us,
> As the days come and go,
> And still, Titus,
> You long for your Berenice,
> And I, Berenice,
> Am denied my Titus.

Just before bed, I would stand in front of the mirror with a candle, seeking to create interesting shadows in my peachy skin and
plump cheeks, which had fleshed out now that food was no longer
scarce. I cried inconsolably when I heard that we would soon be leaving for good and accused my father of ruining my life, without ex-
plaining why. He had bigger worries on his mind and drily requested
that I stop behaving like a damsel in distress.

A terrible storm lashed the cargo ship that conveyed us from
Norrköping to England and from there to France, nearly fulfilling
my sinister predictions of a violent early death. The ship, by one of
those odd coincidences of which the period was so fond, was carrying theatrical sets, and during the entire ten-day crossing in turbulent waters, we had to continually push back the bundled-up stage
curtains and backdrops that were constantly falling on us. As I entered the dining room, a small gold chair struck my legs, pushing
me against a wall and into a cardboard urn decorated with Greek
nymphs. My mother moaned on her bunk in our cabin, and when
we brought her a cup of tea we got nothing out of her except for
some floridly suggestive groans. Neither my father nor I suffered
from seasickness and we were proud to be the only clients at the bar.
I did my best to get closer to André by drowning my sorrows in
drink, despite my father's weak protests. The tiny bar had an upright
piano on which the bartender, a Polish student, banged out Chopin

pieces to pay his passage, struggling to be heard over the noise of the storm.

One night the Polish student simply gave up; the screaming wind was just too loud. The boat's rickety boards vibrated and creaked all around us. The boat no longer rolled from side to side; instead, the bow rose up almost vertical and then fell with a thud, followed by the stern. The tables and chairs were tossed from one side to the other. Cups, saucers, and glasses flew off the tables, like cumbersome riders thrown from a horse. Quite drunk, I easily persuaded my father, who was himself more than a little tipsy, that it would be more dignified to drown on deck than to be crushed by the piano or a piece of scenery. With great difficulty, we climbed a small slippery ladder rendered even more treacherous by the water gushing down and attached ourselves to the mast with our belts. The sea was an inky black, with a greenish light filtering through the leaden clouds, outlining them with a lurid clarity. The false daylight bathed everything—the stays, the rigging, and the guardrails—in a phosphorescent glow. Slapped by the surges of seawater, I recited verses by my beloved Chénier, opening my mouth wide and swallowing salty tears:

> But alone on the prow, as she invokes the stars
> The impetuous wind which fills the sails
> Envelops her. Stunned, and far from the sailors
> She cries out, she falls, she floats on the bosom of the sea.*

The storm became so intense that the captain came out and ordered us to detach ourselves from the mast and return to our cabins, where I fell asleep like a lump. The next morning the wind had died down and we could see the outline of the white cliffs of Dover in the distance.

It was early July. The peace treaty that the parties had been negotiating since January had finally been signed a few days earlier, on June 28, at Versailles. The coastline was illuminated with strings of

Chinese lanterns running from one village to the next. Flairs rocketed into the air, crisscrossing the bolts of lightning that zigzagged across the black sky. The wind carried the sound of marches and oompah bands. On deck, the passengers, now revived, congratulated and kissed each other, soaked in rain and spray. The sea was so swollen that after our brief stop on the British coast and the still-rocky but joyful crossing of the Channel, we were unable to dock at Le Havre. We could just make out the harbor with the captain's binoculars. It was crowded with people dancing to the popular song "La Madelon." Our adopted country was welcoming us with great fanfare.

The following day, the weather was glorious. We floated down the Seine estuary to Rouen through the quiet countryside beneath a porcelain sky flecked with fluffy clouds. The orchards were full of trees, branches weighed down with ripe fruit; in the fields, horses sauntered lazily and spotted cows dozed in groups beneath the trees; there were large country homes with peaked rooftops and latticed walls covered in flowers, and in the middle of the lawns young girls in white dresses played croquet. I was transfixed by this peaceful spectacle, which awoke in me a mixture of relief and bitterness. I was relieved because it seemed that we were at last arriving at our final destination and because, despite my protestations at the start of the trip, I secretly craved peace and security. But I was also bitter because I could still remember similar scenes back home in Russia, at Tsarskoye Selo, for example, whose gardens I knew well from our many picnics there while we were living in St. Petersburg. I thought of my country, once as carefree as this, now devastated and buried beneath ashes and ruins, pillaged, destroyed, torn asunder by rival bands. I thought of the dead, the bodies of young men decomposing in the dry earth all over Europe, in the trenches of Verdun, across the steppes of Ukraine, in the forests of the Urals. Perhaps André was among them. I asked myself, seriously this time, whether this peace which now seemed within reach would reveal itself to be concrete and durable, or whether it would one day be taken from us once again. I swore to myself that no matter what happened, I would never again become an exile.

After arriving at the Gare Saint-Lazare, we traversed a sad, deserted wartime Paris, sporadically lit by dim streetlamps. I had trouble recognizing the city, which had changed so much from the luminous, colorful place I recalled from before the war. With the help of a local branch of his bank, my father had located a private house built in the early part of the century, on avenue du Président Wilson. The large rooms were illuminated by tall, narrow windows framed by thick prune-colored velvet curtains; heavy mantelpieces supported enormous golden mirrors decorated with garlands; and there was expensive furniture of a vague Directoire style. It all seemed a bit generic, as if the previous tenants had only been passing through and had made little effort to create a personal decor. A butler, two maids, and a cook awaited our arrival. My mother was too tired to comment; she disappeared into her room and stayed there for a week. She did not even come with me to watch the victory parade on July 14; I went with a servant instead. Field marshals Joffre and Foch rode by on horseback beneath the Arc de Triomphe, leading the twenty-one corps of the French army. The crowd, who had been waiting since three o'clock in the morning, exploded into cheers. I was unable to repress a shudder; such enthusiasm awoke troubling memories.

My father immediately returned to work at the bank. He would soon have to leave for New York on business, which was once again flourishing. Money was flooding in at an extraordinary rate and all he had to do, he said, was bend down and pick it up. He wanted us to get settled quickly into our new life so that he could depart without having to worry. As soon as my mother had the chance to replace her old sable coat with a mink—so that she could leave the house without feeling completely ridiculous—we began to hold a series of family discussions on such subjects as my immediate future. The essential thing, in her mind, was to find a governess, even though it seemed to me that at sixteen I could do without this outmoded accessory. I had gone to Mademoiselle Rose's last known address; not only did I not find her but there was absolutely no trace of her having ever lived there. Because my French was already perfect, my father suggested an English governess. One was quickly found, thanks to one of the innumerable agencies that were popping up all over town, and one day a new governess arrived at our house. She had been warmly recommended by an aristocratic family whose daughter had just been married off and therefore no longer required her services. This strange and precious bird was my dear Miss Matthews.

It would be hard to imagine anyone more different from my previous governess than this angular redhead with large, deep-set eyes and inward-pointing eyebrows. She was very pale, with a long, pointy nose and curly hair parted on the side and combed back loosely into a chignon at the nape of the neck. She was dressed in the latest fashion, wearing a long jacket over a collarless, sleeveless, pale green silk dress that was loosely belted at the waist; there was nothing immodest about it, though, since it revealed just ten centimeters or so of white stocking above the ankle. I was slightly intrigued by the smell of ether that surrounded her, but was still too naïve to guess its source. I was won over by the firmness of her handshake and her gentle solemnity. I admitted my almost total ignorance of her language and my admiration for her compatriot Oscar Wilde, a declaration that she greeted with a mysterious smile. My mother interviewed her briefly, declared her to be "quite acceptable," and hired her on the spot.

Miss Matthews kept a discreet distance from the somewhat stormy discussions that followed. I had no intention of leading the life of a society lady, which was what my mother apparently had in mind: visits to boutiques and tea shops with my mother, dressed like a little girl, and selling sweets at bake sales on behalf of destitute émigrés under my governess's supervision, while awaiting a suitable marriage. This was not for me. I wanted to continue my studies, pass the *baccalauréat*, and work toward a degree in literature. My mother cried out in horror, spewing every cliché about what was and was not done and how I would become an old maid like every bluestocking.

I had enough self-control not to reveal my plans to become a writer. My father, who saw no trouble with me continuing my studies, advised me to study law. He said that later on, if I still wanted to work, he would be able to find me a job connected to his line of business. I did not back down, and it was decided that I would study with tutors so that I could take the *baccalauréat* in two years. Because our adventures in Finland had made me appreciate the company of people my own age, I suggested, without much conviction, that I might simply register at a secondary school. This idea was met with a great guffaw, after which my mother shrugged her shoulders and left the room, her ample cream-colored silk housecoat fluttering behind her. Her hair was now black—her natural color—but haloed with auburn highlights which owed little to nature.

Perhaps her lack of resistance to this plan can be further explained by another: It was decided that in order to restore her health, so sorely tested during our long odyssey, my mother would spend the winter and the rest of the fall in Nice, where my father would join her upon his return from America at Christmastime. Miss Matthews and I would also join her then. The social season in Nice began around the middle of October. From Cannes to Monaco, the hotels and public establishments closed at the end of May, after which only a handful of solitary military officers remained, sitting glumly and drinking glasses of pastis at one of the few cafés still open on the Place Masséna in Nice. The vogue of the Côte d'Azur in summer began only a few years ago, after sand beaches were created, casinos opened, and artists such as Colette—ensconced with Maurice Goudeket in her villa, la Treille Muscate, in Saint-Tropez—made it popular. Before and just after the war, it would never have crossed anyone's mind to roast in the sun on the pebbly coves of the Riviera or to spend the hottest months anywhere except in the country or on the boardwalk at Deauville or the windy beaches of the North Sea.

My mother would not hear of staying at the Hotel Régina, the marble-and-stucco pile that loomed over the Cimiez neighborhood, Queen Victoria's preferred lodgings in Nice, where my parents had often stayed in the early days of their marriage. She had glittering memories of the Negresco, built, in accordance with the latest trend, directly on the Promenade des Anglais, like the new Hotel Ruhl, whose inauguration she had attended in January 1913. The Negresco had been used as a hospital during the war, and reopened as a hotel shortly after the armistice. The fortune of its founder was depleted, and he was no longer the single owner, but its luxury was still unparalleled. My mother departed in September soon after my father left for America, leaving me with my governess and a cortege of tutors, all of them of a venerable age. We got to work bringing me up-to-date in all subjects, especially Latin and Greek, where I had fallen behind in the preceding two years.

I attacked my studies relentlessly. I had not realized to what extent the imposed idleness had weighed on me over the last year, and this renewed intellectual activity filled me with delight. My professors of French literature and history found me to be at an acceptable level, almost ready for the exam—for which I had Mademoiselle Rose to thank—but the situation was quite different for the poor elderly gentleman who tutored me in math and science, subjects I detested and had always neglected. I did not socialize much and was still dreaming of André and hoping to hear news of his fate, but I had renewed my friendship with Marie Obolensky, who had recently arrived in Paris. I spent deliciously melancholy Sunday afternoons with her discussing my tragic love affair. She was quite shocked at first by my detailed account, which was considerably embellished by my imagination, but the story seemed to fascinate her. In any case, she listened with polite attention.

The day after he came back from America, in late December, my father arrived at the apartment in an astonishing car whose wheels, trim, and headlamps glistened like gold. He wanted to surprise his wife, and it was in this car that we drove to the Riviera. During the entire trip he told stories about America, about New York and its buildings, which were so tall that on Wall Street one could barely make out a sliver of sky. And the stock market, where fortunes could be made and lost over the course of a few days. We arrived in Nice on the evening of December 31. At the Negresco, which resembled a giant pastry, pink and pastel green like a sugared almond, we had trouble locating my mother. We finally found her in the Salon Royal, beneath the enormous cupola designed by Gustave Eiffel and decorated with chubby-cheeked angels with pink behinds. She stood under the dazzling glow of a gigantic Baccarat chandelier—I was told there was only one other chandelier like it, designed for the czar—in the midst of a flurry of ladies in evening gowns and brilliantined young men. I remember she was wearing a lamé tunic whose back was cut in a V down to the waist, a style, she informed me, known as the "Victory décolleté." She had just enough time to kiss us both and disappear under a shower of confetti, drawn away by a dark sleeve which revealed the edge of a bright white cuff. My father and I rang in 1920 alone at the Empire Bar with its mahogany-paneled walls, balustrades, arcaded balcony, and white columns crowned by acanthus leaves beneath a marquetry ceiling. As my mother danced beyond a door sculpted in the style of a confessional, my father and I sat across from each other at a marble pedestal table and dejectedly raised our champagne glasses to the memory of the emperor whom I had so loved as a child and whose initial had been usurped by the grand Negresco.

SEPTEMBER 1945

Neatly dressed in skirts and sweaters supplied by an organization of charitable ladies, the elder sister expresses her gratitude with great dignity—"Mother will send chocolates for your little girls as soon as she returns." The girls are standing on the platform at the station. They hold up white cardboard signs on which the names of their parents are carefully written. When the smoke from the train begins to dissipate, figures appear. Some of them lie on stretchers under brown blankets, their bony hands emerging from striped sleeves. Their heads are like skulls, like the one the teacher displayed in science class at Issy-l'Évêque. These crania have large, unseeing eyes, set deep in their sockets. The little one turns around and begins to hop from one foot to the other, obsessively humming a tune: "Monday morning / the emperor, his wife, and the little prince, / Came to my house and took me by the wrist..." She sees her elder sister go pale and shudder, and worries that, like Anna Karenina, she will slip under the wheels of an oncoming train.

8

AFTER my mother returned from Nice, and during the two years I was studying for the *baccalauréat*, we mixed almost exclusively with the Russian émigré community. All the new arrivals stuck together desperately, despite their different backgrounds. The families who had gone into exile first—some at the very beginning of the Revolution—or who were already in France and decided to stay, presided over welcome committees and associations and organized charity balls, concerts, gatherings, and fund-raising events for the most destitute families. The disparity of social origins, fortunes, and political outlooks disappeared in an exalted sentimentalism, dissolving the rigid boundaries which had been strictly respected in Russia. One of the Gagarin princes, for example, seemed to have forgotten that we were Jewish and invited us to a reception. In Russia, we would automatically have been excluded from such an event. My father often mused about the visits he received at the bank from interested grand dukes, whose IOUs—always in rubles—he carefully kept. In the past, they would have sent a deputy.

It was becoming difficult to remember the old social order. Alongside families like ours, who had managed to conserve their fortunes and were able to live in luxurious circumstances—often in the Étoile neighborhood—similar to those they had enjoyed before the Revolution, there were countless others who eked out an existence under the most squalid conditions. There was an aristocrat, a godson of the czarina and heir to one of the most illustrious names in Russia, who was working as a hotel concierge; in the evenings he dusted off his ten-year-old smoking jacket in order to kiss the hand of a grocer's wife. His wife sold hats at a fashion house; his daughter played small roles at the Tabarin cabaret. In 1922, a story circulated about Colonel Ignatiev, a colossus who attended all our gatherings wearing a gala uniform. His epaulettes were tarnished and his cuffs were frayed, but his chest was covered with military decorations. During the day he drove a taxi. One morning he picked up a young woman with a baby at the Invalides Railway Station and drove her to the Gare Montparnasse. As she got out of the taxi she realized that she had lost her purse and began to cry. Not only could she not pay him, but she would not be able to buy the ticket to take her sick child to Brittany to improve his health. "How much does the ticket cost?" Ignatiev asked. "Fifty francs, monsieur." "Here you go." "But why…who are you?" He got out of the car and, stretching to his full height, held out his card: "Colonel Ignatiev, Military Attaché to the Czar." After which he saluted, got back into the taxi, and disappeared. That, as they say, is how a true Russian behaves.

There was much to fear at these charity events. Only my parents were invited to Ida Rubinstein's gala performance at the Opéra and the great costume balls thrown by the aristocracy. Whereas I was asked to participate in "poetry mornings" at which horse-faced poetesses neighed verses with approximate rhyme schemes, or "musical afternoons" featuring spotty adolescents and elderly bespectacled countesses mistreating the cello or the piano, or asked to sell lottery tickets at charity auctions, or, in the best case, invited to dance performances by folk groups with costumes made out of crepe paper and gold-colored tulle during which the boys tapped the floor half-heartedly with their worn boots and the girls waved gauze scarves, exhibiting an apathy surely born of malnourishment.

Miss Matthews gently reprimanded me for my lack of interest in my mother's plans, and I let myself be dragged all over town, in spite of my revulsion for these gatherings. I became friendly with other young girls, many of them as bored as myself, who were looked after by governesses from Miss Matthews's "set." Among them were the Gordon sisters, the eldest of whom, Mila, became my closest Russian friend. I met another Jewish banker's daughter, Daria Kamenka, whose chaperone was an intimate of my own, and to whom I owe my introduction a few months later to Michel, my future husband. Often we took advantage of intermissions to slip out and drink hot chocolate at a nearby teahouse, returning only for the final ovation.

Two things in particular irritated me. First, I hated the fact that my mother insisted on treating me like a little girl, dressing me up in childish outfits with my hair down over my shoulders. This made me look no older than thirteen or fourteen, which was the age she gave whenever asked, unless I was within earshot. But what exasperated me even more was the unflappable optimism of all these people. There was not a single person among them who did not believe that our exile was temporary and that in a few months or years at the most, they would return to a miraculously preserved estate where their repentant, mollified muzhiks would welcome them with open arms. They argued about the Russian news reports, interpreting every item in the most positive light, while refusing to believe what the French papers said because, obviously, they were all Socialist sympathizers. They even welcomed the arrival of Supreme Ottoman Symon Petlyura, whose brutality in 1919 was described by Bulgakov in his novel *The White Guard*. It was not until Petlyura's murder in 1926 by a Jewish watchmaker from Belleville—whose entire family had been massacred during one of Petlyura's pogroms—and then Joseph Kessel's articles in defense of the watchmaker and Henry Torrès's testimony on his behalf, that the exile community understood who this man they had embraced really was. No one was concerned with the moral fiber or past behavior of the new arrivals; it was enough that they had fought against the Reds—an indistinct mass—for them to be embraced as heroes. After the execution of Admiral Kolchak, who had pompously declared himself Supreme Regent of Russia, in February 1920, and the defeat of Denikin in March, everyone's hopes turned to General Baron Pyotr Wrangel, who was gathering the remains of his army in the Crimea. He had led a few successful raids, described optimistically as triumphs. His August counteroffensive, coming after the so-called Miracle at the Vistula at which Marshal Pilsudski had managed to chase the Soviet troops out of Warsaw with the help of French officers, was interpreted as the "beginning of the end" for the Reds. But by November Wrangel had been pushed back to the coast, and the allies had been forced to send a hundred boats to evacuate his troops to Turkey in order to prevent a massacre.

This would turn out to be the last action taken by the Western powers on behalf of the Whites. Even those who did not read the local press—I myself devoured the French newspapers, especially *Le Matin*, where Colette was now the literary editor—soon realized that, contrary to the exiles' hopes, the French government would no longer intervene in the struggle against the Bolsheviks. The French bourgeois resigned themselves to the fact that they would never again see the money they had invested in loans to the Russian government. True, during the previous year's election the Rightists' propaganda had centered on the battle against the "Bright Glimmer in the East," which was seducing workers and provoking riots and strikes. I remember well my surprise when I saw a poster in the Gare Saint-Lazare depicting a muzhik with a shock of black hair hanging over a red face and clutching a large knife between his teeth. The slogan read: "This is how we must vote against Bolshevism." But Clemenceau's government knew all too well that the situation of the White generals was desperate and that the war was lost; it was not willing to waste any more men or resources, which were already in short supply for the reconstruction of France. Soon, Foreign Minister Stéphen Pichon signed on to the creation of a cordon sanitaire to isolate Red Russia without taking any further action against it. During the presidency of Paul Deschanel, the Blue Horizon Chamber and Millerand's administration were interested only in obtaining reparations from Germany, which was growing increasingly defiant. The game was up for the exiles, but they refused to see it. Even when the sailor rebellion at Kronstadt was crushed, they continued to hope. In the spring of 1922, they reacted indignantly to the Treaty of Rapallo, whereby Germany recognized the de facto revolutionary government. Even so, they argued that because these two countries were the pariahs of the Treaty of Versailles, an alliance between them was to be expected. It did not occur to them that other West-ern governments might follow. By 1924, this too had come to pass.

This was the attitude of the adults in our circle. The younger peo-ple mainly shared my point of view, completely detached and utterly cynical. Like the adolescents at the hotel in Finland, they believed in nothing. They simply wanted to live, to seize the moment, which recent experience had shown to be so precious and fleeting. They were tired of hearing about the terrible toll of the last war: the mil-lion and a half dead; the stories in the newspapers about families visiting ossuaries in order to identify the remains of their loved ones among the piles of desiccated body parts and hollow-eyed skulls; the monuments, columns, steles, statues, cenotaphs, each more pomp-ous than the last, that were being erected everywhere, even in the smallest village; and the ever-present war veterans, disfigured, miss-ing limbs. They felt that the world was filled with cripples and old people. The press and politicians constantly made patriotic declara-tions and war was everywhere: in movies (such as Abel Gance's *J'accuse*, which had frozen me with horror) as well as books, at least the ones we were allowed to read, like Montherlant's *The Dream* and Roland Dorgelès's *Wooden Crosses*, which, to my great joy, had been passed over by the jury of the Goncourt Prize in favor of my most recent discovery, Marcel Proust's *In the Shadow of Young Girls in Flower*. It was true that, as Clemenceau had said of the widows, or-phans, and gassed soldiers of the last war, "we owe them something," but it must also be said that the younger generation of rootless, ex-hausted Russians, tossed between the world of their parents—for-ever lost in memories, illusions, and dreams—and that of their French professors, who assailed them day after day with the "lessons of the disaster," preferred to leave this burden to others.

Of course we were not the only ones who took refuge in this selfish attitude, and in fact some of the adults agreed with us. I did not see much of my mother during this period. She had definitively chosen the Negresco as her winter residence and I joined her there for short periods. Looking out at the Baie des Anges nestled amid the misty mountains, I dreamed of Marie Bashkirtseff and the joy she had felt upon meeting Guy de Maupassant. I imagined that I had caught a glimpse of his *Bel-Ami*. I went to see the old Villa Snegurochka, which had been decorated in marble, alabaster, and crystal by a Frenchman in love with a very blond Russian actress who only liked the color white. The villa was surrounded by a garden filled exclusively with plants that produced white flowers—tuberoses, camellias, carnations, and lilies—and there were three ponds in which white swans drifted serenely. Among the palm trees on the Promenade des Anglais, I watched the flower-covered carnival floats and Miss Matthews reminisced about the little gray donkey that had drawn Queen Victoria's cart.

Usually I rode the train down to Nice with my father after he returned from one of his increasingly frequent trips to New York, Poland, Sweden—where he had purchased a successful match factory—and even China. His travel trunks were covered with exotic stickers, his desk with ivory and jade figurines. He was making money hand over fist. Faced with his wife's indifference to his affairs, he had taken a lady companion who performed the services of a personal secretary and accompanied him on his travels. Her name was Julie Dumot, and she was an astonishing woman from a small village in the Landes who had gone to work for Sacha Guitry in 1902 at the age of seventeen; later, Guitry had passed her along to Tristan Bernard. I loved to hear her stories about them and asked endless questions about their eccentricities and obsessions. She answered with her characteristic even temper and seriousness, the typical attributes of a country girl with a good head on her shoulders.

Of course, the real reason these writers fascinated me was a secret that I kept from everyone, including my parents, my friends, and my governess: I had begun to write stories, and in fact since we had left Finland I was writing incessantly. I had even been published. One day I gathered my courage and sent some short stories, fairy tales, and comic dialogues to the humor magazine *Fantasio*. They were accepted. I was shocked. A few weeks later, I received a note from the director of the magazine, Félix Juven, asking me to come by his office to pick up my payment. This surprised me even more. When I sent the stories, my only fear was that I would have to pay for the honor of having them published, and I worried about needing to tell my parents what I had done in order to obtain the necessary funds. Monsieur Juven's surprise when I showed up at his office was at least equal to my own. I was seventeen years old and looked fifteen. What he did not know was that I had only eluded my governess's supervision with great difficulty. I had sent her on an errand, claiming a sudden wave of fatigue; on the stairs on the way to his office I tucked my hair into my hat in order to look a little bit older. He tried to get me to reveal more about myself but was faced with an obstinate silence. And that was how our collaboration continued for several years, with the greatest discretion. The tiny sums I earned were nothing compared to the sumptuous allowance my father gave me when I went to live on my own, but this was the first money I had ever earned and I was extremely proud.

I quickly realized that my mother was held in very low regard by the posh Russian set, even though she was invited to all of their charity events—on which occasions her checkbook was considered more important than her morals. One day when my friend Daria refused my invitation to tea for the hundredth time, she finally confessed with some embarrassment that though her parents had given her permission to see me, they had forbidden her to set foot in our apartment on the avenue du Président Wilson. The rumor was that Madame Némirovsky led an extravagant lifestyle—daily baths in fresh donkey's milk brought in from the country by the bucketful, daily massages by a masseur who was reputed have a side business as a procurer, and risqué evenings in houses of ill repute. People whispered that she had been seen in compromising situations with gigolos, possibly Argentineans. I couldn't argue. It was all true, more or less: the milk baths, the masseur, and the outings. As for the gigolos, all I knew was that in the middle of the night I often heard music, laughter, and suspicious sounds coming from her bedroom, which she had redecorated in the style of a nineteenth-century cocotte.

When she went out in the evenings she wore heavy makeup, her face covered in creams and powders, cheekbones highlighted with bright red blush, eyelashes stiff with mascara, eyes elongated and rimmed with heavy black eyeliner. The brutal flattening of the hips, breasts, and thighs mandated by the fashion of the period posed enormous challenges for a woman who had long fought a losing battle against her natural plumpness. I can still see her in a midnight-blue velvet dress with a deep décolleté—she had beautiful shoulders—embellished by a light-colored silk lace shawl meant to trail behind her but which could also be draped obliquely over the bust, veiling the rolls of flesh that neither her masseur nor her girdle could altogether efface. Sometimes I also caught a glimpse of her in the morning when she returned, exhausted, dragging her shawl behind her, high heels in one hand, her face looking like a cracking gray mask, the fissures stained with dark eye makeup. Her empty eyes fled mine as we sat together at the breakfast table, and I felt her shudder as she saw me sitting there pink-cheeked in my innocent-looking cotton robe with feather-stitch embroidery.

In February 1921 we had a tragicomic scene in our house. Even though as far as I could tell my father allowed his wife to live as she pleased during his absences, he could be very insistent about certain things. He was adamant that his daughter should have an official coming-out for her eighteenth birthday. At first, my mother seemed truly shocked to discover my actual age; after hiding hers for so long, I think she had convinced herself that I was two or three years younger. Then she began to create obstacles: It was an old-fashioned ritual. It was a waste of money. I was an intellectual and didn't care about such things, just look at my wardrobe! (Of course she did not mention that she was the one who chose my dresses, with great care and against my wishes.) My physical and mental age did not correspond with the date on my birth certificate. I still needed a few years to mature so that I could present myself in society to best advantage. With my awkward, childish body and my glasses, she argued, I would discourage any suitor.

I listened to her arguments in silence. Even though, deep down, I had no desire to play the role of debutante which, as she rightly pointed out, belonged to a lost world, and though I sadly realized that I shared her view of me, a cold rage took hold as I heard her pronounce her cruel, transparent logic. But I also felt a sense of jubilation; this compulsion to point out my childishness and immaturity was not only the result of a refusal to reveal her true age by admitting that she was the mother of an eighteen-year-old but a sign that she considered me a potential rival. The scene at her dressing table in Finland on the night after my first kiss, which had begun to fade from memory, returned triumphantly to my mind. My father held firm. The party took place. It was a grand affair, just as he had wanted. He even took an interest in my clothes, vetoing the predictably frilly, high-necked taffeta dress that my mother had selected. I wore a sea-green draped tunic by Patou, which exposed my neck and arms; it was fastened by a simple crystal clasp on the side and my only jewelry was a marvelous chased gold necklace, a gift from my father, which I still wear and will wear until the day I die. The only disappointment was that he asked me not to cut my hair short because he said he loved my "Gypsy" curls, and I did not have the heart to argue.

The scene that truly epitomized my relations with my mother took place the night of the party, next to the buffet. In the center of the table sat a pheasant, glassily contemplating the silver trays bearing caviar sandwiches, foie gras tartlets, oysters, and jellied fish, all of this framed by two pyramids of exotic fruit. Six waiters in white tails served champagne and cocktails. There were scores of guests; my father had invited all of his business relations, and the entire Russian colony was there, eagerly gulping down food. There were no less than two grand dukes present: Aleksander and Boris. When I caught a glimpse of my reflection I found myself beautiful, perhaps because I was not wearing my glasses and thus the image I saw was a blur. Miss Matthews and my father complimented me on my dress, though my mother said that it did not flatter my complexion and claimed, paradoxically, that it made me look older. During the party I went over to her with one of our friends who had just arrived. Pink, sleek, and ravishing in a mauve silk dress decorated with rhinestones and wearing diamonds in her jet-black hair, she played with a long strand of pearls with one hand while with the other she waved an infinitely long cigarette, bracelets clicking, and roared with laughter as she conversed with a young man whose dark skin contrasted sharply with his white collar. He turned politely toward me with a questioning expression. My mother flushed, hesitated, and said, "Allow me to introduce you to my younger sister." There was an awkward silence. In a second, the story made its way around the room. My father probably heard it as well but made no reference to it, though after the party I heard the sound of raised voices in the empty sitting room.

A few months later, I was allowed to move into an apartment on the second floor with Miss Matthews. I had just passed my *baccalauréat* and was registered to study literature at the Sorbonne the following year. I would no longer have daily contact with my mother, except during the summer of 1921, which I spent with my parents in Biarritz. I fell in love with the Basque Country that year, especially Hendaye, where I went every afternoon with Miss Matthews to tan on the slender arc of beach beneath a ferocious sun that left the bathers' skin looking like gilded copper. Miss Matthews was a romantic; she loved to describe the pyre that Byron had built on a beach just like this one for the body of his adored Shelley after his death by drowning. She told me that he had rolled in the poet's ashes in order to return them to the sea as he bathed in the waves. At night, before returning home, we walked along the barrier by the Bidasoa, which became a low wall with thorny bushes growing between the stones. Fishing boats glided by silently on the smooth river, in whose waters the pink clouds were reflected. The breeze carried the cries of tennis players and music from the small orchestra that accompanied the dancing couples on a terrace built on piles over the water. Across the way, the colored lights of Fontarabie were just coming on. When the wind blew in from Spain, it brought with it the fragrance of cinnamon and orange blossoms from Andalusia. With heavy hearts, we boarded a taxi to take us back to our palace in Biarritz, our lips coated in salt, the folds of our white dresses heavy with sand.

My parents often went out in the evenings, and sometimes they brought me along. At the time, the stock market was constantly going up. Capital traveled from market to market in search of advantageous exchange rates; people bought everything and anything and then sold it just as quickly. The hotels, restaurants, and nightclubs we frequented were bursting with the ultrarich and the parasites who lived at their expense. Luxury was displayed with a crazed arrogance. Ladies in their fifties wore dresses known as *"gosses de riches"** that skimmed their wide hips and revealed pink thighs when they sat down; rivers of diamonds coiled around their sagging necks.

A Russian cabaret opened on the road between Biarritz and Bidart, frequented by Grand Duke Dmitri Pavlovich and his court, which was composed of more or less impoverished members of the Romanov family, haggard old countesses, former pupils of the Page Corps now working as professional ballroom dancers, and ladies-in-waiting wrapped in yellowing lace. The young grand duke was tall, slender, and pale—Gabrielle Chanel was said to be completely in love with him—and whenever he entered the room, preceded by a powdered lackey carrying a silver candelabrum, the jazz trumpets and banjos would pause to play "God Save the Czar." The sudden change of rhythm would cause confusion among a group of drunk Americans, who were frenetically dancing the fox-trot. Then they would dive into a deep reverence, referring to him as "Your Imperial Majesty." Everyone in the club, including international financiers and men who owned gold, platinum, and emerald mines—as well as opium and arms traffickers—would rise, including, of course, the three of us. The grand duke would then sketch a vague greeting with his hand and disappear into the thick fog of cigar smoke. Some nights my father grew tired of this moldy atmosphere and went to the casino. I enjoyed going with him, but I had to wait in one of the sitting rooms because I was too young to gamble. One night he left me there and did not return until dawn. He found me sleeping on a couch, covered in a plaid blanket. I was awakened by a shower of banknotes, his version of an apology.

The move to my own apartment and the start of my university studies changed my life and transformed my character. As I sit here today, a loving wife and indulgent mother, I look back with astonishment, irony, and tenderness at the awkward, prudish girl with her eyeglasses, infantile dresses, and long hair, who was transformed overnight into a frivolous, sparkling young woman, much loved by her companions and surrounded by friends. At the Sorbonne, which I attended halfheartedly from 1922 to 1925, I was not a very diligent student. Our professors, who were for the most part old bores who had been teaching there since before the war, offered the most arid and academic lessons one could imagine: as far as they were concerned, modern literature ended with the Symbolists and the Parnasse. Their lectures contrasted markedly with our own reading habits, which ranged from books that scandalized the bourgeoisie—like Victor Margueritte's *The Bachelor Girl* or, a little later, Radiguet's *The Devil in the Flesh*—to books that also would have outraged them, had they ever heard of them, like the surrealists, Cocteau, and Gide. Gide's *The Fruits of the Earth* had been published twenty years earlier, but the words "families, I detest you" still rang out like a trumpet call with diabolical overtones. Not that I was particularly attracted to the avant-garde. My experiences in Moscow had left me with a secret hatred of violence and excess, and the brutality of the Ballets Russes and, later, the crudeness of *art nègre* troubled me. Secretly, I still read Anna de Noailles, adored Proust, and had discovered and had great admiration for the books of Katherine Mansfield. In short, my tastes were not at all in line with fashion but this did not keep me from joining my fellow students' condemnation of our elderly professors.

Mostly I had an intense social life in which I took great delight. In general I enjoyed myself immensely during the first two trimesters of the year and worked like a dog the last trimester. And the system seemed to work well; at the end-of-year exams, I received a score of nineteen out of twenty. Thanks to Miss Matthews's efforts, I now spoke perfect English, in addition to Russian and French, and had a relatively firm grasp of Finnish and Swedish. My curiosity led me to Spanish and Italian next.

At first, my friends at the Sorbonne were all Russian and mixed well with the friends I already had. We frequented the cafés of the Latin Quarter and played billiards at a club near the university that also functioned as a bistro. We had tea at each other's apartments, often at mine since most of my friends envied my independence. I had furnished my apartment in a style that was highly personal and very comfortable, with low tables and deep couches covered with cushions. Miss Matthews did not interfere; I knew that her long siestas and late mornings were the result of morphine—or ether, when funds were low—but I did not love her any less for it. Often we went dancing. I had discovered a frenetic passion and reasonable aptitude for this activity. At my place, we danced the shimmy and the tango to records we played on the gramophone. We went dancing at the Château de Madrid in the Bois de Boulogne. We danced at our parents' parties, and I can still remember young Mila Gordon, bursting with pride as she waltzed at the Cirque d'Hiver in the arms of the elderly Prince Gagarin. We went dancing in Deauville and Honfleur on the weekends, and in Nice, Juan-les-Pins, Hendaye, and Saint-Jean-de-Luz during the holidays. We danced at the *bals musettes* of the Latin Quarter, and sometimes we went slumming in Montmartre where old Frédé still held court in the small garden of the Lapin Agile. We paid a few visits to some of the classier spots, too, like Le Boeuf sur le Toit, where Picabia's *L'Oeil cacodylate* looked out kindly over this small flock of confused, innocent sparrows who had alighted in this strange aviary, quite convinced of our own sophistication and surrounded by high-class lovebirds, peacocks, pheasants, and hummingbirds.

I also went dancing in spa towns like Vittel and Plombières where on the advice of Professor Vallery-Radot, who was now responsible for my health, I went to be treated for my asthma. One night in Le

Touquet I dressed up like a Gypsy for a fancy-dress ball. I have a picture from that night. I tied a string of coins around my forehead and wore a black velvet blouse decorated with gold-colored braid, a lace bodice embellished with costume jewelry, and flowery skirts. In the photo I am holding a tambourine in one hand, but I am wearing a wristwatch, which clashes with the rest of my getup.

Recently I reread a package of letters I wrote to my friend Madeleine Avot from late 1921 until 1926. She returned these letters to me when she attended my wedding, thinking I would be amused by them. I was amazed that I—yes, I—had written the following words from Vittel:

My dear sweet friend,

In all my life I have never enjoyed myself more than in this adorable place. First of all we dance every evening until one, and twice a week we dance all night. There are six of us, including three young men, who are twenty-one, twenty, and eighteen. They answer to the harmonious names of Fink (a large blond fellow, the butt of every joke, who for some reason is known as Sphynx); Victor Aumont (known as Totoche, and terribly witty); and my flame, Henry La Rochelle, who is twenty. The girls are Henry's sister, who is twenty-two; a charming girl my age, Loulou de Vignoles; and myself. We are all a bit mad! If you only knew all the mischief we get up to! I'll tell you the latest episode. The day before I left, we went to a farm nearby for a nibble. When we arrived, we saw there was an enormous barn filled with hay. We decided to have our chocolate right there, in the hay! You can imagine the look on the maid's face! The hay had a minty smell and we climbed ladders into it; our snacks were carried up there as well, and everything got mixed together, chocolate and bread, butter and hay. I have never enjoyed a meal so much. Then the boys built toboggans out of bales of hay and we slid down like kids. It was charming. The rest of the afternoon, the three couples drifted off to different corners of the barn and we lay in the hay... flirting so happily that we forgot the time and by the time we emerged from the barn we discovered it had been dark for hours! Even so, we went to the casino that night. That is where I got up to my mischief. It was a beautiful night and we went for a walk in the gardens; Totoche and Loulou flirted shamelessly and so did Henry and I. The moral of the story is this: when you go out flirting in the evening, dress warmly. I forgot to do so and here I am, spending the end of my holidays like I did last Easter, in other words, in bed.

The romance with Henry La Rochelle had ended in melodrama. "Dear sweet Madeleine, last Sunday, Choura"—a friend of Daria Kamenka's who had become our closest confidante—"came to see me, and lectured me for two hours: it seems I 'flirt' too much, and it is wrong to excite boys the way I do, etc., etc. You know I had to send Henry away the other day? He came to see me, pale and wild-eyed, with an angry look and a pistol in his pocket. It certainly did not put my mind at ease, I assure you. That madman could just as easily have shot me in the head as himself! In any case, his friends arrived and they all left. But I'm coming to realize that one should really not play with love... at least other people's!" My mischief did not end there and I was in danger of following in my mother's footsteps: "Can you believe it, my sweet Madeleine, once again I've bumped into the gigolo—I think I mentioned him to you once? He is a professional dancer in Nice, and a handsome boy, a little bit like Maurice, do you remember him? He has developed a crush on me and dances with me most of the time. I wanted to pay him, but it made him angry, and instead he pulls me very close when we dance and showers me with all sorts of compliments. That's a price I don't mind paying! But the best thing is that when he found out I was going to Saint-Jean, he arranged to find a job dancing at the Réserve de Ciboure and I'm quite pleased. I have my dancing partner. Mademoiselle and her dancing partner! If you only knew how nice he is! I would have quite a crush on him if he belonged to our set, I swear!!! I don't want to *scandalize* you any further, my darling. Write soon! Please give my respects to your parents." Luckily my future husband arrived on the scene: "I don't know if you remember Michel Epstein; he is smallish and dark-skinned and he shared a taxi with Choura last New Year, on that memorable night, or rather that memorable morning. He has begun to woo me and, I must admit, I find him to my liking. Our crush has become quite intense, so please don't ask me to leave, all right?"

Somehow I was able to complete my degree, with honorable mention. But what these wild years gave me, in addition to my engagement to the sweetest, funniest, loveliest man I could ever have hoped to marry, my husband of three years, was my friendship with Madeleine. She lived in Lumbres, a small town in Pas-de-Calais near Saint-Omer, with her father—a stationer—and a warm, loving mother who showered her with attention. We had met through her brother René, who was studying engineering in Paris. I invited her to my place, and I have to admit I played the role of the Parisienne introducing the impressionable country mouse to her domain and her court. I liked to consider myself extremely daring and, as this correspondence shows, I did my best to shock her.

Madeleine invited me into her home. I spent several short holidays there, often during Christmastime. And my experiences with this French family, prosperous but scornful of excess, tranquil and happy, genuinely devoted to one another, untouched by the slightest shadow of conflict or envy, left a profound impression on me. It convinced me once and for all that France was the place where I belonged, a country of moderation, freedom, and generosity that had embraced me, just as I had adopted it as my own. We named our fair-haired daughter Denise because Michel loves the name and finds it very Parisian; when I gaze at her in her crib, I am profoundly grateful that we did not listen to my father's advice back in 1926 when he suggested we should leave with him for America. I know I made the right choice by opting for security, peace, and moderation. Neither we nor our daughter have anything to fear here.

FEBRUARY 1953

The child is in her room, sitting at her desk and reading a forbidden book, concealed beneath the jacket of a philosophy textbook: it is Irène Némirovsky's Two. *In it, the author describes, with some irony but also enormous tenderness, the tranquil contentment of the French bourgeoisie. The fifteen-year-old girl lifts her head and looks around distractedly at the white bedspread, the varnished dresser, and the window facing a freshly mowed lawn surrounded by a row of well-trimmed boxwood hedges. The previous day, at the entrance to the boarding school in the crush of parents and students, a dark-haired woman with wild eyes had grabbed her wrist and said, "Come with me!" The nuns intervened, in a great fluttering of veils, and sent the woman away. Earlier that month, the kidnapping of the Finaly children* had created a great commotion across France.*

PART II

Irène Némirovsky–*June, 1942*

9

I AM SITTING on my blue sweater with my legs folded under me, as if on a raft in the middle of an ocean of rotting leaves, still drenched from last night's storm. As I look up I can see a corner of sky, crisscrossed with dark green. The sky is the same pale, fragile color as my daughter Denise's scout scarf, a faded rag that she insists on wearing because it reminds her of a time when things were normal. Now that the children's voices have faded in the distance, the silence around me is filled with tiny sounds and movements: the distant whir of a saw against the trunk of an oak tree, woodcutters' voices, and, closer to where I am sitting, the insistent drone of a bumblebee that flies in tireless circles above my flowered dress; the sharp chirping of a bird, a bubble bursting on the surface of a pond coated with greenish muck, the cracking of pine bark. The air smells of sap and wet grass. Heavy, cold drops fall on my forehead from the shimmering underside of a leaf still resplendent with rain. My neck is sore from craning, weighed down by my heavy hair, which is gathered in a snood. My elbows begin to sink into the saturated earth. I am a bit light-headed from staring up at the sky. The world seems too fresh and young to plunge into darkness so soon.

My mood is somber but calm after yesterday's panic, which was followed by an asthma attack during the night: yesterday afternoon, in this same copse, heavy with the heat that comes before a storm, I made the mistake of rereading the rubbish I wrote at the age of twenty-six. What a ridiculous idea it was to drag these self-indulgent pages all the way to Issy-l'Évêque, the small village in Saône-et-Loire where we sought refuge two years ago! I felt as if I were suffocating with impotent fury as I contemplated my image in this selfish, credulous, vain mirror, and I admit that I cried with rage, stretched out on the dry earth, pounding at the dirt with my fists. No, a "quiet happiness" does not appear to be the most likely outcome for my daughter, whose blond head I just saw bobbing down the path away from me. The yellow star she has worn on her chest for the past month demonstrates that France, which I described as a "country of moderation and freedom, and of generosity," has a unique way of adopting those who love it. I try to draw comfort from the thought that in 1915 when I was twelve, as she is now, the situation appeared equally somber, and yet I survived. But as I think back on all the criticisms my generation heaped upon our parents back in 1919— blindness, mental laziness, selfishness—I realize that we have been as blind as they were!

I feel no nostalgia for this "frivolous, sparkling young woman," too caught up in her pleasures to realize what was happening around her. Had I not noticed, in 1921 or 1922, the appearance of royalist militants wearing berets and carrying lead-tipped canes, who walked up and down the boulevard Saint-Michel just outside the Sorbonne, or the Action Française agitators who disturbed the courses taught by Jewish professors? Had I felt no inkling when our troops occupied the Ruhr in 1923? I am horrified to admit that my only memory of that year, the year I turned twenty, was a sparkling dinner at the Dôme with my parents. That night we discussed the recent scandal caused by Isadora Duncan's visit to Paris with her unlikely husband, the redheaded Yesenin, an old acquaintance, who had been thrown out of his hotel after drunkenly destroying the furniture in his room. When we emerged, somewhat tipsy, onto the boulevard Montparnasse, we were suddenly engulfed in a stampede of young trade unionists protesting the deployment of French troops in Germany, pursued by members of Pierre Taittinger's Jeunesses Patriotes. I can still remember how my father took my arm as I stumbled in my high heels, adjusted his glasses, and brushed off the sleeve of his dinner jacket with the back of his hand. A police officer wearing a cape and gripping a truncheon politely stopped to pick up my father's hat, and my father thanked him. This scene, which contains all the actors in the current drama, now seems surreal.

When I left the house a short while ago to walk toward the copse of trees, a group of village children with nothing to do on a Thursday followed me gaily down the road. On either side, the almost ripe wheat waved its blond tufts. I held the hand of my youngest, Babet. The others ran alongside us, playing catch and hopscotch, the lines of the game only slightly smudged by the rain. I picked two blades of grass from the side of the road, one long and one short, and placed them between my fingers. I asked Babet to draw straws in the Russian manner and she won the game. As a prize, I gave her a poppy. Her round face broke into a smile and she slid the flower between two baby teeth. Little Lulu, her best friend, who is also five years old and with whom she gets into all sorts of mischief, began to sing in a high voice: *"Gentil coquelicot, Mesdames! Gentil coquelicot, messieurs!"** Everyone laughed. And for once, when I told the children to go and play at the edge of the copse, Denise did not ask if she could stay behind; instead she took her sister's hand and ran off gaily with the others, her blond hair fluttering in the breeze. She is used to leaving me alone to work, but recently our anxiety has rubbed off on her and it has been difficult for her to leave our side.

I have a feeling that once again today my work on this book, *Suite Française*, will go nowhere. It is a terribly ambitious project in three volumes which I see as a kind of *War and Peace* based on the current conflict. Earlier I opened the large, leather-bound notebook, whose pages I am filling completely, leaving no margins, in a minuscule spidery scrawl that my husband will have trouble transcribing on his typewriter, if he has the chance. He does this with all my manuscripts. I have to economize because it is impossible to find such thick, white, luxurious paper here. I cannot get used to the idea of resorting to the cheap school workbooks which are the only thing available at the town bazaar. I unscrewed my last fountain pen, the one Michel gave me in 1937 with a silly, tender note: "My name is Doret. I hope Maman Minouche will like me! I was created for her and trust that she will use me as she does my older brother, Bel Azur, and hope that he will be able to rest from time to time." There was also another note: "We are five hundred French francs. We beg Maman Minouche to spend us on pretty clothes to wear, for my darling whom I adore." I filled Doret with my favorite ink, which is the color of the southern seas; it has become impossible to find, too.

Today I sat there daydreaming, pen in hand. The passage I read yesterday still haunts me, though the rage is gone. I think about my daughters. If things turn out badly, truly badly, what will they think of me? What faults will they legitimately accuse me of in ten or twenty years, when they have become women? The blindness that yesterday seemed to me so unforgivable in the "frivolous young woman" I once was, and which can be explained only by the fact that I had seen death at such a young age and had sought to banish such thoughts from my mind by pursuing nervous pleasures, seems criminal in the happy and contented adult—with access to multiple sources of information—I was in 1929 and remained until my arrival here. Hadn't I read the newspapers? I remember that yesterday, when I came across the passage in my journal in which I congratulated myself for not following my father's advice when he suggested that we join him in the United States, I trembled and rocked back and forth desperately, my arms clutching my chest—in the same way that I sometimes console Michel when he is overcome with terror and sadness. If my father had not died of a heart attack in Nice in 1932 at the age of sixty-four, I am sure he would have convinced me in the end, that he would have saved us. I can imagine myself in New York, standing under the Statue of Liberty which he had so often described and greeting my dear childhood friend Mila. After she left, she was joined there by her sister Hélène and her husband, the journalist Pierre Lazareff. She had tried in vain to convince us to go.

If I can find excuses for the twenty-year-old Irène, then perhaps the author of *David Golder* had an excuse of her own: she was blinded by her success. When I gave birth in November 1929, I was still unaware of the future that awaited my manuscript and how it would change my life. It had taken me four years to write the book. The idea had come to me in Biarritz, where part of the novel is set, in the milieu of shady businessmen, gigolos, and courtesans that I had frequented with my parents before my marriage. I can pinpoint the precise day the character of Joyce took shape in my imagination. She is the selfish, spoiled daughter of an aging banker who, ill and financially ruined, is forced to rebuild his fortune for her sake, dying in the process. The idea came to me during the long night I had spent waiting for my father at the casino, watching ruddy-faced men smoking cigars and ladies wearing a reliquary worth of jewels coming and going among the tables, until finally I fell asleep. I had already published a short novel, *The Misunderstanding*, with Fayard, in their Oeuvres Libres series; it was the story of an affair that was destined to fail. The main character was a penniless man who, on his return from the trenches, falls in love with the wife of a rich businessman. He does not see that the difference in their status renders their love affair impossible. The book was a respectable if clumsy first effort and received no attention from the critics.

David Golder was more complicated. I had a clear idea of the banker, whose personality, behavior, and language were familiar from observing my father's business associates. Now that I no longer feel the need to spare my mother's feelings, I can confess what all my friends already know: that she was the model for the character of the wife, Gloria, an aging, rapacious, and tired woman, greedy for lovers and jewels, who pushes her husband to his demise. But I had to create a credible business scenario, because in the book Golder loses a fortune and creates another one. I leafed through the *Revue Pétrolière*, a much-handled issue of which I still have in my Paris apartment. I also read a British book entitled, I believe, *The Empire of Oil*, which I pored over for hours. I did not want to consult my father because I was afraid of his opinion. I asked him only to read the final proofs. He returned them to me with the comment: "I expected worse. Well, you've surprised me. You didn't say too many silly things."

Most important, I wanted to write a modern novel, strong and spare, stripped of anything unrelated to the plot, without commentary or analysis, a work that would allow the reader to hear and to see, as in a film. To accomplish this, I employed Turgenev's method, which I still use, and which consists of imagining the life of each of the protagonists and secondary characters chronologically, filling in the periods before and after the events described in the story in infinite detail. I was also happy with the opening line, which was hard and neat, and felt that it immediately established the tone and psychology of the character: " 'No,' said Golder."

As soon as I finished the book, I sent it to Oeuvres Libres. The reader, Monsieur Foucault, informed me that he liked it. But it was too long for them and he asked me to cut fifty pages. I could not bring myself to amputate the book in this way. Instead, I decided to proceed as I had before, in other words send it to a publisher via the post without the slightest recommendation. I bypassed *La Nouvelle Revue française*, which had made the mistake of turning down Marcel Proust, and instead chose Monsieur Bernard Grasset's "Protestant temple," much in the news at the time, and the publisher of such excellent writers as Paul Morand, with whose writing I felt a certain affinity. To protect myself from possible failure, I sent the book under my husband's name, Michel Epstein, requesting that the response be sent general delivery. My pregnancy was already very advanced. Two months before the end of my term, the doctor ordered bed rest, and it was not until a few weeks after my daughter's birth that I was able to pick up my mail. I found a bundle of letters and telegrams, more and more frenzied, imploring me to come to the Grasset headquarters on rue des Saints-Pères. The publisher later informed me that they had gone so far as to place an ad in all the major newspapers: "Seeking author who sent a manuscript to Éditions Grasset under the name Epstein."

I arrived at the rue des Saints-Pères and climbed a narrow, filthy stairway, after which I was admitted to a large, chaotic room filled with dusty books, proofs, and manuscripts. A painted wooden bust of a woman wearing a beret on top of a crooked wig presided over the mantelpiece. There were ashtrays overflowing with cigarettes all over the room, even on the threadbare carpet. The air was filled with the stench of stale smoke. A man burst in. He had a pasty complexion, pomaded hair parted to one side, a toothbrush mustache, a handkerchief bursting out of one jacket pocket, and a cigarette holder between his lips. He froze, mouth agape, staring at me in utter confusion, which I had expected. Bernard Grasset was expecting a middle-aged man, perhaps a retired banker. Instead, standing before him he saw a petite, young, shy, and curiously dressed woman, peering at him nearsightedly. I was still recovering from the birth of my daughter and had not yet replenished my wardrobe which, it must be said, I had somewhat neglected since my marriage. He stammered a few comments. I blushed. We were equally at a loss. He called in the reader, Monsieur Henry Muller, who stared at me as confusedly as Grasset had. The entire office—his associate Monsieur Brun, the editors, and the press agent, Monsieur Poulailles—came through Grasset's office to peer at this exotic young phenomenon as I signed the contract that had been prepared three months earlier. Grasset recovered enough sangfroid to inform me that he would not be publishing the book as part of the Cahiers Verts, directed by Daniel Halévy, but rather in the series Pour Mon Plaisir, which he had just created and which he planned to devote to writers for whom he felt a particular enthusiasm.

By our second meeting he had recovered his wits and even asked me to tell interviewers that I was younger than my actual age. I was twenty-six at the time. He suggested that I admit to being no older than twenty-four. "The launching of a book," he said, "requires an angle, something that inspires curiosity among readers. In your case, it is twofold: First of all you are Russian but you write in French. This could be a possible plug but it does not seem sufficient because there are so many of your compatriots now in France. So we will also publicize your age. Unfortunately I can't claim that you are a young girl of seventeen, as Radiguet was when I launched *The Devil in the Flesh*, though you look no older than he did. But you are a wife and a mother. We will simply shave two years off of your actual age." And from that day forward, I became two years younger in all my interviews. After all the books I have written, it must be said that this ploy has required great mental effort on my part, and that under the current circumstances, it has only served to further complicate the question of my civil status.

I don't think even Grasset imagined that the book would be such a success. I doubt I have ever experienced a shock comparable to the emotion I felt upon opening *Le Temps* on January 10, 1930, and reading the first sentence of a long review by André Thérive, the most respected and feared critic of the time: "There is no doubt that *David Golder* is a masterpiece." On January 31, Pawlowski was equally definitive in his review in *Les Lettres*: "This is a beautiful book that blossoms like a flowering tree in the midst of the literary forest. It has its place, solid and full of life, next to the dark cypress planted by Leo Tolstoy, *The Death of Ivan Ilych*, and Dostoyevsky's funereal willow, 'A Gentle Creature.'" Other critics went so far as to make comparisons to Balzac's *Père Goriot*. They waxed lyrical about my age, just as Grasset had expected. Others were amazed at the ease with which a Russian wrote in the language of Racine, after living in France only ten years. This fact was celebrated as if it were an apotheosis, definitive proof of the superiority of the French language, as if its vocabulary and syntax were so powerful that I had absorbed them with no effort on my part. Secretly I thanked the shadow of Mademoiselle Rose, whose death now seemed certain; had she been alive, the clamor surrounding my name would have reached her even in the deepest provinces.

Grasset inundated the press with ads and sent me to call on all the literary and academic eminences; he threw me into the arms of Cocteau and Morand, Montherlant and Halévy, and dragged me to all the literary salons, like the ones held at the homes of Princess Bibesco and Marie de Régnier. I was the toast of Paris. The book was selling tens of thousands of copies. At the apartment on avenue Daniel Lesueur where we had moved after our wedding, the doorbell rang constantly. I had exiled my daughter to a room in the back of the apartment so that she could sleep undisturbed. Reporters vied for my attention.

Some reporters suspected that I was not really the author of this "man's novel." I had the honor of being interviewed by the famous Frédéric Lefèvre, who was published by Les Nouvelles Littéraires, and whose attitude reflected a certain incredulity:

I was looking forward to paying a visit to Madame Irène Némirovsky. My joy was mixed with curiosity and some concern regarding an issue that, I felt, needed clarification. Like many other readers, I am sure, I felt some uncertainty about the true identity of the author of *David Golder*. To put it simply, I found it difficult to believe that a book so rich in personal experience, and which reflects such a deep knowledge of the business world, could be the work of a twenty-four-year-old woman. As soon as I found myself in her presence, however, my doubts and hesitancies melted away. It is not that the writer appears any older than her twenty-four years; on the contrary, this young mother has the air of a young girl. She is an attractive Semitic type. In her appearance, there is a perfect and rare harmony between the intellectual Slav—familiar to habitués of the Sorbonne—and the *femme du monde*. Of medium height, with a svelte figure, she was wearing a purple velvet sheath; her hair, which is the color of jet or of a crow's feathers—as black as you can imagine—is cut short, in a boyish style. Her eyes are as black as her hair; they have a strangely gentle, flickering quality, a result of her nearsightedness. Her gestures are as calm and gentle as her gaze.

The usual banalities were repeated everywhere regarding my Russian banking magnate father and the Russian Revolution. I told reporters about my time in Moscow at the home of the young man in the Horse Guards, my discovery of Maupassant and Oscar Wilde, and, on the advice of Bernard Grasset, my enthusiastic reaction to Plato, whose *Symposium* I claimed to have read "curled up on a couch while bullets whistled outside even as my mother, outraged by my indifference, assailed me with reprimands each time she entered the room." And finally came the compliments: "A fine objectivity, sharp insight into people and things, a sense of reality so powerful that an atmosphere can be evoked with a word and the reader is able to pass from one situation to the next without the slightest effort. An ease of storytelling, a gift for dialogue, bringing to bear the weight of destiny; this is a strong, virile, brutal book." Even *La Nouvelle Revue française*, openly at war with Grasset, conceded, despite criticizing a slight superficiality on my part, that "the book is always touching and the author's ability to create dialogue makes all the characters appear equally endowed with a burning life."

A few months later, the book was adapted simultaneously for the stage and the screen. The play, directed by Fernand Nozière, was a huge success at the Théâtre de la Porte Saint-Martin. Madame Paule Andral played the role of Gloria. The opening of the play may have marked the moment of my true rupture with my mother. I had not yet forgiven her for her terrible reaction to my announcement that I was pregnant two years earlier, when she had begged me, on her knees, to have an abortion. But still, at my father's request, I had continued to see her. She was far more astute than we were, and already in 1939 she saw the dangers we would face and ran off to Nice without warning. Because she and my father had spent a brief period in Riga during the Revolution she was somehow able to obtain Latvian refugee status; it must be quite an advantage these days given the pro-Nazi sympathies of the Baltic countries. I have her address. A year and a half ago when our resources began to dry up, I wrote asking for help: she has a large fortune, as well as her jewelry. She communicated her refusal in a dry letter written by her lover, an Italian count. I still have the key to her apartment on the Quai de Passy, where she has lived since her husband's death. I sent my brother-in-law Paul to the house. He took all her furs and her silver and brought them to me. I have them here, in our suitcases, and will sell them without a shadow of regret when the time comes.

After the publication of *David Golder*, my mother was forced to accept the idea that I had become famous, believing that my glory would spill over on her. The night of the theatrical première, she held court at the theater in a sumptuous white satin brocade dress from Patou, wearing a river of diamonds. My father sat to her right and her Argentinean lover to the left, both in tails. During the performance, at the moment Paule Andrale began to go through Harry Baur's wallet as he lay dying after his heart attack, and he awoke and began to reproach her bitterly for all the titles and jewels he had given her during their life together, the audience turned toward my mother, inspecting her necklace and rings. The theater was filled with whispers. It was worse yet when Andrale announced to her husband that Joyce, his beloved daughter was not his child, and that the real father was Hoyos, her aging lover. I saw my mother lean toward her left and whisper something in her neighbor's ear. She turned completely red, down to the depths of her cleavage, which was still as firm as marble, and hid behind her fan, above which she flashed me a murderous glance. I gripped Michel's hand as tightly as I could.

Harry Baur played the role of Golder in the movie as well as on-stage. All the newspapers praised his performance. "Last night, he was admirable for his detailed precision, and at the same time, for the amplitude of his interpretation," *Comoedia* reported. "He exhibited a stunning naturalness and that ability to reveal the soul which is particular to him." But the critics were even more impressed by his appearance in the film, directed by Julien Duvivier. "From the start, it was clear that he is among the highest rank of screen actors. He captures each and every aspect of the character, physical and moral, creating unforgettable images. In quick succession he becomes the resigned slave, an aging unemployed clown, a peasant defending his home... In his dressing gown, he looks like a character from a Daumier print; in Moscow, after his success, he becomes Ingres's Bertin the Elder... There is a contained pathos, a highly internalized intensity in him. No, I do not see among the current international roster of stars of the cinema anyone who can be compared to this prodigious artist." Dear Harry Baur! After our shared triumph, he overcame his usual shyness and grasped me to his enormous chest. This man, whose brutish appearance was tempered only slightly by a very soigné style, liked to call me his Russian dove, his sweet bird of the Orient. Now, it seems, the authorities have turned against him: He is suspected of being Jewish, perhaps because he played the character of Golder so well. Dear God, please see that nothing happens to him, and certainly not because of me! I have moments of dizziness, when I am plagued with guilt for having written this book, and I ask myself whether by denouncing this detested milieu—my own—I furthered the arguments of the anti-Semites. I wonder how I could have acted with such suicidal thoughtlessness and irresponsibility.

Frédéric Lefèvre had described me as "an attractive Semitic type." Just last September the Institute for the Study of the Jewish Question organized an exhibit at the Palais Berlitz. It was attended by more than one hundred thousand people over the course of three days, and the minister of education suggested that teachers take their students to see it before the Christmas holiday. I read the well-illustrated reviews of the show. "A giant spider at the entrance of the gallery grabs our attention. Its legs are enmeshed in the enormous web it has woven over the world. This spider is Jewry, feasting on the blood of our France." This was followed by horribly altered photographs of filmmakers, journalists, politicians, and intellectuals, among them Pierre Lazareff, Tristan Bernard, Jean Cassou, and André Maurois. We writers were subjected to special treatment: "Above all, Jewish authors transmit their social unease and sexual perversions. They are temperamentally destructive and take aim at our ideals, our French customs, the honest morals of the provinces, our respect for the fatherland and its beliefs. Plagiarism and scandal are nothing but a means to advance their fame. This race infiltrates our society like a serpent and poisons everything it touches... The Jewish writer *produces, promotes, and sells.*"

Did you see this exhibit, dear Bernard Grasset, you who in 1930 promoted me as a great novelty? Your Aryan roots are beyond dispute and this allows you to continue your publishing business in Paris, where you have created the series À la Recherche de la France in order to publish the collaborationist pamphlets of Drieu La Rochelle, Georges Suarez, and Jacques Doriot. Is this why you have refused to respond to my letters in the last two years? Have you forgotten the letter my husband, Michel, sent to your lawyer in 1934 when your own staff, discouraged by your repeated absences and attacks, attempted to have you banned from your offices? He wrote: "Monsieur Bernard Grasset, who is my friend, as well as my wife's first publisher, has asked me to testify in this affair... It seems that the house continues to do everything in its power to isolate him. Is there anything you can do to put a stop to these activities, which make Bernard Grasset's status in the company completely untenable?"

Have you forgotten how, in 1935, your family attempted to have you declared incompetent, and how we testified on your behalf, Michel and I? Benjamin Crémieux and Marie-Anne Comnène composed a manifesto in your defense which none of your famous writers, neither Montherlant, nor Maurois, Mauriac, or Morand— your beloved "four M's"—nor Chardonne, Châteaubriant, or Giraudoux were willing to sign. When your famous friends abandoned you, I did not, and this despite the fact that I had already left your publishing house for Albin Michel. Do you think of me from time to time, when your eye happens to come across one of my books, one of the few copies you have not yet destroyed, eagerly outpacing German orders? I hear you are known as the Caesar of Garchtesgaden and that you have begun to cultivate a Hitlerian forelock. Have you eliminated the name Irène Némirovsky from your memory, just as you have from your catalogue? Have I changed so much, once deliciously and exotically Slavic, now an unrecognizable Yid? Do I fit Professor Montandon's description of "the Jew": "Powerfully convex nose, fleshy lips, protruding eyes, a slight puffiness of all the soft tissues which constitutes the Jewish mask; frizzy hair, large ears detached from the head, slightly stooped shoulders, often wide or heavy haunches, flat feet, clawlike arms, gangly or shuffling gait."

It is true that neither I nor my husband—though he is quite athletic—bear much resemblance to Arno Breker's colossal statues, which were recently exhibited at the Orangerie. I read about them in *Comoedia* a month ago. Several of your authors, including of course Jacques Chardonne and the bleating Alphonse de Châteaubriant, attended the exhibition of works by this trashy mystic who has become the minstrel of National Socialism. The flamboyant Cocteau was also there. I remember well when he dedicated his poem "Le Bilboquet d'Irène" to me, his eyes misted over with opium. It is partly due to him and his *Enfants terribles* that I named my youngest daughter Élisabeth, though of course the main reason was that I wanted her to have her grandmother's name, in honor of that marvelous woman. All I can now hope is that her luck will equal that of Cocteau's eponymous heroine: "She was accustomed to miracles, and accepted them without amazement. She expected them and they always came true."

These days, she will truly need a miracle. If Cocteau brings her luck, perhaps I will forgive his ode to this "model sculptor," which appeared on the front page of a literary journal:

> I salute you, Breker
> I salute you from the poets' lofty realm
> A realm where nations do not exist, except in that which
>   each man supplies of his nation's labor
> In this lofty realm where we are all brothers, you speak to
>   me of France.

Perhaps he has taken a line from his own play *Les Mariés de la tour Eiffel* too much to heart: "Since these mysteries confound me, I'll just pretend I organized them." Julie Dumot, my father's one-time traveling companion, who once worked for Sacha Guitry, made me laugh when she told me that she had recently spoken with Guitry, who had also seen the Breker exhibit, and who had publicly declared: "Let's hope these statues do not become aroused, or else it will be impossible to circulate!" His quip reminded me of something dear old Tristan Bernard had once said: "Back in '14, we said: 'We'll get them!' Well, now we've got them."

Yes, Julie is here. She is our governess. Exactly one year ago, on June 22, 1941, I wrote to her:

My dear Julie,

As soon as we heard that Russia and Germany were at war, we began to worry about the possibility that we might be put in a concentration camp, and I sent you a card asking you to come as soon as possible. If we are not here when you arrive, please move into the Hotel des Voyageurs with the children, where we have been living for the past year. It is a modest little auberge, but you will be well fed and the owners, Monsieur and Madame Loctin, are completely trustworthy. We have placed a box containing some small jewels in their care, the most significant of which are my diamond ring and a brooch with small diamonds. They also have my father's gold cigarette case, the one you gave us (the smaller one has been sold). The box also contains approximately twenty-five thousand francs in banknotes.

We will also leave, either with Maître Vernet—the notary of Issy-l'Évêque, and a good man—or with the aforementioned Monsieur Loctin, around sixty thousand francs, to do with as you see fit.

On November 11, you will be able to move into the house we have rented on a 3-6-9 lease from Monsieur Marius Simon, at the price of 4,500 francs per year. The house is not furnished, but we have made arrangements to rent all the necessary furniture from Monsieur Billand, a local cabinetmaker, and Maître Vernet. You can simply contact them. If it were possible, the best solution would obviously be to have our furniture brought down from the apartment in Paris, even if it is expensive to do so. We were recently informed that it would cost five thousand francs to complete the move, if it were done by a company from Nevers recommended by Vernet—the Chautard Company. Do whatever seems best to you. If you decide to bring the furniture down from Paris, you will find attached a letter from me for the building manager.

I have bought and *paid* three thousand francs for fifteen crates of wood from Monsieur Frachot, in Issy. He will deliver them as soon as you call him. You will not need to worry about heating.

I've asked Monsieur Fontaine, the ironmonger, to locate a stove, which should cost around two thousand francs.

You should hire someone to look after the garden, which will produce a good quantity of fruits and vegetables. Ask Marius Simon, the landlord, or Monsieur Loctin to advise you. I think that the money I am leaving will be enough to live on for quite some time.

Once the money is gone, sell the furs, which you will find in our suitcases and which you will surely recognize... You will find some fabrics, also taken from Quai de Passy. Keep the sables as long as you can. Then there is the silver. Sell it after the furs, and before the jewels.

And finally, in the worst case, at the Loctins' hotel you will find the manuscript of a novel which I will perhaps not have time to finish, entitled *Storm in June*. Here are some instructions regarding what should be done with it:

1. I've written to Éditions de France, 20 avenue Rapp, Paris, 7th arrondissement (the owners of the journal *Gringoire*), to the attention of Monsieur Horace de Carbuccia, offering the novel to them for publication in the journal. If they accept, they will write to you directly. You can send the manuscript via registered mail and they will hopefully pay approximately fifty thousand francs for it.

2. I've also written to my editor, Albin Michel, 22 rue Huyghens, Paris (14th arrondissement), asking him to send you three to four thousand francs per month through the end of 1942. It is possible that in exchange Albin Michel will want the manuscript of *Storm in June*; if so, send it to him if you have not already sent it to Éditions de France. But if Éditions de France has already received it, tell Albin Michel to contact them directly.

You will probably receive a request for back taxes from Paris. Above all, pay nothing. If you can get my mother to fork up the money, please do, but that seems unlikely. The doctor here, Benoît-Gouin, is excellent. Do not hesitate to call him if you have the slightest concern. For more important matters, you can contact Dr. Pierre Delafontaine, 15 avenue d'Iéna, Paris (16th arrondissement), or Professor Pasteur Vallery-Radot, 49 bis avenue Victor Emmanuel III, Paris (8th arrondissement). Do not hesitate to call them, even for advice or protection, should the need arise.

In February 1942 Denise has an appointment with the eye doctor—she has already seen Dr. Murard, in Creusot.

The children have been vaccinated against diphtheria. Babet has also been given a tetanus shot, and Denise was given a typhoid vaccine. I believe this was done in 1937.

They are both in good health, thank God, except that Babet has a slight case of enteritis; she does not drink unpasteurized milk or eat cream cheese, but a soft-boiled egg from time to time won't do any harm. Madame Loctin is aware of her diet.

Both girls go to school; they should continue to do so, but Babet should stay home on particularly cold days.

You are completely free, of course, to organize the house as you please and in general to make whatever decisions you believe are for the best. For this reason I have left a letter with Maître Vernet, the notary, giving you complete power of attorney.

That is all, my dear Julie. You will understand how unhappy I am as I write this, but I am reassured that if the children are with you, they will be all right, because I know that you will not abandon them. I leave them in your hands.

With my warm embrace,

Irène Némirovsky-Epstein

P.S. Regarding our Paris apartment, I think my preference would be to bring the furniture to Issy but to keep the apartment itself for better times, while paying as few expenses as possible. At the moment, we pay 1,350 francs per trimester, which is half what we paid before the war. Try to work out a price with the building manager. But if things continue to worsen, you will have to let the apartment go.

This letter still exists, but the money, jewels, and furs are long since gone, sucked into the vortex of our debt caused by the anti-Jewish laws which deprive me of most of my royalties. But Julie is indeed here, tall as ever, with her white hair, her glasses, and her mutilated leg, which so fascinates Babet. In the evening, when I emerge from my bucolic retreat with pine needles in my hair, like Ronsard's nymph who has eluded the woodcutter's ax—"Hold still your arm, oh lumberjack / It is not just wood you are cutting"*—and return to the house, leather notebook in hand and blue sweater knotted around my shoulders, I see the rambling manse on the town square, across from the monument to the unknown soldier. My husband anxiously awaits me at the door. Julie gazes at me with the same expression she once reserved for my father after his first heart attack, when he returned exhausted from his foreign travels. The children run out to me, exclaiming joyfully. She takes them gently by the hand and leads them away to dinner, leaving the two of us alone to our joy and our sorrow.

The child emerges from the cinema, blinded by her tears. On a whim, she had gone alone to see Night and Fog. *This is the first time she has faltered. Until now, she had stubbornly refused to know. For fourteen years, without a word, even to her sister, she has awaited her parents' return. One day she thought she recognized her mother on a sunny street. Another time, her father's silhouette appeared to her in the middle of a Russian crowd in a documentary film. Didn't people say that the deportees had disappeared into the east? She had blocked even the memory of their faces, but she had waited. But no, they would not return. Her mother's hair, which was curly like her own, was surely there, on those gray plains. Her father's ashes had been buried, with those of thousands of others, in those mass graves.*

10

MICHEL drinks. It's extraordinary that I have never really noticed this before. Tonight he returned from a long session at the Café des Voyageurs, unsteady and very late for dinner. He slurred his words and made awkward gestures, and his eyelids were heavier than usual, his mouth set in a strange grimace. Denise, who in Paris had sometimes accompanied him to Harry's Bar—where she was surely the youngest customer—and who has often seen him tipsy, recoiled from his pungent breath when he kissed her. He sat down heavily at the table and immediately reached out for the bottle of red wine. He ate very little and drank a lot, and became irritated with Babet, whom I had given permission to sit at the table and who kept spitting out the spinach that Julie was trying to force her to eat. Once the children had gone to bed, he fell asleep, mumbling in his chair, after gulping down one final glass, and I had trouble taking him to our room. I had to undress him; he had collapsed, fully dressed, on the bed. He snored all night long.

I won't mince words here: If his *alcoholism* has eluded my notice until now, it is because I have always seen men warm their blood with alcohol during difficult times. And also because before, when he drank, it was with insouciance and high spirits, with the elegant nonchalance that is his natural state but which now surfaces only rarely. There is an enormous difference between the way he drinks now and the way he drank before, as unalike as the rough, twenty-four-proof red wine he is now forced to drink and the champagne—consumed ice cold, in the Russian manner—which he loved to uncork after a Sunday family lunch. On the beach at Hendaye, where we spent our summer holidays during the thirties, he and his brother Paul would order a bottle of cognac and finish it off in an afternoon. Cheekily, they would offer a glass to my dear Cécile, Denise's nurse, as she sat on the sand beneath our beach tent, her head whipped by the windswept fabric. She scolded them in her thick Burgundian accent, tucking a lock of brown hair beneath her kerchief and clutching her dark-blue striped skirt tightly around her wide hips. Michel and Paul would rest their wet heads against my knees as they swirled the amber liquid in their brandy glasses. Eventually they would fall asleep despite the children's screaming and the seagulls' calls, engulfed in the roar of the sea. I read my book, from time to time shaking out the sand that crunched between its pages.

In Paris, after a day of writing, I would meet Michel near his bank at a little English pub with mahogany walls, on avenue Henri Martin. Michel, who bought fresh flowers for his secretary every morning and sent her home in a taxi every evening, was incapable of ending a workday without laughter and conversation. My brother-in-law Paul would meet us after a day at the Banque Lazard. He splashed seltzer water into our whiskey glasses while recounting the most recent chapter of his campaign to accomplish the impossible: he wanted to become a member of the Jockey Club despite being a Jew, following in the footsteps of Proust's Swann and the man on which he was based, Charles Haas. In the pub, the elderly habitués read newspapers, spread across large wooden newspaper holders, in the light of small lamps placed on pedestal tables. They barely looked up when weary-looking prostitutes came in and collapsed onto the tall barstools. I drank little, lingering over my Americano as I conversed with the ladies in the reddish half-light. In exchange for the address of a milliner or seamstress, they told me anecdotes which I would often use in a story the following day. I owe a good portion of my collection *Talking Pictures* to these conversations. We would stay for an hour or two and then Michel and I would depart arm in arm, Michel with his coat tossed over his shoulder and a cigarette in one hand, I in my little tweed suit and cloche. We hailed a taxi and went home, and on the way I would tell him some of the stories the girls had imparted to me.

Whiskey, champagne, vodka, or fine wine, people drank an awful lot back then. Some memorable evenings come to mind. The Revue Nègre at the Théâtre des Champs-Élysées in 1925, for example, where Michel took me to celebrate our engagement, and the unforgettable sight of Josephine Baker, a glorious ebony statue carried onstage by her black partner, completely in the nude and upside down, legs open wide and wearing only a pink flamingo feather between her thighs. Baker strutting about the stage, serenaded by Sidney Bechet's clarinet. The room froze in astonishment, then suddenly burst into an endless ovation that drowned out the syncopated rhythms of the music. We ended the night at Fouquet's, drinking plumed multicolor cocktails in a crowd so excited by what it had just seen that they simply refused to leave. That same year, we went with my parents to hear Maurice Chevalier at the Casino de Paris, which had not yet hung the sign that read FORBIDDEN TO DOGS AND JEWS; that did not appear until July 1940.

Later, when Michel felt nostalgic for his Russian adolescence, especially in winter, the hardest season for the exiles, when we dreamt of snow, real snow, a magical swirling of heavy, silent flakes and the bitter cold that cuts the lungs, we spent many wild nights in Russian bars, restaurants, and cabarets. They were beginning to pop up all over Montmartre, around the rue Pigalle, the rue Fontaine, and the rue de Douai. We often saw our friend Joseph Kessel, lips bloodied from chewing glass for tourists, his large head bent over a tablecloth scattered with mismatched silverware decorated with the arms of aristocratic families, sold by impoverished émigrés. He would sleep, arms crossed, his leonine hair brushing against an almost empty vodka bottle. Only his fingers moved on the table while a violinist— perhaps a descendant of the highest aristocracy, or just as easily a real, chicken-stealing Gypsy—scratched away or a dancer brushed his head teasingly with a fold of her red skirt. In a corner, an aging singer, eyes burning dully in her sunken face, croaked out the words to "Otchi-Tchor-Ni-Ya" in a raspy voice.

I had practically stopped frequenting literary salons since 1933. In that year, tired of Bernard Grasset's manias, I had followed one of his advisers, André Sabatier, to Albin Michel. My mother, who still ordered her chauffeur to drive her over to our apartment for a visit from time to time, reproached me. "You don't dress the part," she said disdainfully, finding me at home in a plain skirt and brown sweater, hair messy from pulling at it while searching for a word that escaped me. I was tired of the old academicians who still treated me like a child prodigy and the mediocre scribblers who were always asking me to write articles for their journals. But we often went to see Sacha Guitry, who invited us to his "intimate dinners." He would hide his growing paunch beneath purple silk pajamas and hold out a fat hand on which he wore an enormous ring with his initials engraved in gold beneath the stone. We took Denise to tea with Tristan Bernard's granddaughter; I found his ferocious sense of humor charming. We always accepted invitations from my friend Marie de Régnier. I knew her children's books, which she wrote under the pen name Gérard d'Houville, by heart because my daughter loved them, especially *Les Rêves de Rikiki*, which she had begged me to read over and over before going to bed. I was spoiled by both Marie's lover and her husband. The former, André Chaumeix, praised each of my books and introduced me to the *Revue des Deux Mondes*, and the latter, Henri de Régnier, wrote a very favorable review of my novel *Jezebel* which appeared in *Le Figaro* on the very day he died. We enjoyed ourselves immensely amid the Venetian decor at 24 rue Boissière. I would gently scold Marie's boy, Tigre, who described his father as an old bore and refused to call him anything but "the Immortal." Meanwhile, my husband proposed toasts to our olive-skinned hostess's beautiful Spanish eyes.

Back at the house, Michel would open another bottle of champagne for an intimate dinner of caviar and foie gras, or a more modest repast of cold chicken plundered from the icebox, which we then consumed in bed, listening to Michel's beloved popular songs on the gramophone: "*Elle avait de tout petits petons, Valentine, Valentine, / Elle avait de tout petits tétons que je tâtais a tâtons*" [She had tiny little footsies, Valentine, Valentine / She had tiny little titties, which I tenderly tickled]. Or if we were feeling more wistful: "*Parlez-moi d'amour, redites-moi des choses tendres, / Votre beau discours, / Mon Coeur n'est pas las de l'entendre*" [Speak to me of love, whisper to me once more that you love me, / Your loving words, / My heart aches to hear once more]. He sang along, imitating Maurice Chevalier's guttural argot or Lucienne Boyer's beautiful husky voice, dancing around the room and swaying his hips with a worldly air, a champagne flute pressed against his chest. He made up mischievous lyrics—using his amazing gift for prosody to come up with an alexandrine in no time at all. He demonstrated these uncanny abilities later on as well. When we arrived in Issy-l'Évêque in 1940, Michel realized that Denise, then ten years old, was still struggling with arithmetic. So he created math problems for her in verse:

> There once was a dwarf
> Who felt out of sorts.
> He went to the doc
> And paid three francs ten.
> He bought him some pills,
> Paid forty and nil.
> Then had a massage
> For twelve eighty-five.
> So what did he pay
> To make him okay?

And another:

> One day a jaunty sailor
> Went off to buy a sweater.
> At the store they declared,
> "We've got one right there,

It'll cost you a hundred four francs, sir."
He answered, distraught,
"Eighty-eight's all I got."
So how much did the sailor still owe her?

These games usually ended with a crazed waltz in her father's arms. Ours ended in the silk sheets that had been our wedding gift from Mavlik.

Samuel, Paul, Mavlik . . . Michel's brothers and sister. It is June 1942 and we know they are still in Paris, and we tremble for them. Like us, they are forced to wear the yellow star and I fear that the dangers are even greater in the streets of the capital than they are here in this small village in Saône-et-Loire. It has become more common for neighbors to turn in neighbors, and raids and arrests are becoming ever more frequent. Back in the days when we could easily call them, we wasted our breath begging them to join us here. We had endless discussions about the situation with Paul the last time he drove down, for Denise's communion. He brought a wonderful gift, especially considering that these days even warm sweaters and socks are hard to come by: a white leather desk blotter with a pen and matching portfolio. He implored us to return to Paris, arguing that should the need arise, it would be easier to hide in a large city than in a tiny village where everyone knows everyone else.

I met Michel's family in 1925, when we were engaged. Parents, grandparents, children, and grandchildren lived together in an enormous apartment on avenue Victor Emmanuel II. Everyone, including the governesses, had their own room. The Epsteins were originally from Moscow, then St. Petersburg, where my husband's father had worked as the managing director of the Azov-Don Commercial Bank, the third-largest banking institution in Russia, and held the post of vice president of the Central Committee of Banking and Commerce. His direct superior was Boris Kamenka, my friend Daria's father. It turned out that Daria's brother, Hippolyte, had been a childhood friend of Michel's. When the Epsteins decided to leave Russia in 1920, they took a different route than we had, toward the south. On the first evening I dined at their home, Michel's sister-in-law Alexandra (née Ginzbourg), who was married to his older brother Sam, left the table to console her screaming daughter. Her icon-like beauty fascinated me. Earlier that evening, when I arrived, I had stumbled upon little Natasha, a nine-year-old with very dark hair and extraordinary green eyes; she was wearing a tussah silk dress and ankle boots, and learning how to ride a bicycle in the long hallway while her cousin Victor, a pale, sickly boy of sixteen or seventeen, teased her sarcastically. Their governesses intervened to keep the two from arguing, and ordered the little girl, who had accidentally brushed my leg, to apologize. She obliged in strongly accented French, but only after much cajoling.

While her mother was consoling her, the others explained that the child was tormented by a recurring nightmare. In 1919, when she was three, her parents had taken refuge in the Crimea. In early March, the Red Army had captured the peninsula. They had suffered fear, famine, typhus, and constant harassment by the Chekists, who would periodically burst into their apartment in Yalta in the middle of the night, rifling through closets and suitcases in order to make sure that they did not contain any requisitioned items. Each person was allowed only two shirts, two dresses, and two pairs of underwear; Alexandra had hidden her lace handkerchiefs—which she did not have the heart to give away—under the floorboards.

In June, the Whites chased the Soviets out of the Crimea and several British warships reappeared in Yalta. But by the end of the war it became more and more clear that General Wrangel's volunteers could not hold out much longer against the Reds, who had begun an unstoppable takeover of southern Russia. Samuel and his wife attempted to find space on one of the last British destroyers carrying refugees to Constantinople, but it was impossible. They bought false travel papers and crossed the Caucasus by train, traveling from Batumi to Baku. A small oil tanker picked them up and dropped them off in British Mesopotamia. They reached Baghdad, and from there they went to Basra with the intention of traveling to Bombay and being repatriated to England. A series of misadventures led to their having to cross part of Persia on horseback, with little Natasha tied onto a saddle amid the luggage and in her nightgown. Her horse was carrying a load that turned out to be too heavy and stumbled down a ravine. When they found the child she was unhurt but completely silent; her eyes were wide open and her hands gripped the horse's mane with a desperate strength. They had to cut the mane in order to unlock her fingers. From that day on she could not stand to touch any kind of hair and if at night a lock of her own hair—which was carefully gathered in a sleeping bonnet—came loose and brushed her cheek she would relive the experience and wake up screaming.

There was a vast age difference, almost a generation, between Michel and his eldest brother Samuel. But he was very close to his younger brother Paul and to his sister, Sophie, who was known as Mavlik because even as a child she had manifested an immoderate passion for elephants, and at the time there was an elephant by that name in the St. Petersburg zoo. She did not have a pretty face, but she was shapely, witty, and charming. I went to her room, which contained a large divan upholstered in damask silk littered with numerous multicolor cushions and a small dresser covered with bibelots, books, and perfume bottles. There, dressed in black silk pajamas, she would tell me of her amorous adventures. Her husband, Victor's father, had succumbed to septicemia at the beginning of the First World War, in Russia. Since her arrival in Paris she had accumulated several lovers, both male and female; as they say, she played all the angles. Though I had transformed myself, since my marriage to Michel, into a virtuous wife, I took enormous pleasure in hearing the stories of her shocking escapades, some of which ended at the police station after raids at certain nightclubs for ladies, which she frequented. She adored Madame Colette, all of whose books she had read and whom she was proud to have met on several occasions.

One particular story made me roar with laughter. It is less amusing now that we are forced to count every penny, but perhaps one day, depending on what the gods have in store for us, it will amuse our children and grandchildren—or perhaps it will fill them with bitterness. During the Great War, Sweden could not pay its debt to the Red Cross and asked the czar for an advance. The Azov-Don Bank agreed to make the loan. A train departed for Stockholm, transporting a tidy sum: seventeen tons of gold bars. In the early twenties, as soon as they arrived in Paris, the owners of the bank, Boris Kamenka and my father-in-law, Efim Epstein, reconvened the board of directors and asked the Swedish government to repay its loan. There were three lawsuits; the last was presided over by the king of Sweden. The outcome was that the debtor country requested that the two associates—Kamenka and Epstein—prove that they were the legitimate representatives of the banking institution in question and that the reimbursement would not damage any other possible beneficiaries. It goes without saying that, in their hasty departure, neither associate had dreamed of burdening himself with the bank archives. The matter went no further and thus, should my daughters survive the war, they may find themselves the possessors, after subtracting Kamenka's share, of four and a quarter tons of gold each.

It will probably disappoint many anti-Semites to hear of the joyous indifference the family exhibited each time it received discouraging news from Sweden, and of the dark humor that accompanied preparations for the final lawsuit, which was to be settled by the International Court in the Hague. But in September 1939, war was declared—a war which my father-in-law would not survive—and other more pressing issues dominated the attention of this august institution. While they awaited their hypothetical inheritance, each of the siblings had been put to work. Natasha's father, Samuel, had taken up cinema; his production company had produced René Clair's *The Italian Straw Hat* and Jacques Feyder's films. He was constantly scolding his daughter, who skipped classes at the Lycée Victor Duruy to attend screenings at the Colisée and the Marignan and took advantage of her connections to sneak in fifteen of her schoolmates. Little Natasha was extremely strong-willed; at a young age, following in the footsteps of her aunt and uncles, she had managed to convince the pastry shop Rollet to open an account in her name. For months she had treated her friends to strawberry tarts, until one day the bill arrived. When she was an adolescent, I cannot remember a Sunday when she did not make a scene during lunch, her large green eyes turning a stormy gray as she stomped off to her room and slammed the door violently because her father would not let her take a screen test. Her delightful grandmother Élisabeth, a tiny round woman who loved to sing Russian ballads during dessert, accompanied on the violin by her husband, would readjust her hairpiece, displaced by the tumult, and sneak off to take her granddaughter a slice of cake.

Michel, who had studied physics and math at the university in St. Petersburg and had later gone to business school before beginning a career at the ministry of finance in 1919, registered to study at the college of public works in Paris, specializing in electromechanics, while continuing to study mathematics and classical mechanics at the college of sciences. When I met him he had just accepted a position at the Banque des Pays du Nord, whose director had placed him in charge of French and foreign projects and servicing credit documents. For the first time in my life, I, an only child with a wonderful but absent father, rejected by a mother from whom I expected nothing, felt completely safe. This generous and colorful family had surrounded me with affection the moment it knew that I was loved by one of its members.

Should I have foreseen Michel's future problems with alcohol when, on our wedding day, he was unable to break the ritual glass? It was replaced by a crystal—and thus, more delicate—goblet, which the rabbi's maid brought down after my father-in-law slipped her a few banknotes. The chunky tumblers into which he now pours the rough local wine suit him less than the translucent flutes, cups, or goblets he once drank from and their more sophisticated contents. The last time I saw him drink for the joy of it and not in order to deaden the senses, for pleasure rather than out of need, was, ironically, the day of the strange party on the lake organized by the German soldiers stationed at Issy-l'Évêque, on June 21, 1941.

When this terrible war is finally over, no matter the outcome, events will surely be distorted, and the truth, which is never black or white, will be reshaped by those who write the history, depending on whether they are the victors or the vanquished. A year ago Michel, the children, and I were still living at the Hotel des Voyageurs. A unit of the Wehrmacht had been billeted there for several months. For the most part, the villagers received them with a dignified reserve mixed with mistrust. The shutters that faced the main road were always closed when the soldiers passed on the way to and from their maneuvers. People looked away when the soldiers walked by and spoke to them only when it was absolutely necessary. Fathers did not allow their daughters to go outside unless they were under the strict supervision of their mother or a neighbor. Children who accepted candy from the *Boches*, *Frisés*, *Fritzes*, *Beetles*, or *Vert-de-Gris**

were punished with a slap. The owners of occupied houses removed anything of value—good furniture, family heirlooms—and the officers had to demand a few comforts to make their empty rooms livable. Pigs, horses, cows, and fowl disappeared from farms practically overnight and pantries in this prosperous little town were suddenly emptied of sausages, pâtés, and cheeses. Only a faint trace of their fragrance was left. In every barn, rifles were hidden beneath the hay. The village went through the motions of praising Marshal Pétain and quietly violated all the *Verbotens* listed on the posters pasted up halfheartedly by the town policeman.

But these German soldiers were just boys, cheerful, blond-haired and pink-cheeked youths. In the mornings we saw them gather water from the well in the town square, pulling energetically on the squeaky chain to bring up buckets of ice-cold water which they splashed over their bare chests. They placed their pocket mirrors on tree branches and swirled their shaving brushes, their faces contorted like clowns covered in makeup. They ambled shyly into shops, innocently purchasing, at hugely inflated prices, dresses in styles long out of fashion, hideous lingerie, and quantities of trashy jewelry which had gathered dust in storerooms for years. Despite orders, they could not help ogling every pair of legs that went by. In short, they resembled the town's own boys, many of whom were prisoners in Germany and were greatly missed by their wives, mothers, and sisters. Without realizing it, the women found it increasingly difficult to fend off the impulse to treat them kindly, just as they hoped someone would treat their men on the other side where they waited, crouched in the snow behind barbed wire.

Little by little, the town began to come out of its shell. Recipes and clog-making techniques were exchanged in a mixture of German and French. Or a farmer would agree, with some lingering hesitation, to allow one of the youths, a farmer's son who clearly knew what he was doing, to help in the fields or in the stables. He would be offered a cup of coffee or a drop of wine at the farmer's oilcloth-covered kitchen table. One or two farmer's wives went so far as to look on with tender astonishment as one of the soldiers gulped down a twelve-egg omelet, as long as he gathered the eggs and prepared them himself. Behind his back, they might even use his real name: Karl, Heinrich, Fritz, or Willy. The girls were no longer scolded if they were heard to laugh in response to a comment by one of the youths. The children were allowed to hang around them all day long. The soldiers were even allowed to pick up the babies; they bounced them on their knees and let them play with their belt buckles.

Despite our unique situation, my husband's reserve did not last. I was working relentlessly on my novel and had no time to feel idle, but one could not say the same about Michel, who was having great difficulty compiling data for the biography of Pushkin that I was planning to write. After a decree was passed restricting the movement of Jews, he was no longer allowed to travel to Autun to use the library, the only establishment worthy of that name in the entire region. He was a Germanophile, like most of my male compatriots; in addition to French, it was typical in Russia for girls to learn English and for boys to learn German, especially if they were planning on a career in business. As a young man, he had traveled to

Germany many times. In the early days, I watched him with tenderness and some pity as he pretended to read the paper, glasses on his
forehead, chair pushed back, straining to hear the conversations of
our German occupiers outside. It was clear that he would have liked
to join in.

When he could resist no longer, he offered to act as interpreter
one day in the hall of the hotel. The owner, who could not understand what was being asked of him, shrugged impotently at the soldiers' requests. The officers did not seem to know that we were
Jewish or else pretended not to care. Michel became friendly with
one of them, Lieutenant Hohman; they discussed music and literature and played long games of billiards in a large smoky room filled
with chalk dust. Denise, who followed him around like a shadow,
tallied the points. I did not like the idea of my children hanging
around there, so I often went down to fetch them. I would find Babet sucking her thumb in the lap of one of the green-uniformed soldiers, his cap and holster on a side table next to a foamy pint of beer.
The officers' spurs clicked amid the noise of laughter and exclamations. The thin, flaxen-haired boy adopted by my youngest daughter
looked no older than eighteen. He was of vaguely Alsatian extrac-
tion and spoke perfect French. Babet called him *mon petit chéri*.

Like everyone else in the town, we participated in the festivities
of June 21, albeit from a distance. The commotion began in the
morning. The soldiers borrowed long wooden planks from the cabinetmaker and placed them on homemade trestles in a vast field that
descended to the edge of a lake. The hotel provided tablecloths, napkins, and silverware. That morning, the regimental cook had set up
shop on the main square to make an enormous cake, closely watched
by the town women who could not resist giving bits of advice. Cart-
loads of beer, champagne, and wine were carried down the streets of
the town. Then, in the late afternoon, the soldiers went back to the
camp to get ready; they reappeared at dusk, well-dressed, hair slicked
back, boots shiny, belts and medals gleaming, their large peasant
hands patting down impeccably creased green trousers and their
cheeks red from so much scrubbing.

The evening was like something out of a dream, warm and mild. A yellow moon worthy of Henri de Régnier rose slowly above the poplar trees. The scent of cut wood and freshly mowed hay filled the air. The aroma of grilled pork reached the clearing where the inhabitants of the town had congregated to watch the party. A few boats, which at midnight would be used to launch the fireworks, bobbed up and down in the shimmering water. Bats crisscrossed the grayish-blue sky. A toad sang itself hoarse in a puddle somewhere. Denise sat with her father, who was dressed in a tennis shirt and white trousers. He put his arm around her shoulders. Babet, wearing a pink apron, her face bearing the traces of the strawberries she had secretly devoured during the afternoon, ran around with the other children. I stopped her from time to time and kissed her curly hair, moist with sweat.

From where we sat, we could hear only an indistinct clamor of voices, the clink of silverware, and the crash of glasses each time the soldiers said a toast. But after the cake arrived, to great acclaim, the crowd went silent; in the quiet of the evening, a pure, youthful voice began to sing "Einsamkeit," a lied by Schubert: *"Wie eine trübe Wolke / Durch heit're Lüfte geht, / Wenn in der Tanne Wipfel / Ein mattes Lüftchen weht..."* (As a dark cloud / Drifts through clear skies, / When a faint breeze blows / In the fir tops...). As the melody traveled from one table to the next, an admirable chorus wove its magical cocoon. All around us, the French townsfolk had gone silent. Even the children stopped their games, and Babet lay down in the grass and placed her head on my lap, just as I had placed mine on my father's years ago on the coast of Finland. Tears filled my eyes.

Suddenly, just before midnight, we heard horse hooves beating against the paving stones and a courier appeared in the field. The rider jumped down from his steed, handed the reins to another soldier, and rushed to the head table, where he clicked his heels and stood at attention. The singing stopped. The officers stood and called out orders. The tables emptied. We thought that they were preparing for the fireworks. But instead of running toward the boats on the lake, the young men readjusted their loosened belts and straightened their caps. A voice bellowed "Heil, Hitler" and a sea of arms went up as the cry echoed around the field, cutting through the night air. The soldiers lined up and marched out of the field singing *"Deutschland, Deutschland über alles, über alles in der Welt,"* as their superiors, gathered in a small tight group, exclaimed and moved their arms animatedly. Catching our eye as he rushed by, Hohman hesitated for a moment but then approached us and said to my husband, in German, "Russia has declared war on Germany. We leave tomorrow at dawn for the eastern front."

The following day, I wrote a few lines in my large leather-bound notebook, which I was constantly filling with notes, mixed in with the draft of my novel:

> They are leaving. For twenty-four hours they were gloomy. Now they are gay once again, especially when they are together. But *le petit chéri* says that "the happy days are over." They send packages home. They are overexcited, that is clear. But they exhibit admirable discipline, and I think that, deep down, they do not rebel against their orders. I hereby swear never again to feel rancor—with or without justification—toward any group of men, no matter what their race, religion, convictions, prejudices, or errors. I feel sorry for these young men.

Would I still write these words today, as I feel danger approaching and have a terrible sense of foreboding regarding what the Führer has in store for us? And would Michel be so nonchalant now as to write to the German headquarters, as he did then, signing the letter with his very Jewish name, Epstein? He had tried to reach Lieutenant Hohman in order to send him his watch, which he had left at the repair shop. The town hall of Issy-l'Évêque is no longer occupied by soldiers of the Wehrmacht but rather by the Gestapo, with their black uniforms. Arrogant SS officers wearing jackets with a skull embroidered on the biceps drive through the town at breakneck speed, screaming the "Horst Wessel Lied" as they go. Last year we could still hear messages from London and the odd obscenity over the wireless, but no longer: all the radios have been confiscated. Some of the prisoners who had been released were once again taken in and accused of "planning terrorist acts." The mayor, a friend, was relieved of his post and replaced by a large landowner who treats us with contempt and insolence at every opportunity. Our neighbors are uncomfortable around us and turn their heads whenever they see us pass with our yellow stars sewn onto our lapels. These days, little Babet hums a tune that the school principal, after much hesitation, was forced to teach to the children: "*Maréchal*, here we stand before you, the savior of Fra-an-ce."

Hair pulled back in a ponytail, wearing jeans, ballerina flats, and a borrowed leather jacket, the young girl grasps the subway pole with one hand as she reads Jean-Paul Sartre's Anti-Semite and Jew. *So this is the answer? Are we only Jewish in the eyes of the Other? She catches her reflection in the glass: frizzy hair, hooked nose. She remembers a line her mother wrote in* David Golder. *It had struck her: "Much later, Soifer would die all alone, like a dog, without a friend, without a single wreath on his grave, buried in the cheapest cemetery in Paris by his family who hated him, and whom he had hated, but to whom he nevertheless left a fortune of some thirty million francs, thus fulfilling till the end the incomprehensible destiny of every good Jew on this earth."* She wants to understand. But the Sartrian explanation cannot explain the profound sense of belonging she has recently begun to feel, despite being an atheist, this powerful sense of pride at belonging to a people who, despite persecutions and massacres, never ceased to procreate, even in sadness.*

II

"The Earth is a sphere, supported by nothing." Babet chants these words in a singsong voice as she bounces a ball against the garden wall. The garden is decked out in its summer colors: azure, tender green, and pink. I watch her from a shallow tiled balcony on the second floor where I like to sit before dinner with my knitting while there is still some light. Her silhouetted frizzy hair, which the town hairdresser has never been able to tame, looks like a crown of thorns. My youngest daughter is like a little savage; she disappears for hours and likes nothing better than to roll around in the fields with the town children. The local policeman has dragged her home by the ear several times when she was cutting school. I think back on her older sister's pampered upbringing—too pampered, perhaps. I can remember when Michel scolded the director of the Lycée Victor Duruy after Denise grazed her knee on the first day of school. We had registered her in the school with some reservations; up to then she had always studied at home, under the mentorship of Miss Matthews. After this incident we took her out and once again placed her in the care of my old governess.

Babet was able to enjoy only two years of being pushed down the boulevard des Invalides by a uniformed nurse in her gleaming navy-blue and chrome pram, dressed in little embroidered linen dresses and lace bonnets. Her red-and-white gingham apron, too short now, reveals a corner of her dirty knickers, her socks droop over dusty sandals. All this is in sharp contrast with her sister's delicate gray coats and matching hats, the kilts and muffs bought at Old England, in the days when we went to Rumplemeyer's for frozen meringue. Is

Babet less happy for it? I have no idea what goes on in that little head of hers. Has our fear contaminated her, as it has Denise, who understands too much? I have tried in vain to reassure Denise; sometimes I see her wearing a worried expression like an old woman, inappropriate to her thirteen years. Is it only due to the restlessness typical of Babet's tender age—she is still a baby—that she struggles whenever we pick her up in our arms? She breaks free as quickly as possible, as if her nose perceives a whiff of pleasure coming from some other place, a fragrance more appealing than our stench of sadness. In any event, the first line of her geography textbook is a more tolerable chant than the previous one—"You put your left leg in, you put your left leg out, you put your left leg in, and shake it all about"—which she had been singing nonstop for days.

On March 20 of last year, when she turned five, she surprised us by revealing that she already knew how to read. After the ritual blowing out of the candles on a cake which—in the absence of flour—had been concocted out of rice thickened with cornstarch and covered in ersatz chocolate, she curled up on her father's lap. He was leafing through the local newspaper, *Le Progrès de l'Allier*, in a half-empty sitting room where we gather around the fireplace in the evenings; it is the only warm room in the drafty house. I was pulling apart a sweater, winding the wool around Denise's outstretched hands. We thought the little one was asleep in her fluffy red plush dressing gown, and I was about to carry her up to bed where a hot water bottle—or "friar" as they call them in these parts—awaited, when she removed her thumb from her mouth, pointed at the headline with a soggy finger, and deciphered the words. We asked her to go on, which she did fluidly, if struggling with a few of the more difficult words. The next day we visited her teacher, who had not noticed a thing; her students, who were of different ages, worked together in the same room, and Babet had probably learned how to read by listening to the older pupils. After the Easter holiday, she was moved into a higher class. Perhaps she will not become a milkmaid as I once feared might happen if the war dragged on.

We are waiting for dinner, which is being prepared by our corpulent cook, Francine. She is of a respectable age, since it is illegal for Jews to employ servants under the age of forty-five. In April, Denise and Julie went to Paris to try make arrangements for the apartment, because we can no longer pay the rent, and to have the furniture sent down. They were able to find a corset large enough to encompass Francine's considerable girth. Ever since, she has cooked for us with great affection, using ingredients that only she is capable of obtaining from the surrounding farms. Once again, tarts made with real flour began to appear on our table. Thanks to her and to my maid Cécile, who was born in the town, I have even been able to send packages of food to my in-laws. Michel, wearing a black undershirt and white trousers and holding an aperitif—a glass of red wine—in one hand, inspects his lettuce plants which will never reach maturity because he continually pulls them out to check their progress. Meanwhile, Denise sits next to me in her black pinafore, on which is sewn a yellow star. She repeats: "France, mother of the arts, of arms, and of laws, / Long have you nourished me with the milk of your breast. / Now, like a lamb who calls out to her nurse / I fill caverns and forests with your name."*

This poem, which Mademoiselle Rose taught me during our sojourn in Paris in 1912, could hardly be more appropriate than today. On my lap I have the first volume of Joseph Caillaux's memoirs, which he sent to me last December with a letter written on Senate letterhead. He was the chairman of the finance committee. "Dear Madame, please be assured that the two or three volumes of my Memoirs will all be autographed and dedicated to you as they are published. I would like to express here the admiration I feel for you, as a great writer, as well as the enormous friendship my wife feels for your person. I am honored to present to you this tribute, my happiest remembrances. Madame Caillaux sends her warmest regards." In this book, I read the following words: "It is difficult to deny that the principal actors in the Russian upheaval were Jews who, having dominated other Oriental peoples such as the cross-eyed Scythians, and having set them against the West and against the laws that govern our civilization, have attempted to weaken the European fortress by encouraging other Israelites, also haunted by age-old dreams handed down to them from ancient Asia, to attack from the inside. More generally, one must be blind to ignore the fact that the Jew, in every sphere which he touches, carries inside him the will to destroy, the thirst for domination, the appetite to reach a precise or vague ideal."

Michel, who knows how much such writings upset me, normally leafs through the few books that still come to us and conceals them when he believes they will be too painful for me to read. But who would have expected this from our friend, the former radical Joseph Caillaux? And besides, one would have to stop reading altogether—novels, essays, even newspapers—to avoid the constant flood of insults and rants. And I do not mean only the traditionally anti-Semitic press, like *Je suis partout* or *Pilori* or *Gringoire*, which in 1940 serialized my novel, but rather such widely read newspapers as *Paris-Soir* or *Le Matin*. And not only writers like Abel Bonnard or Alphonse de Châteaubriant, both of whom consider themselves Drumont's heirs, or madmen like Louis-Ferdinand Céline, whose *L'École des cadavres* I refused to read in 1933 and who has, it seems, committed another crime in the form of a terrible pamphlet, a call to murder entitled *Bagatelles pour un massacre*,* but also real writers, writers whose work I have loved and who loved my books or at least pretended to: Brasillach, Drieu, Chardonne, Giraudoux, Morand, and many others.

What happened? The other day, when I reread those naïve words I wrote just after the birth of my daughter, I was furious at my own stupidity. For the past two years I have continually sought to understand the reasons behind this stupidity. Hadn't these people, whose current ferocity terrifies me, revealed symptoms of their malady before now? The other day, in the modest town library, I found a book by Paul Morand, *I Burn Moscow*, a book I had read without batting an eyelash in 1925 when it was published. How could I not have been shocked by some of the lines he places in the mouths of his Jewish characters, lines which now leap off the page? "The great reservoirs of Jews all over the world have cracked open. We have spread out in all directions, ardent, intolerant, Talmudic. Ezekiel said, 'You will live in houses you did not build; you will drink at wells you did not dig!' The houses and the wells are here. There is another continent left, the greatest laboratory in the world, and it is the promised land: Eurasia."

In February or March 1933—I can no longer remember the exact date, but it was just after Hitler had been named chancellor of the Reich—there was an animated dinner at our house. Among the guests were my husband's uncle, the great psychiatrist Alfred Adler, who was traveling through Paris with his wife, Rhaïssa, as well as Daniel Halévy and the philosopher Emmanuel Berl whom I have known since 1930. His book *Mort de la pensée bourgeoise* and my *David Golder* were published at roughly the same time. I had debated whether or not to hold this dinner, knowing that Adler—whom Michel's family rarely saw because they felt him to be too close to the Communists—and the other guests were at opposite ends of the political spectrum. But everyone was curious to meet Freud's disciple, who was seldom in Paris, since he lived and taught in New York. Despite my efforts, the conversation quickly turned to the burning subject of the German Jews who were being driven out of their homes, and the problems caused by their presence in France. Adler had brought an article from the newspaper *L'Ami du Peuple* in which the perfumer François Coty called upon the French government to create "concentration camps" in order to quarantine the immigrants, as during outbreaks of cholera or plague. He read it to us indignantly. Berl stroked his chin as he listened. Then he sat up, pushed back a lock of hair, and declared calmly that though he did not agree with the terms described in this article, he believed that the French government should not accord citizenship to the refugees "with such wild generosity." If they did, the Jews who had integrated into French life for generations, like his own family, would only be worse off. Halévy was even more extreme; Alfred and Rhaïssa called him a Fascist and angrily threatened to leave the table. Denise's tears—she had been awoken by the commotion—and her sleepy face when I cannily brought her to the table in order to smooth everyone's feathers, created a diversion. After the other two guests had departed, Adler removed his pince-nez, took me in his arms, and furrowing his thick black eyebrows, implored Michel and me to leave Europe as soon as possible. I can still feel his salt-and-pepper mustache tickling my neck when he kissed me goodbye. He and Rhaïssa wrote to us several times from the United States, pleading with us to leave. But we never listened.

I must admit that I shared Berl's opinion: I did not take measure of his blindness or my own until 1940, when I was told that he had followed Pétain to Vichy and had even written two of the marshal's famous speeches, including the well-known line "I hate the lies that have done you such harm." But my arrival in France after the Great War had convinced me that anti-Semitism no longer existed there. We foreigners had an exalted opinion of this country, the land of the Revolution, of liberty, of the rights of man. And let's not forget it was the time of the Sacred Union. The Jews, whose circles had been destabilized a few years earlier by the Dreyfus affair, were happy to reconquer everyone's respect through demonstrations of patriotism. They were recognized as French through the rights of kinship. Even Maurice Barrès beat his breast and proclaimed their virtues. Former anti-Semites told the story of a rabbi who had been killed on the battlefield while bringing a cross to a Catholic soldier to ease his agony. Everyone around me, including my father, believed that complete and definitive assimilation was possible, and I remember how shocked I was by an ironic poem by André Spire which circulated in those days:

> You are happy, you are happy!
> Your nose is almost straight, by Jove.
> And after all, so many Christians have crooked noses, too.
> You are happy, you are happy.

Your hair is barely frizzy, by Jove.
And after all, so many Christians don't have straight hair...

Secular families like ours, who considered Judaism a relic of the past, were convinced that, except for a handful of extremists, enlightened France would see the situation as clearly as we did. It never occurred to us that France might betray us.

We did not hold a monopoly on trustfulness. Polish and Italian immigrants who had fled pogroms and poverty had also been welcomed with open arms by a war-battered country in need of labor. Wealthy families from all over Europe sent their children to France to perfect their educations. Paris in the twenties boasted of its cosmopolitanism. Both the poorer areas and the rich neighborhoods were filled with foreigners. In cafés and restaurants, from dives to the most luxurious establishments, one could hear people speaking all the dialects of the world: Russian in Belleville and Montmartre and all the way to the *caves* of the George V and the Closerie des Lilas; English on the terraces at La Coupole and La Rotonde, both of which were crammed with Americans; Spanish on the Grand Boulevards. In 1925, the Exposition Internationale des Arts Décoratifs was the apex of this intermingling. Only a few staunch but isolated voices complained that Paris, overrun by half-breeds, was becoming "Chanaan-sur-Seine."

At the time, the White Russians were the height of fashion. The French bourgeoisie, half bankrupted by the Bolsheviks who left them no hope of recovering the capital on their loans, sympathized with our plight. Gabrielle Chanel, seduced by the Slavic charms of Grand Duke Dmitri, made us all the rage. The man who had assassinated Rasputin, Prince Yusupov, had opened his own fashion house. Henry Torrès's defense of a young Jewish clockmaker who tried to avenge his coreligionists killed in the Ukrainian pogroms by shooting Ataman Symon Petlyura, moved the French to tears. In 1930, the kidnapping in central Paris of the White general Alexander Kutepov, who had fought alongside Denikin and Wrangel, caused widespread indignation toward a government which had not been capable of protecting him. Adulated and celebrated, all wealthy Russians, including Jews, were assumed to be aristocrats; all poor Russians were seen as the victims of Communism, which had briefly seemed close to victory in France as well, with the rise of the Cartel des Gauches and later the great strikes. At the time, we had completely forgotten that we were Israelites.

I was at the Hôtel Salomon de Rothschild on rue Berryer on May 6, 1932, when Pavel Gorgulov assassinated the president of the republic, Paul Doumer. I was signing copies of my latest book, *Snow in Autumn*, as part of a benefit for writers who had fought in the war. My table was quite far from the counter where Claude Farrère was signing his book *The Battle* for Doumer, when I heard five shots. I saw the bald head and dark eyes of a colossus dragged to the door by two policemen, while the limp body of the illustrious gentleman was hastily carried away. In the confusion that followed, the Grasset representatives quickly spirited me off. When it became known that the assassin was a Russian, a wave of panic washed over the émigré community. And rightly so. I can now see that this was the moment when the public began to look at us with suspicion. The right saw the hand of the Bolsheviks and the left was convinced that the crime was the work of the Fascists. Many newspapers advised the police to pay closer attention to the "cosmopolitan circles" in which, they argued, agents were plotting on behalf of either Berlin or Moscow, depending on the political tendency of the publication. The extremists argued that these foreigners were all Jews, just like Trotsky-Bronstein.

In Jewish circles like my own, the order of the day was discretion. Jérôme and Jean Tharaud, members of the Académie Française, advised us: "If the thousands of German Jews who are emigrating here do not bring with them a suitcase full of discretion—but this is the virtue you most lack!—we must fear the reawakening of a terrifying, age-old passion which you have unleashed time and time again..."

This was in fact what we feared the most. Among our friends, everyone insisted on the distinction made by Maurras, between "well-born Jews" who had lived in France for generations and had given their blood for the motherland, and those who we thought of as "the dregs." We were the first to worry that the French people's capacity for welcome might reach a point of saturation. There was talk of instituting quotas on immigration and several decrees were passed which were meant to protect French workers who feared unfair competition from cheap foreign labor. One of these decrees greatly amused Joseph Kessel at the time: "Only fifteen percent of the musicians in a Russian balalaika orchestra, and only ten percent of the singers in a Russian religious choir, may be Russian."

The notion that the number of foreigners had reached its limit started to take hold. The worry began to grow that what was taking place was not simply an intrusion that caused unemployment, problematic because it imposed upon this refined country, polished by the patina of centuries and habit, certain sounds and smells that were unfamiliar and even discordant and dangerous to the French identity, which was at risk of being diluted by excessive, reckless naturalization, but something rather more sinister: a veritable "invasion." Frightening images began to appear in the papers, such as Iribe's drawing of Léon Blum playing the flute, calling all the German Jews to France. The Jews were depicted as rats, their fur bearing the image of the hammer and sickle.

Then, to top it all, in 1934 the Stavisky affair exploded. Stavisky was a Ukrainian Jew like my family, but naturalized French. He lived in the Hotel Claridge in grand style and owned a racehorse. He had already committed a number of swindles but his highly placed protectors, both on the left and on the right—including his close friend the chief of police Jean Chiappe—had prevented the many complaints against him from being investigated. In December 1933 his most recent fraud, so massive that it could not be covered up, was revealed: the Crédit Municipal de Bayonne, which he had founded, had issued two hundred million francs of false bonds. Stavisky disappeared. On January 8, 1934, it came to light that he had committed suicide in a chalet in Chamonix. No one believed that he had died by his own hand, and the *Canard Enchaîné* ran an article with the title: "Stavisky Commits Suicide with a Pistol Shot from Close Range." According to the left, Chiappe had had him killed to avoid any compromising revelations; according to the right, it was obvious that those responsible belonged to the circles of foreign finance linked to the Masonic demimonde, personified by Premier Camille Chautemps and his brother-in-law, Georges Pressard, the state prosecutor. During the entire month of January, the Jeunesses Patriotes, Croix de Feu, and Camelots du Roi swept through the Latin Quarter screaming slogans against the "Jewish plutocracy."

The chief of police, who had done nothing to control the riots, was dismissed. At the time we were still living on avenue Daniel Lesueur, one of two small cul-de-sacs that open out onto the boulevard des Invalides on one side and the gardens of the Frères Hospitaliers de St. Jean de Dieu on the other. On the evening of February 6, my husband, my daughter, and I were at home when we heard a report on Radio Paris describing the overexcited hordes converging near the Place de la Concorde. They were attacking the police with bottles and using the glass to cut the horses of the mounted police as they marched toward the Palais Bourbon where Daladier, with the backing of Léon Blum, had asked for the support of the National Assembly. I felt that we had been transported thirty years into the past, to 1905, to the day when the Black Hundreds attacked the Pechersk neighborhood. I ran to Denise's room and held her in my arms so tightly that she began to scream, and then I was literally choked by an asthma attack. Michel called Professor Vallery-Radot who, despite the danger, managed to traverse Paris and come to my bedside. Once I had begun to breathe normally again, he told me that the antiriot police who had cordoned off the Pont de la Concorde had held strong. Colonel de La Rocque had not ordered his Croix de Feu followers to attack the National Assembly. A few days later, the left marched in the streets, heeding the call of the Socialists and the Communists. Gaston Doumergue, who had been named prime minister, created a national unity government and Paris was once again peaceful.

My fears were allayed, and once again I buried myself in my work. I liked my new publisher, Albin Michel, a charming and witty elderly gentleman. Here is an example of his sense of humor: in October 1933 I signed a contract giving him the rights to publish all of my literary output for the next twenty years, but in November I asked for permission to give a collection of stories to Paul Morand, who had requested it for his collection at *La Nouvelle Revue française*. "Dear Madam," Albin Michel had written, "our spiritual marriage is still too recent and it would be painful for me to allow you such indiscretions even before our first child has seen the light of day!" In the spirit of fair play, I answered: "My dear Editor, a wife must obey her husband, and it is for this reason that I happily bow to your decision, in the hopes that you will feel the same way about our offspring once they are born as you do today when they are still in the embryonic stage."

I gave Morand some other texts, and my "spiritual husband" was not offended. I wrote one book each year for Albin Michel except in 1937, the year my second daughter was born. After *The Wine of Solitude*—my most autobiographical novel—I once again turned to my mother for inspiration. In the novel *Jezebel*, I depicted her as a woman who refuses to grow old and who causes the death of her own daughter by forcing her to give birth in secret. Twenty years later her grandson seeks her out and she kills him, too, terrified that he might reveal her real age to her lover. "Honesty is Madame Némirovsky's greatest gift," Jean-Pierre Maxence wrote. "Her lucid eye, her steady hand, her spare, clean, nervous style give us not only an impression of virility but one of presence. It is enough for the author of *Jezebel* to imagine an event for it to seem real, or to describe a character for it to feel as if we have known him. In passages where, in another writer's work, we might be overly conscious of the will of the creator, here we are conscious only of the internal exigencies of the characters. Nothing more clearly reveals the gift of the story-teller."

Book after book, the critics, no matter what their political sympathies, praised me to the skies. Driven by a sense of urgency, I worked compulsively. We moved to another cul-de-sac, at 10 avenue Constant Coquelin, because the top-floor apartment there had two balconies, one of which was enclosed and could be used as an office. I loved to shut myself in to write, lying on a couch or sitting at my table, which was covered with a green blanket under which Denise was allowed to play with her dolls as long as she was quiet. She would eventually fall asleep on the floor and the sensation of her warm skin against my leg helped me to focus even more. My short stories were published in the *Revue des Deux Mondes* and *Candide*. My novels appeared as serials in *Gringoire*, edited by Hector de Carbuccia, whom I had met through Joseph Kessel.

This Carbuccia was an extraordinary character, a giant Corsican with a taste for cigars and good wine, who happened to be the brother-in-law of the infamous Chiappe, the chief of police. Even if I never heard him personally express flagrantly anti-Semitic opinions and though he is one of the few people who has returned my letters and attempted to help me since my exile to Issy-l'Évêque, it must be said that he has allowed the basest filth to be published in the political pages of his journal. It sells copies, he said, without giving it the slightest importance. No expression was vulgar enough, no tirade incendiary enough for his editorial writer Henri Béraud when referring to the Jews. Kessel broke off relations with Béraud immediately after the Stavisky affair, as a reaction to an outrageous article he had written. Béraud repeated the offense a few months later when a Croatian separatist assassinated King Alexander of Yugoslavia along with the French foreign minister Louis Barthou. Béraud was content to paint everyone with the same brush, treating those who in his eyes were insufficiently anti-Semitic as half-breeds or traitors.

It was almost as if there were no connection between the political pages and the literary section of the journal. In 1934, on the same day that Béraud was foaming at the mouth about the Judeo-Masonic conspiracy, the famous novelist Marcel Prévost, Carbuccia's cousin and patron, praised my book *The Pawn on the Chessboard*. I have the clip here in front of me. In this article he wrote, on the subject of a biography of Heine:

> Nothing resembles the current Hitlerian period more than the period following the so-called War of Deliverance, in other words, the defeat of Napoleon. Heinrich Heine was eighteen at the time. He admired Napoleon rapturously. As a Jew, he had welcomed France's liberal treatment of the persecuted. The defeat of the French upset him, and he was not the only one! Germany at the time began to look and feel as it does today. There were the same appeals to the grandeur of the German race. The same persecution of Jews: bonfires were built, books and newspapers gathered from every corner of the land. Because they did not have every condemned book in hand, they wrote out their titles on sheets of paper which they threw into the fire. The torches stirred restlessly; the flames rose up to the heavens; young voices went hoarse from crying out: *Pereat!* And the following day the newspapers reported that it had been an event in which the people of Germany would take pride for centuries. There are times when Germany wraps itself in liberalism and fraternity, but deep down it cannot change. One century later, the recurrence of these events proves this to be true.

I didn't realize at the time but I see now that in this period the word "Israelite" suddenly disappeared from all the articles in which my name was mentioned. Scrupulously observing rules of discretion which I, like most Jews, had accepted, I avoided the subject of Judaism in my books. I imagined plots set in France, within the Catholic, bourgeois circles to which my friend Madeleine had introduced me. These old, prudishly prosperous French families, whom I had come to know more intimately after becoming a well-known writer, inspired more mistrust in me than they once had. I did not hide their vices, their avarice, their stinginess, their pettiness but described them from the inside, placing myself squarely in their midst. Critics saw French qualities in these books while still judging that I exhibited characteristics that were, if not Jewish, then very Russian. "A temperament, an anxiety about the world and about its inhabitants that is very Slavic, combined with a very French clarity and sense of composition," a journalist wrote in an article entitled "Russia on the Boulevard des Invalides." She added: "In this setting, where one could well imagine a shy bourgeoise or a provincial lady, Irène Némirovsky appears even more Russian, more profoundly mysterious than she would if one could make out the slightest hint of exoticism in her dress or way of life."

We experienced two years of seeming tranquility. The monstrosity of Hitler's measures against the Jews—the Nuremberg Laws banning them from all prominent posts, outlawing marriages or out-of-wedlock relations with Aryans, and denying them all electoral rights, the daily attacks against people and property—inspired indignation in France and silenced the more moderate anti-Semites. Israelites like myself were careful not to make the slightest reference to that which they refused to see as a French problem and left it to others to denounce the excesses of the new Führer, afraid that they would be considered warmongers, eager to drag all of Europe into a bloodbath for the sole purpose of avenging their fellow Jews.

But with the success of the Popular Front and especially with the election of Léon Blum to the post of prime minister, the floodgates opened. He filled us with worry: born of a family which had been in France for several generations, secular and Socialist, he nevertheless asserted his Jewish identity. To those who considered this a reason to insult him, like Léon Daudet—who in 1920 had called him "the spokesman for high finance and Semitic plundering... a Semite with a sissy expression who makes prissy little gestures"—Blum responded: "I am a Jew... This is a fact. It is not an insult to remind me that I belong to the Jewish race, a race that I have never disowned, and for which I feel only gratitude and pride." Not surprisingly, in February 1936 he was the victim of a lynch mob in central Paris: the car that was taking him from the Palais Bourbon to his home on the Île Saint-Louis crossed the funeral cortege of a famous historian, Jacques Bainville, a member of Action Française. As soon as the right-wing militants recognized him, insults began to rain down: "Jewish traitor! Swine! Murderer!" They pulled him out of the car and struck him repeatedly. He was saved only by the intervention of a group of construction workers who climbed down from their scaffolding to defend him. Three months later, he was attacked in the National Assembly by Xavier Vallat, who would later become our commissioner for Jewish Affairs, and who assailed him with these words: "Your coming to power, Mr. President, is incontestably a historic event. For the first time, this ancient Gallo-Roman country will be governed by a Jew." And when Vallat's colleagues attempted to interrupt him: "I say that it would be better for this peasant nation of ours to be governed by someone whose origins, no matter how modest, lie deep in the heart of our soil than by a subtle Talmudist."

After long months spent reflecting on the events of our time and writing *Suite Française*—the first volume, *Storm in June*, recounts the start of the war, the debacle, and the exodus—during which I have been doing my best to comprehend the disaster we are experiencing, I am now convinced of one thing: An uncontrollable process was set in motion when a group of journalists from the extreme right began to compose a list of Blum's cabinet ministers; not content to expose only those who were actually Jewish, they began to invent Jewish ancestors for the others or, when that was not possible, accusing them of being "Jewified." The notion of foreignness had by now become synonymous with Communism. A fear of those who were obviously Jewish—the modest watchmaker with sidecurls accused of stealing the bread of the French, the Stavisky-like businessman whose shady dealings could be blamed for the failure of the economy—was replaced by a fear of the hidden Jew, whose occult influence was perceived as even more threatening. On the right, those who hated Hitler saw the Jews' ploys as the root of the violent madness that was taking hold of the German people; and those who were seduced by Fascism denounced the Jews' links to London bankers and believed them to be responsible for the weakening of the French spirit. On the left, the pacifists disapproved of Jewish calls to fight the rise of Nazism.

In the Senate, Louis Darquier de Pellepoix, who had been chosen by the Vichy government to succeed Xavier Vallat as commissioner for Jewish Affairs, filed a motion in the following terms:

> Considering that there is good reason to be particularly on our guard against the Jews, a nation of wanderers, recruited by the couriers of the international anarchist movement and the nationless powers of international finance ... and considering that our national education system, our religious policy, the integrity of our colonial empire, and even the health of the French family have been and are still powerfully influenced by Jewish intervention (by members of parliament, writers, state employees, etc.) which has as its aim the enslavement and ignorance of the French people ... I put forth a request for the following from the public authorities: 1. The immediate annulment of all naturalizations dated after the armistice of November 11, 1918; 2. The declaration of a statute regulating the right of Jews to vote and stand for public office.

The die had been cast. Two years later, on November 17, 1938, when a seventeen-year-old boy, Herschel Grynszpan, shot the German diplomat Ernst von Rath on the rue de Lille in order to call attention to the deportation of thousands of Jews from Germany to Poland, his action was met with a complete lack of understanding by the police and by public opinion. There was no sign of the compassion that had surrounded the man who had murdered Petlyura. In Germany, his action was used as the pretext for Kristallnacht. In France, it unleashed a deafening clamor against Jews and foreigners, against everyone and everything, which has brought us to where we are today. Shielded from the real world by the thick curtains of my success, cut off from reality by my stubborn will to see myself, despite everything, as French—to the point that I did not even see the point of requesting naturalization—I, like everyone else, did not foresee the impending disaster. Now when I cover my eyes and ears, it is no longer out of a lack of awareness but rather to block out the hideous insults intoned by my former colleagues, from the elderly Châteaubriant to the young Brasillach, from the revolting Céline to the elegant Morand.

When I was the same age as Denise is today, I was moved to tears by a poem by Alfred de Musset; in it, the author of *Les Nuits* paid homage to two of his illustrious precursors, just as many Russian writers have done, to honor their predecessors and contemporaries by maintaining a conversation with them through time and space, filled with tenderness and respect. I do not know of another example in French literature that reveals such a sly sense of camaraderie. The poet attends a performance of a play by Molière at the Théâtre-Français, where he becomes distracted:

> I was lost in my thoughts (though all the time, out of the corner of my eyes, I continued to peruse the gallery), when in front of me, beneath a lock of black hair, I noticed the cheerful poise of a slender and charming neck, and the sight of that ebony encased in ivory made me remember some singing, almost unknown verses from an unfinished poem by André Chénier, lines pure as chance and not so much written as dreamed. I wasn't afraid to speak them out loud, even in the presence of Molière, whose great shade certainly wouldn't take offense. Still listening (still contemplating the unsuspecting girl), I whispered:

> Under your lovely head, your delicate white
> Neck bends, and the whiteness of snow is not so white.*

All that is left of the camp at Pithiviers—which along with the camp at Beaune-la-Rolande "accommodated" sixteen thousand Jewish men, women, and children between May 1941 and September 1942, all of whom were deported to Germany—is an old silo and a rusty train track. Did no one in this quiet town raise a hand to halt the departure of the sealed train cars? The young girl does not feel proud of herself: a few months earlier, racist attacks in the center of Paris caused the death of hundreds of Algerians, and she "knew nothing" of what was happening. She looks around for something she can take with her which might contain some tiny part of her mother's essence, and decides to pick up a small stone from the track bed. Perhaps her mother placed her foot there as she climbed onto the train.

12

I WAS SHAKEN from sleep by an asthma attack. It always begins with a tickling sensation, a tension in every nerve, forcing me to sit up, chest first, hands pushing down on the bed. Air comes into my lungs but does not come out again. My chest swells, becomes blocked, freezes. I felt around blindly for the miraculous inhaler that Professor Vallery-Radot used to order for me from Switzerland— I have only one flask left—and calmed down. I could no longer sleep, so I gently lifted Michel's arm, which lay across my thighs. I wrapped a shawl around my shoulders and walked through the silent house, stopping for a moment in the girls' room. I tucked Babet back under the covers and removed a bag of marbles from her pillow; they had left an indentation on her cheek. Denise moaned in her sleep and her messy hair was matted with sweat. I wiped her face with a moist towel, without waking her.

Dr. Benoît-Gouin prescribed sleeping pills for Denise after her traumatic ordeal last year. She had been complaining of stomachaches and vomiting; he diagnosed appendicitis which, after a few hours, became acute peritonitis. She required an immediate operation, but how could we take her to a hospital or clinic? Jews in the occupied zone were not allowed to travel outside the town in which they lived, or even to leave the house between eight in the evening and six in the morning. Her fever increased; she became delirious and began to cry out in pain, while we wrung our hands desperately. Finally the doctor located a kind man who owned a gas generator and agreed to drive her to Luzy. He wrapped her in a blanket, put her in his automobile, and departed. We had no news until he returned with her, half-conscious, the following day. He recounted their odyssey: because of the yellow star, not a single clinic had been willing to accept the eleven-year-old child in the middle of the night, despite the fact that she might well die. He had knocked on many doors before finding a surgeon who was willing to operate on his dining-room table. When she awoke from the anesthesia she cried out for us, between waves of nausea, and the man had been forced to bring her back despite the dangers because the doctor did not dare keep her in his house any longer.

I go out into the garden and sit under the apple tree. Leaning on the trunk, I look up at the innumerable stars, made brighter by the absence of a moon or lights in the town, plunged into darkness because of the curfew. The peaceful, fragrant night reveals nothing, but I do not allow myself to be seduced by its mildness. I know that danger lurks there and I search for God in the silent sky, not to ask for help but to hurl a blasphemous prayer in his direction, the blasphemy of a converted Jew: "My God, forgive us our offenses as we forgive you yours."

Ten years ago, through the Princess Bibesco, I met Prince Ghika, the Romanian archbishop, a man of great kindness and simplicity despite his position. Denise adored this giant with his long white hair. I had taught her to kiss his ring before climbing into his lap. He often came to tea and spoke of his faith, which radiated from within. He spoke of Max Jacob, who had been converted by Jacques Maritain. I gently teased him by mentioning another of Maritain's converts, Maurice Sachs, whose time in the seminary had apparently taught him little about virtue, at least if one believed Parisian gossip. He did not take offense.

At the time I was tempted to convert but eventually decided not to, despite the fact that I had never practiced the religion of my family. Perhaps, like my father, I had been held back by a mysterious fear of abjuration that I did not quite understand. And then, in 1938, after Hitler invaded Austria and began to threaten Czechoslovakia, when we were finally convinced that war was inevitable, we decided to request naturalization. Our daughters were already French; Michel had easily obtained citizenship for them because they had been born in France. We believed that it would be just as easy for the two of us. My husband had a letter of recommendation from the managing director and the director of his bank, Monsieur de Boisseau and Monsieur de Maizière: "Monsieur Epstein has worked with us since March 1925. He is a faithful collaborator, whose moral and professional qualities we have had the opportunity to observe, and we are convinced of his love of France, as well as his absolute loyalty."

As for me, my guarantors were André Chaumeix, director of the *Revue des Deux Mondes* and a member of the Académie Française, and Jean Vignaud, a commander of the Legion of Honor, Military Cross, and president of the Society of Men of Letters, which I had joined in 1930 under the patronage of Gaston Chéreau and Roland Dorgelès. At the time of my candidacy, Chéreau had written on my behalf: "It is always a precious stroke of luck when a writer can say of a young colleague that she possesses the greatest gifts; it is even more exceptional to have the opportunity to propose to my peers that they should welcome a young author who, at an age when one normally can speak only of potential, has offered for our admiration and critique a work as significant as *David Golder*." Dorgelès seconded Chéreau's opinion: "When a person has written *David Golder*, does she need sponsors? I am very happy to lend my support to Madame Irène Némirovsky's candidature."

Chaumiex personally handed the completed documents to the Minister of Justice, Monsieur Paul Marchandeau, who replied that he had "indicated to his staff that the request should be examined with particular attention and diligence." Nothing happened. Michel was not overly concerned. As usual, he was less pessimistic than I about the political situation, and Daladier's victorious return after the Munich Agreement seemed to support his optimism. Four years later, the sense of relief and blissful hope that followed the signing of what was actually a retreat seems surreal. *Paris-Soir* ran the headline PEACE in giant letters spanning eight columns and even suggested that its readers join together to buy Chamberlain the summerhouse of his dreams. With few exceptions—which did not include us, I am afraid—the population of France, both the left and the right, believed that the country had been saved, granted an enduring peace. Our certificate of naturalization, delayed by unseen obstacles, still did not come.

In February 1939, just before German troops advanced on Prague and as Hitler's anti-Jewish measures in Germany were becoming more heavy-handed and the sense of hope produced by the Munich Conference was beginning to fade, I decided to be baptized. Did I do so out of conviction or opportunism? Today I can no longer say which it was. When the idea first occurred to me, I felt drawn to a religion that would definitively—or so I thought—cut my ties to the past and integrate me into a society which I had felt myself to be part of from the age of sixteen. Like everyone, at times I asked myself certain questions of the kind Tristan Bernard captured so aptly in a quatrain sent to me by his son Jean-Jacques, who had taken refuge in Brittany:

> To leave this world? But what awaits me?
> What could it be, this life beyond?
> I would like to go away... But would it be an ending?
> This nuisance of a soul, could it be immortal?

Most of all, I was tired of the cascade of daily insults against the "warmongering" Jews; if I felt a cowardly desire to sever these final ties to a people whose alien sense of identity I had never understood, it was because I wanted to close the remaining gap between myself and the nationality of my choice, and to protect my children. In Russia, it had been enough to be baptized to be exempt from anti-Semitic laws. I can now see that to the Germans and their followers, it is no longer a question of religion but rather one of race, a word I have used lightly in the past.

What does it mean, exactly, to be a Jew? After spending several years writing exclusively about the French Catholic bourgeoisie among whom I lived, I once again approached this subject in a novel during the fateful year of 1939: *The Dogs and the Wolves*. In it I describe two Israelite families from Kiev. They are distantly related, but one is poor and the other rich. In the book, I explore the fatal reality that weighs upon both families. The poor family is persecuted, mistreated, first in Russia and then in France; the other is treated with contempt and then excluded from society. I say of the character of Ben, a scrawny, feverish boy: "His experience was that of an old man. Perhaps race had something to do with the matter? Perhaps he felt, like all Jews, the dark, slightly frightening sense that he carried in him a past more ancient than that of most men. Where another might feel the need to learn new things, he, Ben, felt the need to remember—or at least this was how he saw it." This was the past I wanted to break away from by being baptized, but as we can see, it has stuck with me to this day.

On September 3, 1939, we were in Hendaye, and the declaration of war surprised us. It would be too heartbreaking to write about our final holiday; I have sealed off my memories of this red-and-gold summer. We did not want to return to Paris with the girls. I called Cécile Michaud, Denise's former nanny who, without a moment's hesitation, agreed to take them to her hometown, Issy-l'Évêque. She is only one year younger than I; I call her Néné and I love her dearly. In the days when I still laughed, we spent hours together devouring popular magazines which I subscribed to in her name—I loved serialized novels as much as she but was afraid that my fans would be shocked if they learned of my passion.

During the war, I traveled to see my daughters as often as possible, either by train or in my brother-in-law, Paul's, car. They were happy at Issy-l'Évêque, though Denise was shocked to discover life without running water or toilets; there was an outhouse at the bottom of the garden. I spent the Whitsuntide holidays there and then decided to stay on. Michel remained in Paris because of his work. In June, when the Germans were at the gates of Paris, his superiors decided to evacuate the bank to the provinces, leaving only an administrator behind. Then my husband fell ill with septicemia and almost died. His brother Paul and sister Mavlik nursed him back to health. I was sick with worry. After he recovered, he was so weak that he had to ask for further sick leave. The administrator, Monsieur Koehl, refused, and because Michel was truly unable to work, he was fired. He joined me at Issy-l'Évêque, where we soon found ourselves in a gentle trap. A few weeks after we arrived the authorities banned Jews who had left Paris from returning. At least we were not separated; I don't think either of us could have survived otherwise. I have a deep love for my children, but if Misha were taken from me I would become a shadow; if I disappeared, he would also be reduced to a shadow; and our two shadows would not rest until they were together again.

Rumors circulated that the government was planning to pass new measures against foreigners and stateless people. The decree of September 28, 1940, threw us into a panic: should we comply or should we disregard this directive instructing all Jews to register by October 20? We exchanged many pneumatic messages with friends and relatives. Some believed that it would be jumping into the wolf's mouth, others that we should continue to respect legal norms, that nothing would happen to us if we scrupulously followed the law. The French authorities pretended to bow to the occupiers' wishes; they claimed that they would use these lists only to protect us. Still unconvinced, I asked Michel to write to the president of his bank, who had close ties to the government. He responded nonchalantly: "My dear Epstein, I have received your letter, but your request puts me in an awkward position. I would be happy to help you, because I remember your excellent work for the bank and, as I have already expressed, I am a great admirer of Madame Epstein's talent, but I do not see what we can do for you. I believe, unfortunately, that you will have to execute the formalities required by the German authorities. No intervention can exempt you from them."

On my husband's insistence, I wrote a long letter to Pétain, through the subprefect of Autun, to whom I pointed out that "I have had the honor of contributing to the same publication as our head of state." I wrote:

Monsieur le Maréchal,

I had intended to ask Monsieur André Chaumeix, the director of the *Revue des Deux Mondes*, in which I have often been published, to draw your attention to the situation in which I find myself. Unfortunately, I cannot reach him because he is currently in the Unoccupied Zone. Even so, I dare to hope that this letter will reach you. This is the matter I would like to discuss with you: I have learned that your government has decided to take measures against stateless persons. I feel a great deal of anxiety regarding the fate that awaits us: my family (my husband, who was recently seriously ill, and daughters, who are ten and three years old), as well as myself. My husband and I are originally Russian; our parents emigrated during the Revolution. Both of our children are French. We have lived in France for the last twenty years, during which time we have never left the country. For fifteen years my husband was a senior banking executive at the Banque des Pays du Nord (which belongs to the Schneider group), a post he was forced to leave due to his illness. If you should care to obtain references from Monsieur Chaumeix, he will confirm that I have been writing for the *Revue des Deux Mondes* for several years. He can also guarantee my character; he was even willing, a few years ago, to support our request for naturalization, a process which no doubt has been interrupted by the war. I am a personal friend of Monsieur René Doumic and his family. Madame René Doumic and Madame de Régnier would, I am sure, be willing to attest to this. It goes without saying that I have never been involved in politics, and that my work is purely literary. In any case, I have done my best to make France known and loved around the world, in the foreign press and on the radio. I cannot believe, Monsieur le Maréchal, that no distinction will be made between undesirables and such honorable foreigners who, having received a royal welcome in France, have done their best to be worthy of it. Thus, I respectfully request that my family and I be understood to belong to the latter category, and that we may be allowed to live freely in France and that I may be able to continue to exercise my profession of novelist. Thanking you in advance for your attention to my letter, allow me to assure you of my deepest respect.

The only response was the decree of October 3, 1940, which was like a lightning bolt. We read it again and again, going over every detail with a fine-tooth comb. According to the definition in the first article, there was no doubt that we were Jews: "For the application of the present law, a person will be considered Jewish if he has at least three grandparents belonging to the Jewish race, or two grandparents of the Jewish race if the spouse is also Jewish." It was implacable, with regards to our children and ourselves. In this document, we were informed of all the professions that were forbidden to us, including government posts and teaching: "Newspaper, magazine, wire service, or periodical writer, editor, or editorial director, except in the case of specialized scientific publications." (Farewell to my hope of earning some money by publishing reviews, as I had been doing for several years.) "Director, administrator, or manager of companies involved in the creation, printing, distribution, or presentation of cinematographic films." (Exit my brother-in-law, Sam.) "Director, cinematographer, screenwriter; managing director, administrator, or manager of a theater or cinema; producer, director, administrator, or manager of any business related to radio broadcasting." Article eight reassured me somewhat: "By decree of each individual Council of State, and with sufficient evidence, the preceding interdictions may be lifted for Jews who have rendered exceptional service to the French State in the literary, scientific, or artistic fields." Michel ran to his typewriter and composed another letter to the Maréchal, in which he summarized the accolades for his wife, "the great writer," accumulated over the years, and respectfully requesting that this clause should be applied to me. We are still awaiting a reply.

The following day, October 4, a second decree was announced. It terrified us: "Foreign nationals belonging to the Jewish race may, as of the declaration of this law, be interned in special camps by decision of the prefecture of the *département* in which they reside." We had terrifying memories of the camps for Spanish refugees we had seen in the Basque Country during the Spanish Civil War. The horrible conditions had been described to us in great detail by a young woman who stayed at our villa in Hendaye with her child while she was visiting her husband in one of the camps. Cécile also remembered her conversations with this unhappy young woman. She begged us to flee. Switzerland was not so far, she pleaded, and the sympathetic villagers would help us find a smuggler who could get us across the border. She has repeated this plea many times since. Until last year, I always responded, "Cécile, why would we flee? We have done nothing wrong." Now it is pointless to even dream of such a thing.

After our arrival at Issy-l'Évêque, we lived with the girls at the Hotel des Voyageurs; we could not leave them with the Michauds in their tiny house. Finally we rented this enormous pile with fourteen rooms on the Place de l'Église, across from the World War I memorial; it is the largest house in the village, impossible to furnish or heat, but it was the only one available. We do not lack for food; meat is scarce, but we have milk, eggs, and cheese, and our garden produces an abundance of vegetables and fruit—cherries, apples, pears, and prunes. That is, when Michel doesn't meddle. But we are cruelly short of money. We can no longer pay the rent on our apartment in Paris, and we have asked the owner to allow one of our old servants to stay there for the time being. My husband has been maintaining a grotesque correspondence with the tax collector, who seems completely unaware of the conditions under which the Jews are living and insists that we must pay taxes that we obviously cannot afford. Michel continues to make desperate attempts to improve our situation, and has once again sought out Lieutenant Hohman, this time to ask for his help. He went so far as to write to Ambassador Abetz. As for me, I arranged for Julie to come here to look after the children, and now I wait.

Even though for some reason my books have not been banned, Grasset, my previous publisher, has removed them from his list without being ordered to do so. In October 1940, I had an interesting confrontation with Jean Fayard, who in April had asked me to serialize a novel in his weekly, which was published in the Free Zone. The fee we had agreed upon was sixty thousand francs, half of which I received when the contract was signed. I sent the manuscript but he refused to pay the balance of the fee, arguing that if he were to publish the book he would be breaking the rule that bars Jews from writing for newspapers. I asked for arbitration from the Society of Men of Letters, who ruled in my favor: "One cannot liken a great writer such as Madame Némirovsky, independent and unattached to the publication, with an employee such as a journalist, and for this reason the contract regulating the publication of her novel in your journal cannot be likened to a normal work contract. Therefore it follows that the law of October 3 does not apply in this case." Still, nothing came of their decision, and instead I received an insulting letter from Monsieur Fayard, in which he said that I should consider myself lucky that he had not demanded reimbursement of the money he had already paid.

On the other hand, I am forever grateful for having left Grasset for Albin Michel. Few letters have touched me as much as the one Albin Michel wrote spontaneously on August 28, 1939, the day before war was declared, and which I received in Hendaye, at our beloved Villa Ene Etchea:

Dear Madame,

We are living through anguishing hours which could become tragic from one day to the next. In addition, you are both Russian and Jewish, and it is possible that those who do not know you—who must be few, given your fame—may create problems for you. For this reason, as it is important to plan ahead as far as one can, it has occurred to me that a letter from me, as your publisher, might be of use to you. I am happy to attest to the fact that you are a woman of letters of enormous talent, a fact which is further proven by the success of your books in France and abroad, where some of them have been translated. I am also more than willing to declare that since October 1933, when you came to me after publishing several books with my colleague Grasset, one of which, *David Golder*, was a dazzling success and became the basis for a remarkable film, I have always enjoyed the most cordial relations with you and your husband, in addition to our professional relationship as publisher and author.

It is Albin Michel who has provided my only subsidy since the beginning of the war. He is ill and has withdrawn to the country-side, but his son-in-law, Robert Esménard, obtained permission from the Germans to publish *The Dogs and the Wolves* and to bring out new editions of some of my previous works. Even though it has become impossible for him to go ahead with the publication of these books, he has maintained my monthly allowance of three thousand francs. Courageously, he defies the ordinance of April 26, 1941, which obliges publishers to place all fees paid to Jewish writers into a frozen bank account. In order to protect his accounting ledgers from official inspections, he has assumed the risk of signing a false contract with Julie for a future novel to be written by me. His ad-viser, André Sabatier, supplies me with books and rarely allows a month to pass without sending me letters, and sees Paul regularly in Paris in order to maintain closer contact with us. I know that no matter what happens, I can count on Esménard and Sabatier. Where would I be today if I had stayed with Fayard or Grasset?

Our existence here is gloomy. Only Denise and Babet enjoy them-selves: Denise because she has our undivided attention and can no longer complain, as she did in Paris, of our too frequent social en-gagements; Babet because she loves this country life, the jaunts in the fields, her wooden clogs. I try to convince myself that all of this will end one day. As I compose *Suite Française*, I tell myself that I must write something important and try to silence the voice in my head that asks: What's the use? All too often, I am even more afraid for my books than I am for myself; I imagine them destroyed, forever erased from human memory.

In my more childish moments, I look to one of Nostradamus's prophecies which says that the end of our troubles will come in 1944. But will I still be here in two years? I read, I take copious notes, and I ask myself constantly how we reached this point. The other day, I wrote this in my leather-bound notebook:

> For several years, every action taken by members of a certain social class in France has had one motive: fear. Fear has been the cause of the war, of the defeat, and of the current peace. A member of this caste feels no hatred, no envy, no disappointed ambition, nor even a real desire for vengeance. He is simply scared stiff. Who will cause him less pain, he asks—not in the future, not in the abstract, but right now, in the form of real punches and kicks? Is it the Germans? The English? The Russians? The Germans defeated him but this reality has now been forgotten, and he can now defend them. Thus he is "for the Germans." The weak schoolboy prefers to be oppressed by a single bully rather than have complete freedom; the bully torments him but defends him from other students who might beat him up for his marbles. If he escapes the bully's dominion, he is alone, abandoned to the crowd.

What I am describing here is the bourgeoisie, not the ideologues. I often think about two writers, both my age, whom I used to know; they are both graduates of the École Normale Supérieure, both extremely talented, but they have chosen diametrically opposed paths. They are Robert Brasillach and Paul Nizan. They published books three years apart: *Before the War* and *The Conspiracy*. The former hates the Jews and is fascinated by Fascism, or rather, shall we say, by the young Fascists (he never mentions the older ones): clearly, he was seduced by their blond hair during his travels in Germany. The latter's book has as its hero a Jew, a student by the name of Rosenthal, and describes his attraction to Communism. But even though they come to opposite conclusions, their premise is the same. In my own books, especially the later ones—*The Pawn on the Chessboard*, *The Prey*, *Two*—I have often expressed my sympathy for the generation who were children during or grew up in the shadow of the Great War. These young people came to realize in the wild twenties that their parents and their elders had died for nothing. Those who were not seduced by easy money became disgusted by politics and quickly accepted the dangerous notion that politicking is the same as politics. There was nothing left for them but the path of extremism.

I am not speaking here of the working classes. The inhabitants of Issy-l'Évêque, this village lost in the fields of Saône-et-Loire, with only one street, reveal their noblesse and generosity to me each day. The priest often stops by for a chat, and he did not hold it against Babet when, on his first visit, he handed her a box of bonbons and she answered, "Thank you, madame." I am speaking of people like the director of the local school, the farmers who bring a rabbit or a chicken for our table, the peasants who tip their hats when they pass me in the street. Many of them have given their children to the Resistance. They all hate the Vichy government. The two men they hate the most are Philippe Henriot and Pierre Laval: the first is considered a tiger, the second, a hyena. And it is true that one emanates a fragrance of fresh blood, the other, the stench of decaying flesh.

But often I think of my former colleagues, the journalists and writers who covered me with accolades, many of whom now court Vichy or the occupiers. I imagine Florence Gould's salon, and the brilliant dinners at which many of the writers who are still in Paris probably gather to this day, despite restrictions. The other day I felt a pang when I saw a photograph in a magazine of Danielle Darrieux, all smiles; she was leaving for Germany with a group of artists. I remember her sitting in my living room, young and shy, during the filming of her first big movie, which was based on my book *The Ball*.

Because of my impending asthma attack I had no appetite and did not eat dinner. Before going up to my room, I stopped in the kitchen to pour myself a glass of milk and cut a slice of the ham that my dear Cécile was able to procure for us. It was wrapped in a page of newspaper which I—being the obsessive reader that I am—mechanically smoothed out and read. It was a page from *Paris-Midi*, dated June 2, with a report signed by a certain André de Laumois on the man-in-the-street reactions of the French to the appearance of the yellow star, decreed by an ordinance of May 29, 1942:

How modest the debut of the little yellow star has been! One hardly saw it, it seemed afraid to show its face, it hid itself away. And people said, "Are there so few, then?"

But it did not take long for it to become more emboldened. First, it emerged from behind the stalls in the Faubourg Montmartre. Then it reached Saint-Lazare, the Madeleine, the Champs-Élysées, and, finally, spread through Passy and Auteuil. Now, the cry is unanimous:

"Who knew there were so many?"

Do not think that those who wore it felt ashamed, or wore it with discretion. Not a bit of it! Especially among these well-fed, well-dressed children of Israel from the well-to-do neighborhoods where the black market flourishes, it was worn with an explosion of arrogance. We saw them in fancy restaurants, wearing provocative expressions, calling out to the manager and waiters in a high and mighty tone. Nothing was ever prepared well enough, the service was never good enough. It was as if the Aryans were the poor relations, almost out of place. How powerful is the force of habit!

Now it is a different story. The Israelite has calculated how to take advantage of the yellow star. He plays the victim. He passes himself off as a martyr.

The plan is executed with great skill. The message makes it way, ferret-like, transmitted by anonymous voices along the line at the grocer's, in loges, and in servants' quarters. They soften up kindhearted, credulous Aryans by speaking of the children. "Poor little innocent Jews," they murmur. "Imagine their misfortune!" And they peddle stories of dramatic scenes in which women and children figure prominently.

Good souls forget what the parents of these children—who will also grow up one day—have done to our France before plunging it into war: they turned it into a cesspool in which its traditions languished and its virtues festered.

The yellow star is perhaps the only way to keep the star of Israel from swallowing up our entire sky.

I returned to the sitting room. Osip Mandelstam once wrote: "This werewolf century flings itself on my shoulders." I closed the doors in order to avoid waking anyone in the house and put on the record of Ernest Bloch's *Baal Shem*, which Alfred Adler brought us from the United States in 1932 when he came for my father's funeral. I listened to it for the first time after the ceremony at the cemetery in Belleville, my head full of memories of this man who had called me Rirette instead of Irotchka after our arrival in France, and who had just been buried, according to his dying wish, in a Jewish grave. The deep, sonorous quality of the music, the heartrending bow-strokes of this Hebrew lament moved me inexplicably. I thought of the shtetls in Poland, where they say that the Jews are sent after being gathered in concentration camps. Then I went back upstairs, seeking Michel's warmth; his arm fell across my chest. But before turning out the light, I picked up my leather-bound notebook and had the strength to write: "My God, what is this country doing to me!"

In 1917—when I was fourteen—my father took me with him to Yalta on one of his business trips. When he had finished his work, we spent two days alone in a hotel in Gurzuf. It is on the other side of Cape Martian, a vast bay filled with roses, at the foot of mountains whose terraced sides are planted with vineyards. There is a story that says that three menacing bears once lived there in the

Babugana mountains. One of these, the Aiu-Dag, is shaped like a bear. The three bears had taken a little girl from a nearby village and held her prisoner for years. She kept house for them. But she grew more and more beautiful and wise. One day a storm brought a handsome young man to those shores; he fell in love with her, and she returned his love. He convinced her to run away with him and they set off together. The three bears realized what had happened and ran down to the shore and began to lap up all the water in the sea. A good fairy came to the lovers' aid. She ordered the bears to return to their mountain. One of them refused, and she turned him into a giant rock, the Aiu-Dag. Pushkin loved to daydream there.

My father and I walked along the shore for a long time. He told me that when Chekhov began to notice the symptoms of tuberculosis, the disease that had killed his beloved brother Nikolai, he traveled around the world and then, after a terrible attack of hemoptysis, went to live in Crimea. Vera Komissarzhevskaya came to see him. She was the most famous Russian actress at the time; when she died, her fragile remains were transported by train from Tashkent to St. Petersburg, from Asia to Europe, and greeted at each station by crowds of people in tears. In the twilight, the sandy-bearded, sickly Chekhov, wearing a pince-nez, and the lady with enormous tragic eyes had paced up and down this beach just as we were doing, surrounded by the fragrance of roses and the ethereal melody of the waves. At his request, she recited Nina's final monologue from *The Seagull*, which had been created for her:

> It was nice in the old days, Kostya! Do you remember? How clear, warm, joyous and pure life was, what feelings we had— feelings like tender, exquisite flowers ... Do you remember? "Men, lions, eagles, and partridges, horned deer, geese, spiders, silent fish that dwell in the water, star-fishes, all living things, all living things, have completed their cycle of sorrow, are extinct ... For thousands of years the earth has borne no liv-

ing creature on its surface, and this poor moon lights its lamp in vain. On the meadow the cranes no longer waken with a cry and there is no sound of the May beetles in the linden trees...”*

The child ceased being a child many years ago. At her age, she could almost be the mother of her mother, who will remain thirty-nine for all eternity. She has undertaken the long voyage and evoked the irrevocable. Today she says to herself, "From this point onward no one, not even her daughters, can follow." She allows History to speak.

After being arrested on July 13, 1942, Irène Némirovsky was transported to Pithiviers, where she arrived on July 16. She gave her date of birth not as February 24 but as February 11, 1903.

She was in convoy number 6, which left for Auschwitz on July 17 with a contingent of 809 men and 119 women. Serge Klarsfeld has determined that there were 18 survivors from this convoy who were alive in 1945. She was not among them. According to a German encyclopedia, she died one month after her arrival. According to the testimony of some, she died of typhus.

Her husband, Michel, who was arrested three months later and confined at Drancy, was deported on November 6 in convoy number 42, which included 478 men, 504 women, and 16 "unspecifieds." Of these, 221 were children under 18, of which 113 were under 12. Only 4 were alive in 1945.

Her two brothers-in-law, Samuel and Paul, and her sisters-in-law, Alexandra and Mavlik, who were arrested in July, died during the deportation. Her niece, Natasha, was eventually able to reach North Africa.

Her children, Denise and Élisabeth, who were arrested with their father, were saved.

ACKNOWLEDGMENTS

THIS BOOK was imagined on the basis of other books. Firstly, those of my mother, Irène Némirovsky.*

Le Malentendu (The Misunderstanding), 1926
David Golder, 1929; *David Golder, The Ball, Snow in Autumn, and The Courilof Affair,* translated by Sandra Smith and published in a single volume (Everyman's Library, 2008)
Le Bal, 1930; *The Ball*
Les Mouches d'automne, 1931; *Snow in Autumn*
L'Affaire Courilof, 1933; *The Courilof Affair*
Films parlés (Talking Pictures), 1934
Le Pion sur l'échiquier (The Pawn on the Chessboard), 1934
Le Vin de solitude, 1935; *The Wine of Solitude*, translated by Sandra Smith (Chatto & Windus, 2011)
Jézabel, 1936; *Jezebel*, translated by Sandra Smith (Vintage UK, 2010)
La Proie (The Prey), 1938
Deux (Two), 1939
Les Chiens et les loups, 1940; *The Dogs and the Wolves*, translated by Sandra Smith (Vintage UK, 2010)
La Vie de Tchekhov, 1946; *A Life of Chekhov*, Translated by Erik de Mauny (Haskell House, 1974)

---

*The first date following each title is the date of first French publication; the second date, that of most recent translation into English. Titles of books that are not available in English are also translated and have been employed throughout the book.

Les Biens de ce monde, 1947; *All Our Worldly Goods*, translated by
    Sandra Smith (Vintage, 2011)
Les Feux de l'automne (Autumn Fires), 1957

[Published subsequent to the writing of *The Mirador* and the death
of Élisabeth Gille]

Dimanche, 2000; *Dimanche and Other Stories*, translated by
    Bridget Patterson, (Vintage, 2010)
Destinées et autres nouvelles (Destinations and Other Stories), 2004
Suite Française, 2004; (Vintage, 2006)
Le maître des âmes (The Master of Souls; serialized in *Gringoire* as
    Les Échelles du Levant [The Ports of the Levant] May–August
    1939), 2005
Chaleur du sang, 2007; *Fire in the Blood*, translated by Sandra
    Smith (Vintage, 2008)

Also, Konstantin Georgiyevich Paustovsky's *Story of a Life*, especially the first three volumes, *The Faraway Years*, *Restless Youth*, and
The Start of an Extraordinary Era.

Also Sholem Asch's trilogy, especially *Petersburg* and *Moscow*.
The scenes I describe at the Hotel Metropol are inspired by the
latter.

In addition, I thank Anna Akhmatova, Sholem Aleichem, Yuri
Annenkov, Pierre Assouline, Isaac Babel, Jean-Jacques Becker, Serge
Bernstein, Andrei Bely, Alexander Blok, Dominique Borne, Jean
Bothorel, Mikhail Bulgakov, Ivan Bunin, André Chénier, Jean Coc-
teau, Yves Courrière, Fyodor Dostoyevsky, Joachim du Bellay,
Henri Dubief, Ilya Ehrenburg, Marc Ferro, Janet Flanner, Robert
Fleury, Philippe Ganier-Raymond, André Gide, Nikolai Gogol,
Ivan Goncharov, Maxim Gorky, Raul Hilberg, André Kaspi, Joseph
Kessel, Serge Klarsfeld, Alexander Kuprin, Gaston Leroux, Osip
Mandelstam, Jean Barabini, Michael R. Marrus, Guy de Maupas-
sant, Sergei Mintslov, Alfred de Musset, Robert O. Paxton, Georges
Perec, Leon Poliakov, Alexander Pushkin, Henri Raczymow, Gilles

Ragache, Jean-Robert Ragache, Nicholas Riasanovsky, Zeev Sternhell, Anton Chekhov, Leo Tolstoy, Ivan Turgenev, Henri Troyat, Gustave Welter, and Oscar Wilde.

I thank Francis Esménard for entrusting me with Irène Némirovsky's dossier, carefully conserved since 1933, so that I could study it at my leisure. The file contained a note written by Robert Esménard, dated January 13, 1986, and addressed to his son, which began with these words:

I am leaving you this small dossier regarding Irène Némirovsky, with whom I always had friendly relations, just as Albin Michel had before me. In addition to her talent, he appreciated her rectitude, her simplicity, and her qualities as a person. Peruse it when you have a moment.

You will see what a terrible situation she found herself in due to her Nazi tormentors, and you will see the courage and dignity that she maintained until the end. This is the drama of the Jewish people, persecuted by Nazi hatred. You will also see all that was done to save her from the worst and to ensure, after her deportation, the safety and education of her children.

May this book be a testimony and an homage to Albin Michel, Robert Esménard, André Sabatier, and Francis Esménard.

Above all others, I thank my sister, Denise Epstein-Dauplé, without whom this book could not have been written. Not only did she open her memory to me, but she did an enormous amount of research in order to decipher our mother's documents and gather correspondence and press accounts.

And finally, I add that though this book has been "dreamed," the letters and all citations by Irène Némirovsky come from unpublished notes, and are authentic. A few of her phrases have also slipped, like marks of love, into my writing.

NOTES

Unless otherwise noted, all translations of quoted material have been made by the translator.

5   The highly compressed opening lines of Valéry's long poem "The Young Fate." Their sense can be rendered as "Who is it weeping if not simply the wind / Alone this late with the last diamonds of all? / But who is it, weeping, so close to me / On the verge of weeping myself?"

7   George Perec, from *W., or the Memory of Childhood*, translated by David Bellos (Harvill, 1975).

34   Konstantin Paustovsky, Russian writer who lived from 1892 to 1968. His celebrated memoirs are one of Gille's sources.

59   Mikhail Lermontov, from "Smert Poeta," in *Mikhail Lermontov: Selected Works* (Moscow: Progress Publishers, 1976).

59   From Osip Mandelstam's *Stone*, translated by Robert Tracy, (Princeton University Press, 1981).

63   Sholem Aleichem, *The Adventures of Menahem-Mendl*, translated by Tamara Kahana (Putnam, 1969).

66   Alexander Blok, from *The Rose and the Cross*.

68   Aleksandr Pushkin, from "The Bronze Horseman," in *Eugene Onegin and Other Poems*, translated by Charles Johnston (Everyman's Library, 1999).

78   Anton Chekhov, from *Virgin Soil*, translated by Constance Garnett (New York Review Books, 2000).

94   Andrei Bely, from *Petersburg*, translated by Robert A. Maguire (Indiana University Press, 1979).

98   Chekhov, from "The Steppe," in *The Steppe and Other Stories*, translated by Ronald Wilks (Penguin Classics, 2001).

102 "The bearded king advancing / Is Aga, Agamemnon." From Jacques Offenbach, *La Belle Hélène*.

104 Blok, from "Autumn Day," in *The Twelve and Other Poems*,

translated by John Stallworthy and Peter France (Oxford University Press, 1970).

105 Blok, from "The Twelve, " ibid.

119 André Chénier, from "La Jeune Tarentine."

137 Literally, "rich spoiled brats."

144 After their parents were arrested by the Gestapo, Robert and Gerard Finaly were sheltered in an orphanage in Grenoble, whose Catholic director had them baptized and then adopted them. In 1953, after an extended legal dispute, France's highest court ordered that the boys be returned to the care of Jewish relatives. Before they could be, they were kidnapped and smuggled into Spain with the help of Catholic priests, leading to a major conflict between the French government and the Catholic church.

149 "Pretty poppy, ladies! Pretty poppy, sirs!" The lines are from a traditional French children's song.

160 "Iréne's Toy."

164 Pierre Ronsard, from "Against the Woodcutters of the Gastine Forest."

176 Derogatory French slang for German soldiers.

182 Translation by Sandra Smith (Everyman's Library, 2008).

185 Joachin du Bellay, from "Les Regrets."

186 Gille is mistaken: *Bagatelles pour un massacre* came out first, in 1937. *L'École des cadavres* appeared in 1938.

199 Alfred de Musset, from "Une Soirée Perdue."

217 Chekhov, from *The Seagull*, translated by Constance Garnett (Modern Library, 2001)

AFTERWORD

ÉLISABETH Gille waited until she was over fifty to measure her-self against her mother. By deciding to devote her first book, *The Mirador*, to the story of Irène Némirovsky's life and by deciding to tell that story in the first person, she also made it clear that what had held up her own career as a writer for so long was the problem of having been a writer's daughter. And not just any writer, rather one who at the peak of her career had fallen prey to a murderous anti-Semitism.

Which meant that Gille had to decide to confront the Shoah as well, while also having to come to terms with the fact that not only had she survived her mother, who died at the age of thirty-nine, but she had outlived her. Her daunting literary legacy, Auschwitz, being a survivor (and ending up as a kind of mother to her mother): Gille hesitated for years before confronting these intractable issues. They went to the heart of her existence.

Gille's talent as a writer emerged late but with a burst of brilliance. When it was published, *The Mirador* was immediately proclaimed as an important and original work of biography. By this time, however, Gille had only a few years left to live—something that she both did and didn't know. Her health was fragile and the cancer that would eventually kill her was beginning to spread.

Her amazing energy, her refusal to complain, the vast amount of editorial work she undertook, her almost religious devotion to her friends (she preferred to care for others than to feel sorry for herself) soon inspired a second book, *Le Crabe sur la banquette arrière* (The Crab in the Backseat): a work in the form of dialogue that is more a satiric broadside than a tale of woe. Instead of railing against her sickness, Gille attacked the harmful changes in attitude that sick people encounter in the world around them. This book was also a success, astonishing both critics and readers with its comic, corrosive, unsparing tone, and its yoking of sorrow and compassion.

After this there was time for Gille to write one last book, *Shadows of a Childhood*, a novel about her youth after her mother's death. It is a work whose outlines, faint as a watermark, can already be discerned in *The Mirador*.

The Mirador is interspersed with short italicized entries that are like sketches for a self-portrait: to bring out the tragedy of her mother's deportation, Gille also had to describe her plight as a little girl and that of her older sister, Denise Epstein-Dauplé (for whom preserving the memory of the Shoah was to become the work of a lifetime). The understated way in which the book counterpoints these narratives is more than an exercise in literary artifice. Gille, in picking up her mother's pen, was trying to see herself from the outside, and she became closer to her mother than to herself.

By casting the largely autobiographical *Shadows of a Childhood* as a novel, Gille returned to a project that had begun to take shape in *The Mirador*. Inevitably the book alters the details of her life. Lea, the main character, is not identical to Élisabeth, though they have much in common: the same life story and the same warm, engaging personality, a shared passion for friendship, a similar outlook on politics. But strictly speaking the book is a work of fiction, a free variation on autobiographical themes, with the language, structure, and style of a novel. And from the very first word of the book, an interjected "No," Gille was nodding to Némirovsky. *David Golder*, the novel that made her mother famous, begins in the same way.

In four years, Gille had written and published three greatly admired books, and having worked in publishing her entire life, she was aware of how utterly unpredictable a book's critical or commercial success could be. She was surprised and delighted by the reception of *The Mirador*, but she was also wary. Over the years, she had formed all sorts of ties in publishing and to the press, and she knew perfectly well how self-seeking, prejudiced, and hypocritical those worlds could be. Her mother, as Gille is at pains to show in *The Mirador*, had been more credulous and had paid dearly for it, finding herself abandoned in her hour of need by the editors and critics who until then had treated her as a star. So Gille was careful to put into perspective the praise that now came her way.

By the time *Shadows of a Childhood* appeared, she was in the hospital fighting for her life. She fell into a coma that appeared to be terminal, but then she regained consciousness. She had dreamed of her own death, and it was with a certain glee, which gave her a brief reprieve from her pain, that she recounted the dream to her visitors, almost provocatively, with a mixture of sarcasm and irony and surreal poetry, while watching closely to see how her listeners, who would be her survivors, responded. But then the pain came back, and she wanted only her closest and most trusted friends to be at her side.

She often drew a connection between her mother's early death and her own death by cancer, but only to make light of the latter. And though she had always had a powerful sense of humor, this gave way to something else, not so much a softness as a profound clarity of spirit, a recognition of fate. The approach of death also made her that much more aware of her Jewishness, bringing her back to a religion that, finally, was not hers any more than it had been her mother's, and yet which she could hardly deny, given how it had shaped her childhood and her life.

In writing about her mother in *The Mirador*, and in writing as her mother, Gille was forced to attack an intricate array of problems from several angles. Apart from the issues already mentioned—of taking up writing, of fame and its illusions, of Judaism, of the Shoah—there was the most fundamental issue of all, that of mother and daughter. Némirovsky's best books all feature a hated mother figure. Gille's grandmother, who refused to recognize her granddaughters after the war when the woman who had saved them brought them to her door, was a hated figure, and Némirovsky wrote about her again and again. She is the model for all the grasping, self-ish, frivolous women in Némirovsky's work, but especially in *David Golder* and *The Ball*, not to mention *Jezebel*.

This obsessive struggle between mother and daughter comes up repeatedly in *The Mirador*: Gille has no doubt that this struggle drove her mother throughout her career as a writer. In an important scene in the book, the conflict between these women whose minds will never meet is captured in the image of the two of them reflected in a single mirror. Because of course it was Némirovsky's mother who, by insisting on speaking to her daughter only in French, deter-mined the language she would write in, while providing her with the psychological material for her work and serving as her perfect foil. Némirovsky came to be herself by fighting off her mother. Gille in turn came to be herself by forgetting, and then by remembering, her mother. Had she ever really forgotten? No, but her mother's paralyz-ing shadow had made it impossible to speak for herself. She had to write in her mother's voice to liberate her own voice as a writer.

But in writing about her mother, Gille was also forced to consider other things that she had long ignored: Russia, Judaism, being a survivor. In putting the book together, Russia proved the biggest problem, since she wanted her picture of the country to be both ac-curate and alive. Kiev, St. Petersburg, and Moscow had to be more than words on a page. She was convinced, too, that Némirovsky's Russian background—which, with the exception of a few stories and an unfinished novel, the novelist had written about only early in her career—was crucial. During the war, while working on, among other things, a biography of Chekhov, Némirovsky returned to the subject of Russia, for her inseparable from her mother. And yet dur-ing her lifetime, she was best known for her depictions of the Pari-sian bourgeoisie.

The first part of *The Mirador* evokes a Russia that is riven by con-flict but dazzlingly alive, still vibrant with childhood memories. By imagining these pages as having been written by Némirovsky in 1929, the year of her great triumph, when *David Golder* was adapted for both the stage and the screen, Gille turns Russia into the negative reflection of her mother's imagined Parisian paradise. And yet thirteen years later Némirovsky will pass a very different judgment (or rather her daughter will for her) on the city that had once praised her to the skies.

By this time she is living in isolation in La Nièvre, rejected, ostracized, forgotten, soon to be arrested and deported. Her editors—led by Bernard Grasset—have turned their backs on her. Fortunately, her last publisher, Albin Michel, has not, and Gille quotes a courageous letter from him to her mother. For the false friends, however, the erstwhile "magnificent Slav" has become an "Israelite." A cosmopolitan.

Cosmopolitan was now an insult in France, just as in Italy, as Pavese was to recall after the war. The situation was the same on both sides of the Alps. Rosetta Loy's essays, stories, and novels about prewar Italy complement Gille's description of her mother's France. An enlightened but naïve middle class, having failed to read the writing on the wall, has been rapidly reduced to helplessness. Intellectual circles are distinguished only by their apathy. Gille reminds us that Némirovsky was unquestionably slow to realize what was going on. She didn't pay attention to the slippery sympathies of writers like Paul Morand and Jean Cocteau or, perhaps more seriously, to the incoherent views expressed, whether out of blindness or foolishness, by such friends as Emmanuel Berl or Daniel Halévy.

By writing in the first person, Gille confronted head-on the challenge that lay before her. Némirovsky, the mother of whom she had no memory, had involuntarily cast a spell of silence on her from beyond the grave. And yet thanks to her mother, Gille could now retrieve the words that had been stolen from her by restoring them to her mother. Mother and daughter would equally give each other the power of speech.

Gille read Némirovsky's work with mixed feelings, at once severely critical and admiring. She was charmed by the early stories about Russia, and she couldn't help being dazzled by the murderous elegance of *The Ball*, a novella that is widely recognized as a master-piece of concision. In *The Mirador* Gille echoes the betrayal that takes place in that story when she has Némirovsky conceal from her mother the letter announcing her father's imminent return from Baku.

Otherwise Gille makes no effort to imitate Némirovsky's style or voice in *The Mirador*, apart from the occasional sharp turn of phrase. Némirovsky's style displays a hardness and cynicism of which Gille was incapable. Gille wasn't the least bit cynical. She could be bru-tally straightforward, but she was generous at heart. Thus the self-portrait that Gille "dreamed" on her mother's behalf is much more tender than Némirovsky is in her own books—more thoughtful, less evasive, and more self-aware. Némirovsky's dazzling intelligence found its outlet in the cutting phrase. Gille, curiously, is closer to her mother in the book about her cancer, or in her last book, when de-nouncing the French complicity in the slaughter of innocent Jews, than she is in telling the story of her mother's life.

Each of Gille's three books is an effort to describe something un-describable: the consciousness of death, whether under the guise of genocide or terminal illness. She never attempts to describe the Shoah. *The Mirador* ends, inevitably, with her mother's deportation, since it is Némirovsky who is supposed to be writing it as a final work for posthumous publication.

And yet during her period in Issy-l'Évêque and after the begin-ning of the war, Némirovsky wrote powerfully about what was go-ing on. She could tell what awaited her. "Have you noticed that portraits of those who are condemned to die young or to die vio-lently have a sad, slightly haggard look?" she writes in "Aino" (a story which reaches back to an entirely different period of her life, the months she spent in Finland before moving to France). This is no less true of the pictures that have survived of Némirovsky, whose eyes have the same expression as those of her daughters, Élisabeth and Denise.

A number of Némirovsky's stories take up the topics of the war, of the threat of death, and of anti-Semitism. In "Fraternity" a poor man and a rich bourgeois sit side by side on a bench at the train station. The men share the same name: Rabinovich. The rich man has been thrown back into a Yiddish world that he long ago rejected, and he responds with exceedingly bad grace to his stint of compulsory brotherhood.

"Monsieur Rose" is a very moving story about a self-involved rich man, apathetic and unlikable, who, fleeing from the occupying German forces, grows close to a young hero who teaches him nothing less than how to be a human being, how to live. Here, in a handful of pages, all of Némirovsky's extraordinary skill as a writer is on display, a skill that links her not only to Maupassant and Chekhov but to the American writers, Baldwin above all, that Gille admired so much. And one imagines that if Némirovsky had taken her father's advice and emigrated to the United States, she might have enjoyed a normal writer's life, rather like that of Carson McCullers, a writer she somewhat resembles, in fact. It's because Némirovsky is so good at capturing a character in a few swift strokes that her books translate so easily into film. And she has an emotional range that is not just limited to tragedy.

The stories and novels about love (always linked to, and soiled by, the question of money) are filled with unforgettable descriptions. "The Happy Shores" is a marvelous story about two "prostitutes" who meet in a pickup bar on New Year's Eve. One is a real prostitute, an aging woman waiting for a client who never arrives; the other is a metaphorical one, young and in love with a man who has abandoned her for an older mistress who, for professional reasons, it is inconvenient for him to give up. The encounter between the women and the conversation they have are utterly gripping. Where did Némirovsky come by her knowledge of contempt, in Moravia's sense, that condition of willing debasement? "The closer she drew to the place where he should be waiting for her, the more she realized how, as always, her heart was slowly contracting with sorrow in her chest. She imagined him saying it, his voice low and hesitant, 'love,' murmuring the word as doubtfully as one might the name of a half-recognized passerby."

"The Spectator" is one of Némirovsky's most harrowing stories about the consciousness of death, linked here to the theme of selfish love. A man who is incapable of love is fleeing war-torn Europe and considering going into exile in Uruguay. Before he boards the ocean liner on which he is to cross the Atlantic to the New World, he launches into an angry denunciation of love, in which the war is all mixed up with his past disappointments. "Every evil that descends upon the human race is due, Hugo thought, to those who love others more than themselves and demand gratitude for their love."

He tries to save his skin but he finds death. In the icy sea where his torpedoed ship is sinking he contemplates his end with the cold eyes of a stranger, the indifferent stranger he had been to others whose unhappiness failed to touch him. But now it is his turn. Tragedy has caught up with him. There is no love to save him. Neither his fellow human beings nor his wits can save him from the overwhelming indifference.

It is awful to think that Némirovsky, caught in a storm that would soon sweep her away, is here describing the very indifference that would assure her own fate. There had been clear signs of what was to come, but no one had wanted to read them, or too few had known how. In the final pages of these "dreamed memories" Gille undoubtedly grants Irène Némirovsky more understanding than she had. And yet here and there Némirovsky's work is touched by terror.

–RENÉ DE CECCATTY
Translated by Edwin Frank

Élisabeth Gille and René de Ceccatty
An Interview

This interview with Élisabeth Gille was conducted in January 1992, on the occasion of the publication of *The Mirador*, and appeared in *Il Messaggero*. The Italian publishing house Feltrinelli had just brought out translations of several of Irène Némirovsky's most important works.

Do you think your mother's work has been given its due—like, for example, Nina Berberova's—now that she's being rediscovered throughout the world?

No, I think she is still poorly understood, lumped together with other women writers of her time. I think she's better than Colette, for one thing—especially if you compare her novels to *Chéri* or *Mitsou*. But my mother wrote a lot, more than a book a year. She had a remarkable ability to convey an atmosphere or set a scene in just a few lines. As to Berberova, well she didn't have a painter's eye, though I do like *The Accompanist*. Still, I prefer Yuri Annenkov's *La Révolution derrière la porte* (The Revolution Behind the Door), which does a brilliant job of describing the wretched situation of writers during the Russian Revolution. Berberova's writing doesn't have that kind of visual precision. There is, however, another a Russian-born French novelist from my mother's generation whom I love: Nathalie Sarraute. I visited her while I was writing *The Mirador*, and she was clearly moved. She remembered how in 1942 the news went around that my mother had been arrested and deported. Sarraute never understood why my mother hadn't gone into hiding.

Writing this book about your mother, you set yourself up as a privileged witness to her life, and yet one who'd forgotten a lot...

I deliberately walled myself off—thanks to which I've been able to lead a relatively normal life, get married, raise children, have a career as a translator and editor. But the cost of normality was repression. I was also fighting against various received ideas: all the baggage, for example, that comes along with my mother being Russian. A problem I had was that there was no documentation of her life from between 1903 and 1930. Then one day someone came back from Kiev and told me about all the linden trees there, and for some reason that made me think of my mother's asthma. The first sentence of the book came to me: "I have always found the fragrance of linden blossoms aggressive, though it is in fact quite tender, at least in literature..." I'd just read about a pogrom which had taken place in the wealthier neighborhoods of Kiev. With Bulgakov's *Kiev* and Paustovsky's memoirs as a point of departure, I tried to imagine the life of a young girl caught up in history at the start of the twentieth century.

The hardest thing must have been to write about Irène Némirovsky's all too slow political awakening at the beginning of World War II.

When I was an adolescent, I was angry with her for her lack of political sense. It would have been easy for her to have saved herself, but she didn't even try, and by staying she put my sister and me in danger. We were also picked up and, logically, we should have been sent to Auschwitz just like our parents. She was criminally blind. Looking at her work from the 1930s, you can see that she couldn't have cared less about the plight of the poor Jews in the working-class neighborhoods. And yet my mother wasn't right wing: She defended the Russian Revolution. She lived a life of privilege, though, and she didn't understand what was going on all around her. Apparently the officer who escorted her to police headquarters in 1942 even gave her a chance to escape. She said she wasn't going into exile again. She was French, and that was that. There's nothing to suggest that she was even worried, unless it's the request for French citizenship my parents filed in 1938—too late.

Would you call her a White Russian?

Of course. Her early books, up to *The Dogs and the Wolves*, were entirely inspired by Russia. They're her best books by far. What I love is the spareness of the style, which is very French, but at the same time there's a Slavic dreaminess. My favorite book is *Snow in Autumn*. She was much less original when she stopped writing about Russian subjects, and her later works haven't aged nearly as well. She refused to teach us Russian. She'd closed that door.

And she didn't really think of herself as Jewish?

Her Jewishness was a burden for her. In *The Dogs and the Wolves* she describes her hero as, in a sense, knowing too much—as if he has a past he can't escape. Of course, before the war, it was possible for her to write critically about certain Jewish social circles, as she did in *David Golder* in particular, in a way that she never could have done after Nazism. For her, Jewishness was a relic of ancestral traditions that had lost any meaning. I have no idea why she decided to be baptized; there isn't a trace of religious faith in her books or her letters, apart from one blasphemous remark: "My God, forgive us our offenses as we forgive you yours . . ." She must have done it to fit in . . . That said, even if she was an atheist, you can't look at what it means to be Jewish the same way after Nazism.

What do you think led her to serialize her novel Les Échelles du Levant *(The Ports of the Levant) in the extreme right-wing magazine* Gringoire?

That's something I've always held against her. And yet when you thumb through the magazine you'll notice a complete split between the political articles, which are extremely anti-Semitic, and the literary pages, which could even be anti-German . . . The novel came out in *Gringoire* between May and August 1939. Above each episode it read: "The latest installment of the work of the great Slavic novelist." All her friends went out of their way to forget that she was Jewish. Even she'd forgotten.

How did your sister and you manage to escape?

It's a story worthy of Vercors's *The Silence of the Sea*. The day we were arrested, we were taken to police headquarters. My older sister was very blond, and a German officer noticed her. He pulled out a picture of his own daughter, who was also blond. He said "She looks like her," and he told Julie, our governess: "We're not going to take the children this evening. Go home. We'll come for them tomorrow morning." The governess took the hint. She got in touch with her brother, who was in the Resistance, and we were hidden in a convent in Bordeaux. Later, in a basement. After the liberation, we came back to Paris. Our parents' apartment had been looted. And when Julie took us to our grandmother—my mother's mother, the model for the monstrous mothers in *Le Bal* and *David Golder*—she sent us away, saying, "There are shelters for indigent children." The French Society of Authors, Albin Michel (the publisher), and my father's bank all held a meeting. Albin Michel saw to our education, paying for it with money he'd gotten from selling the film rights to *David Golder* to an American producer.

In your book you compare the prewar period and the current wave of xenophobia in France.

Then as now, there was balkanization abroad and a hatred of foreigners at home. When Fayard refused to publish a manuscript of my mother's—which had been commissioned before the war—because of the new racial laws, he was showing greater zeal than he had to, just as the Vichy government bent over backwards to meet German demands. Then again, Albin Michel did everything he could to continue publishing my mother's work. Even in 1940, he was still publishing her. Her married name, Epstein, is clearly Jewish, but Némirovsky, her maiden name and the name she published under, sounds Slavic more than anything. Her books weren't on the first list of books banned by the German authorities. In the Catholic daily *La Croix* you could read: "The French people are bothered by the noise and smell of foreigners." Just what you hear today from the right! In writing about the life of someone whose life ended so trag-ically, I hoped that my book would, at least in a modest way, lead people to reflect.

Translated by Edwin Frank

TITLES IN SERIES

J.R. ACKERLEY Hindoo Holiday
J.R. ACKERLEY My Dog Tulip
J.R. ACKERLEY My Father and Myself
J.R. ACKERLEY We Think the World of You
HENRY ADAMS The Jeffersonian Transformation
CÉLESTE ALBARET Monsieur Proust
DANTE ALIGHIERI The Inferno
DANTE ALIGHIERI The New Life
WILLIAM ATTAWAY Blood on the Forge
W.H. AUDEN (EDITOR) The Living Thoughts of Kierkegaard
W.H. AUDEN W.H. Auden's Book of Light Verse
ERICH AUERBACH Dante: Poet of the Secular World
DOROTHY BAKER Cassandra at the Wedding
J.A. BAKER The Peregrine
HONORÉ DE BALZAC The Unknown Masterpiece *and* Gambara
MAX BEERBOHM Seven Men
STEPHEN BENATAR Wish Her Safe at Home
FRANS G. BENGTSSON The Long Ships
ALEXANDER BERKMAN Prison Memoirs of an Anarchist
GEORGES BERNANOS Mouchette
ADOLFO BIOY CASARES Asleep in the Sun
ADOLFO BIOY CASARES The Invention of Morel
CAROLINE BLACKWOOD Corrigan
CAROLINE BLACKWOOD Great Granny Webster
NICOLAS BOUVIER The Way of the World
MALCOLM BRALY On the Yard
MILLEN BRAND The Outward Room
JOHN HORNE BURNS The Gallery
ROBERT BURTON The Anatomy of Melancholy
CAMARA LAYE The Radiance of the King
GIROLAMO CARDANO The Book of My Life
DON CARPENTER Hard Rain Falling
J.L. CARR A Month in the Country
BLAISE CENDRARS Moravagine
EILEEN CHANG Love in a Fallen City
UPAMANYU CHATTERJEE English, August: An Indian Story
NIRAD C. CHAUDHURI The Autobiography of an Unknown Indian
ANTON CHEKHOV Peasants and Other Stories
RICHARD COBB Paris and Elsewhere
COLETTE The Pure and the Impure
JOHN COLLIER Fancies and Goodnights
CARLO COLLODI The Adventures of Pinocchio
IVY COMPTON-BURNETT A House and Its Head
IVY COMPTON-BURNETT Manservant and Maidservant
BARBARA COMYNS The Vet's Daughter
EVAN S. CONNELL The Diary of a Rapist
ALBERT COSSERY The Jokers
HAROLD CRUSE The Crisis of the Negro Intellectual
ASTOLPHE DE CUSTINE Letters from Russia

For a complete list of titles, visit www.nyrb.com or write to:
Catalog Requests, NYRB, 435 Hudson Street, New York, NY 10014

LORENZO DA PONTE Memoirs

ELIZABETH DAVID A Book of Mediterranean Food

ELIZABETH DAVID Summer Cooking

L.J. DAVIS A Meaningful Life

VIVANT DENON No Tomorrow/Point de lendemain

MARIA DERMOÛT The Ten Thousand Things

DER NISTER The Family Mashber

TIBOR DÉRY Niki: The Story of a Dog

ARTHUR CONAN DOYLE The Exploits and Adventures of Brigadier Gerard

CHARLES DUFF A Handbook on Hanging

BRUCE DUFFY The World As I Found It

DAPHNE DU MAURIER Don't Look Now: Stories

ELAINE DUNDY The Dud Avocado

ELAINE DUNDY The Old Man and Me

G.B. EDWARDS The Book of Ebenezer Le Page

MARCELLUS EMANTS A Posthumous Confession

EURIPIDES Grief Lessons: Four Plays; translated by Anne Carson

J.G. FARRELL Troubles

J.G. FARRELL The Siege of Krishnapur

J.G. FARRELL The Singapore Grip

ELIZA FAY Original Letters from India

KENNETH FEARING The Big Clock

KENNETH FEARING Clark Gifford's Body

FÉLIX FÉNÉON Novels in Three Lines

M.I. FINLEY The World of Odysseus

THEODOR FONTANE Irretrievable

EDWIN FRANK (EDITOR) Unknown Masterpieces

MASANOBU FUKUOKA The One-Straw Revolution

MARC FUMAROLI When the World Spoke French

CARLO EMILIO GADDA That Awful Mess on the Via Merulana

MAVIS GALLANT The Cost of Living: Early and Uncollected Stories

MAVIS GALLANT Paris Stories

MAVIS GALLANT Varieties of Exile

GABRIEL GARCÍA MÁRQUEZ Clandestine in Chile: The Adventures of Miguel Littín

THÉOPHILE GAUTIER My Fantoms

JEAN GENET Prisoner of Love

ÉLISABETH GILLE The Mirador: Dreamed Memories of Irène Némirovsky by Her Daughter

JOHN GLASSCO Memoirs of Montparnasse

P.V. GLOB The Bog People: Iron-Age Man Preserved

EDMOND AND JULES DE GONCOURT Pages from the Goncourt Journals

EDWARD GOREY (EDITOR) The Haunted Looking Glass

A.C. GRAHAM Poems of the Late T'ang

WILLIAM LINDSAY GRESHAM Nightmare Alley

EMMETT GROGAN Ringolevio: A Life Played for Keeps

VASILY GROSSMAN Everything Flows

VASILY GROSSMAN Life and Fate

VASILY GROSSMAN The Road

OAKLEY HALL Warlock

PATRICK HAMILTON The Slaves of Solitude

PATRICK HAMILTON Twenty Thousand Streets Under the Sky

PETER HANDKE Short Letter, Long Farewell

PETER HANDKE Slow Homecoming

PETER HANDKE A Sorrow Beyond Dreams

ELIZABETH HARDWICK The New York Stories of Elizabeth Hardwick

BOHUMIL HRABAL Dancing Lessons for the Advanced in Age

ELIZABETH HARDWICK Seduction and Betrayal

ELIZABETH HARDWICK Sleepless Nights

L.P. HARTLEY Eustace and Hilda: A Trilogy

L.P. HARTLEY The Go-Between

NATHANIEL HAWTHORNE Twenty Days with Julian & Little Bunny by Papa

GILBERT HIGHET Poets in a Landscape

JANET HOBHOUSE The Furies

HUGO VON HOFMANNSTHAL The Lord Chandos Letter

JAMES HOGG The Private Memoirs and Confessions of a Justified Sinner

RICHARD HOLMES Shelley: The Pursuit

ALISTAIR HORNE A Savage War of Peace: Algeria 1954–1962

WILLIAM DEAN HOWELLS Indian Summer

RICHARD HUGHES A High Wind in Jamaica

RICHARD HUGHES In Hazard

RICHARD HUGHES The Fox in the Attic (The Human Predicament, Vol. 1)

RICHARD HUGHES The Wooden Shepherdess (The Human Predicament, Vol. 2)

MAUDE HUTCHINS Victorine

YASUSHI INOUE Tun-huang

HENRY JAMES The Ivory Tower

HENRY JAMES The New York Stories of Henry James

HENRY JAMES The Other House

HENRY JAMES The Outcry

TOVE JANSSON Fair Play

TOVE JANSSON The Summer Book

TOVE JANSSON The True Deceiver

RANDALL JARRELL (EDITOR) Randall Jarrell's Book of Stories

DAVID JONES In Parenthesis

ERNST JÜNGER The Glass Bees

KABIR Songs of Kabir; translated by Arvind Krishna Mehrotra

HELEN KELLER The World I Live In

FRIGYES KARINTHY A Journey Round My Skull

YASHAR KEMAL Memed, My Hawk

YASHAR KEMAL They Burn the Thistles

MURRAY KEMPTON Part of Our Time: Some Ruins and Monuments of the Thirties

DAVID KIDD Peking Story

ROBERT KIRK The Secret Commonwealth of Elves, Fauns, and Fairies

ARUN KOLATKAR Jejuri

DEZSŐ KOSZTOLÁNYI Skylark

TÉTÉ-MICHEL KPOMASSIE An African in Greenland

GYULA KRÚDY Sunflower

SIGIZMUND KRZHIZHANOVSKY Memories of the Future

MARGARET LEECH Reveille in Washington: 1860–1865

PATRICK LEIGH FERMOR Between the Woods and the Water

PATRICK LEIGH FERMOR Mani: Travels in the Southern Peloponnese

PATRICK LEIGH FERMOR Roumeli: Travels in Northern Greece

PATRICK LEIGH FERMOR A Time of Gifts

PATRICK LEIGH FERMOR A Time to Keep Silence

PATRICK LEIGH FERMOR The Traveller's Tree

D.B. WYNDHAM LEWIS AND CHARLES LEE (EDITORS) The Stuffed Owl

GEORG CHRISTOPH LICHTENBERG The Waste Books
JAKOV LIND Soul of Wood and Other Stories
H.P. LOVECRAFT AND OTHERS The Colour Out of Space
ROSE MACAULAY The Towers of Trebizond
NORMAN MAILER Miami and the Siege of Chicago
JANET MALCOLM In the Freud Archives
JEAN-PATRICK MANCHETTE Fatale
OSIP MANDELSTAM The Selected Poems of Osip Mandelstam
OLIVIA MANNING Fortunes of War: The Balkan Trilogy
OLIVIA MANNING School for Love
GUY DE MAUPASSANT Afloat
GUY DE MAUPASSANT Alien Hearts
JAMES MCCOURT Mawrdew Czgowchwz
HENRI MICHAUX Miserable Miracle
JESSICA MITFORD Hons and Rebels
JESSICA MITFORD Poison Penmanship
NANCY MITFORD Madame de Pompadour
HENRY DE MONTHERLANT Chaos and Night
BRIAN MOORE The Lonely Passion of Judith Hearne
BRIAN MOORE The Mangan Inheritance
ALBERTO MORAVIA Boredom
ALBERTO MORAVIA Contempt
JAN MORRIS Conundrum
PENELOPE MORTIMER The Pumpkin Eater
ÁLVARO MUTIS The Adventures and Misadventures of Maqroll
L.H. MYERS The Root and the Flower
DARCY O'BRIEN A Way of Life, Like Any Other
YURI OLESHA Envy
IONA AND PETER OPIE The Lore and Language of Schoolchildren
IRIS OWENS After Claude
RUSSELL PAGE The Education of a Gardener
ALEXANDROS PAPADIAMANTIS The Murderess
BORIS PASTERNAK, MARINA TSVETAYEVA, AND RAINER MARIA RILKE Letters, Summer 1926
CESARE PAVESE The Moon and the Bonfires
CESARE PAVESE The Selected Works of Cesare Pavese
LUIGI PIRANDELLO The Late Mattia Pascal
ANDREY PLATONOV The Foundation Pit
ANDREY PLATONOV Soul and Other Stories
J.F. POWERS Morte d'Urban
J.F. POWERS The Stories of J.F. Powers
J.F. POWERS Wheat That Springeth Green
CHRISTOPHER PRIEST Inverted World
BOLESŁAW PRUS The Doll
RAYMOND QUENEAU We Always Treat Women Too Well
RAYMOND QUENEAU Witch Grass
RAYMOND RADIGUET Count d'Orgel's Ball
JULES RENARD Nature Stories
JEAN RENOIR Renoir, My Father
GREGOR VON REZZORI Memoirs of an Anti-Semite
GREGOR VON REZZORI The Snows of Yesteryear: Portraits for an Autobiography
TIM ROBINSON Stones of Aran: Labyrinth
TIM ROBINSON Stones of Aran: Pilgrimage

MILTON ROKEACH The Three Christs of Ypsilanti
FR. ROLFE Hadrian the Seventh
GILLIAN ROSE Love's Work
WILLIAM ROUGHEAD Classic Crimes
CONSTANCE ROURKE American Humor: A Study of the National Character
TAYEB SALIH Season of Migration to the North
TAYEB SALIH The Wedding of Zein
GERSHOM SCHOLEM Walter Benjamin: The Story of a Friendship
DANIEL PAUL SCHREBER Memoirs of My Nervous Illness
JAMES SCHUYLER Alfred and Guinevere
JAMES SCHUYLER What's for Dinner?
LEONARDO SCIASCIA The Day of the Owl
LEONARDO SCIASCIA Equal Danger
LEONARDO SCIASCIA The Moro Affair
LEONARDO SCIASCIA To Each His Own
LEONARDO SCIASCIA The Wine-Dark Sea
VICTOR SEGALEN René Leys
PHILIPE-PAUL DE SÉGUR Defeat: Napoleon's Russian Campaign
VICTOR SERGE The Case of Comrade Tulayev
VICTOR SERGE Conquered City
VICTOR SERGE Unforgiving Years
SHCHEDRIN The Golovlyov Family
GEORGES SIMENON Dirty Snow
GEORGES SIMENON The Engagement
GEORGES SIMENON The Man Who Watched Trains Go By
GEORGES SIMENON Monsieur Monde Vanishes
GEORGES SIMENON Pedigree
GEORGES SIMENON Red Lights
GEORGES SIMENON The Strangers in the House
GEORGES SIMENON Three Bedrooms in Manhattan
GEORGES SIMENON Tropic Moon
GEORGES SIMENON The Widow
CHARLES SIMIC Dime-Store Alchemy: The Art of Joseph Cornell
MAY SINCLAIR Mary Olivier: A Life
TESS SLESINGER The Unpossessed: A Novel of the Thirties
VLADIMIR SOROKIN Ice Trilogy
VLADIMIR SOROKIN The Queue
DAVID STACTON The Judges of the Secret Court
JEAN STAFFORD The Mountain Lion
CHRISTINA STEAD Letty Fox: Her Luck
GEORGE R. STEWART Names on the Land
STENDHAL The Life of Henry Brulard
ADALBERT STIFTER Rock Crystal
THEODOR STORM The Rider on the White Horse
HOWARD STURGIS Belchamber
ITALO SVEVO As a Man Grows Older
HARVEY SWADOS Nights in the Gardens of Brooklyn
A.J.A. SYMONS The Quest for Corvo
HENRY DAVID THOREAU The Journal: 1837–1861
TATYANA TOLSTAYA The Slynx
TATYANA TOLSTAYA White Walls: Collected Stories
EDWARD JOHN TRELAWNY Records of Shelley, Byron, and the Author

LIONEL TRILLING The Liberal Imagination
LIONEL TRILLING The Middle of the Journey
IVAN TURGENEV Virgin Soil
JULES VALLÈS The Child
MARK VAN DOREN Shakespeare
CARL VAN VECHTEN The Tiger in the House
ELIZABETH VON ARNIM The Enchanted April
EDWARD LEWIS WALLANT The Tenants of Moonbloom
ROBERT WALSER Jakob von Gunten
ROBERT WALSER Selected Stories
REX WARNER Men and Gods
SYLVIA TOWNSEND WARNER Lolly Willowes
SYLVIA TOWNSEND WARNER Mr. Fortune
SYLVIA TOWNSEND WARNER Summer Will Show
ALEKSANDER WAT My Century
C.V. WEDGWOOD The Thirty Years War
SIMONE WEIL AND RACHEL BESPALOFF War and the Iliad
GLENWAY WESCOTT Apartment in Athens
GLENWAY WESCOTT The Pilgrim Hawk
REBECCA WEST The Fountain Overflows
EDITH WHARTON The New York Stories of Edith Wharton
PATRICK WHITE Riders in the Chariot
T.H. WHITE The Goshawk
JOHN WILLIAMS Butcher's Crossing
JOHN WILLIAMS Stoner
ANGUS WILSON Anglo-Saxon Attitudes
EDMUND WILSON Memoirs of Hecate County
EDMUND WILSON To the Finland Station
RUDOLF AND MARGARET WITTKOWER Born Under Saturn
GEOFFREY WOLFF Black Sun
FRANCIS WYNDHAM The Complete Fiction
JOHN WYNDHAM The Chrysalids
STEFAN ZWEIG Beware of Pity
STEFAN ZWEIG Chess Story
STEFAN ZWEIG Journey Into the Past
STEFAN ZWEIG The Post-Office Girl